An Innocent Girl and a Dangerous Outlaw..."Unforgettable"
—Elizabeth Forsythe Hailey

"I wondered if he were still out there in the night. I thought about his kisses and I touched my own lips, all around, with both my hands, trying to feel them the way he had. Were they soft? Warm like his were? If a kiss was such a wicked thing, if it could lead you down the path of sin and degradation like Brother Parsons preached ... if it were true, and one kiss could ruin a body's soul, then mine was ruined for sure."

—from *Lily*

"Lily's voice—and heart—stay with you."
—*Charlotte Observer*

"Author Cindy Bonner captures Lily to perfection ... a tale tailor-made for the movies."
—*Book World*

"Poignant and new." —*Houston Post*

"Beguiling ... manages to be thoroughly romantic without romanticizing violence."
—*Kirkus Reviews*

"The reader will cheer for Lily to the final page. A believable, engrossing tale of love and violence."

—*Abilene Reporter-News*

Lily

A LOVE STORY

by
Cindy Bonner

AN ONYX BOOK

ONYX
Published by the Penguin Group
Penguin Books USA Inc., 375 Hudson Street,
New York, New York 10014, U.S.A.
Penguin Books Ltd, 27 Wrights Lane,
London W8 5TZ, England
Penguin Books Australia Ltd, Ringwood,
Victoria, Australia
Penguin Books Canada Ltd, 10 Alcorn Avenue,
Toronto, Ontario, Canada M4V 3B2
Penguin Books (N.Z.) Ltd, 182-190 Wairau Road,
Auckland 10, New Zealand

Penguin Books Ltd, Registered Offices:
Harmondsworth, Middlesex, England

Published by Onyx, an imprint of Dutton Signet, a division of Penguin
Books USA Inc. This is an authorized reprint of a hardcover edition published by Algonquin Books of Chapel Hill, a division of Workman Publish-
ing Company, Inc.

First Onyx Printing, February, 1994
10 9 8 7 6 5 4 3 2 1

To Randy, Stuart, and Brandon
for believing I could.
And to Mildred,
whose courage inspires my awe.

Many thanks to Putzie Martin of the Bastrop Public Library, and to Diana Bennett of the Nancy Carol Roberts Memorial Library in Brenham for entrusting me with the priceless microfilm I needed to get the facts straight. Thanks also to the people at the Blinn College Library for their help with the microfilm copiers; and to Susan Rogers Cooper and Karen Weidemann for their enthusiasm. Thanks, guys, for being such good readers. And finally, thanks to Shannon Ravenel for finding merit in my work.

1

*F*olks around here say the Beatty boys were just
plain wild and no good, and that they made
us all look bad here in McDade. Made the whole
county look bad in the eyes of the rest of Texas.
Like we were all wild and no good ourselves, to
have grown up such bad boys, like that Beatty
bunch.

That's Beatty with the *a* sounding out. But not
B-A-T-E-Y, like it was spelled in that newspaper
article that came out three weeks after Christmas.
January 18, 1884. Most everything in that article
was wrong, and I dwelled on it after I got back
home. Just sitting out on the hollow log back of
the barn by the running creek those first days
back, dwelling on how that Beatty name got
spelled wrong. It had been raining. Awful cold.
Enough to make water come out my eyes and
nearly freeze to my face.

The Beattys didn't have a mother. Daddy neither
by the time I knew them. Old man Beatty had died
a year or two before. Some say he poisoned himself with bootjack whiskey and Tutt's pills. Liver
disorder was how Marion explained it to me. But

he never said much about his mama. What she went of. Birthing Marion is what Mrs. Kennedy told me. Plum wore herself out having those last three boys right in a row like she did, one every year till Marion came. I sat on that hollow log by the creek for three days thinking about her, and about how it seemed like they didn't any of them ever exist. I guess I was the only sad one in the whole town.

My own daddy left me alone for those three days. So did my two brothers and my sister. And then the morning of the fourth day, Papa came out to fetch me, saying, "That's all now, Lily. That's all the grieving you got time for. There's bread to bake and hogs to slop, and them little 'uns can't tend to it all alone."

You see, my own mama passed on in childbirth too, so I guess I know what's it's like to come up without your ma. It's hard work, and it's lonely, and there ain't ever anybody there to tuck your covers and pat your head when you're feeling poorly. And even though I'm the oldest, fifteen now, and can take care of the others, I know a little bit how those Beatty boys felt. How come they turned out so wild and misbehaving.

Jack was the oldest, and so I don't remember him much as a little kid. Azberry neither, though he was just two years in front of Marion. The oldest boys were the two roughest, lowest talking. One time, I heard Az tell Mr. Westbrook down at the lumberyard to get off his lazy-ass butt and saw up a board for their wagon. He said it loud enough folks heard all the way down the street to

Billingsley's store. Marion said Az just liked to show off for folks, prove he was a man himself and could say those dirty words. I never heard Marion cuss. Never once. But the rest sure could. Even Haywood, who only outdid Marion in age by ten months or so.

The four of them, I swear to you, were as different as sugar and salt. Az and Haywood had the dark hair. Az kept a kinky beard like coal dust on his cheeks. Those two were blue-eyed. Jack's and Marion's eyes were brown. But Marion had soft eyes, not small and cold, or set deep back in his head like Jack's were. Jack had light hair, but he wore it so dirty it turned to the color of the ground inside a hog pen. Marion's hair was red. Not red like the magnolia seed on the tree by our house. But red like the later end of sunset, spang through with streaks of gold and yellow, and darker shades underneath like heavy, low clouds hanging at the horizon.

When I noticed him again, after years of raising my brothers and my sister, and after growing into womanhood—when I saw him again like it was the first time, standing in the dust and daylight there on the road outside Billingley's store, it was that funny-colored hair of his I noticed, flecking at me like a length from a bolt of the best organdy in Bastrop.

He was standing beside his horse, his hat off, inspecting something inside the crown like a burr had caught up in a seam. He looked up, as if my eyes had stung him somehow, and when he saw me looking, a smile cracked out one corner of his mouth. He cupped his hat back onto his head, covered up that flashy hair, and gave the brim a tip in my direction.

"Well, hello there, Lily DeLony," he said. "Ain't seen you in a while."

It kind of surprised me how he remembered my name. Last I could recall he'd been about twelve years old, stumbling over the words in Miss Huddleton's reading books at the schoolhouse behind the city bank. He wasn't twelve anymore, but he had the same face. Same soft, shy eyes. The spit dried up inside my mouth.

"Hello yourself," I said, pulling Dellie with my free hand towards the spring buggy we used for hauling store goods. Nathan sat behind the mule, waiting on us, popping the leather whip at a ball of flies swirling under Mr. Billingsley's awning.

I stepped off the walk with my sister and my package of sugar, some nickel-plated sewing needles, a twist of tobacco for Papa. It wasn't heavy. I didn't feel a strain. But Marion ducked around the hitching rail and grabbed the package from my arm.

"Lemme help you with this, Lily," he said, even though we weren't but two steps from the buggy. He put the package inside the plunder box, then lifted Dellie under her arms and swung her up to the seat. "This 'un yours?" he said to me as she squealed out a giggle from being swung so high and fast. Her skirt ruffled out around her as she plopped onto the cowhide.

"My sister. I wasn't but eight when she was born, so I ain't old enough to be her mama. She's seven now." I put my foot on the booster and pushed my own self up to the seat. He didn't reach to help.

He slapped the bench beside Nathan. "Hello, Bobbo," he said.

My brother sneered down the length of his nose. "The name's Nathan."

"He's nine," I said.

Marion grinned wide. "Too young to be his ma too, I guess. It don't seem like folks would lose track of each other in such a dinky town, does it, Lily?"

"I hear tales about you and yours." I smoothed at the uncaught hair beside my ears, peeved that the piece of twine wouldn't keep my pigtail in tow. I'd been hoping for hairpins from Mr. Billinglsey. He was still fresh out.

"Can we go now?" Nathan was ready to crack the mule on his back.

"What tales?" Marion said, his grin almost fading.

Somebody whistled from the door of the rock saloon, then catcalled, "Whoo-ee! Come take a look at what Shot's found hisself." After than came some more caterwauling.

I glanced and saw Azberry and a man named Charlie Goodman, and another of Marion's relations, Thad McLemore, who lived down in the bottom with his older brother and sister-in-law. They had a shack on a couple of acres of weeds. No means of livelihood that anybody in McDade could see. The McLemores hadn't been in town long. Only about two months or so. Rumor was

Thad had left a wife and six kids somewheres over in Fayette county.

The three men standing at the saloon door leered at me. They looked half-drunk already, at just a little past high noon. All three of them wore gun belts strapped around their hips, leather thongs tying the holsters onto their thighs. We had a no-gun law in our town, but wasn't anybody with nerve enough to force it on the Beattys.

Azberry cocked his fingers like they were a pair of six-shooters and fired them off in our direction. The two fellows standing beside him hawed with laughter.

I reached to tap Nathan to whip up the mule. Marion walked beside the buggy a few steps. His face had gone purple.

"Don't pay them no mind, Lily," he said. It bothered me how he kept saying my name. It seemed impolite some way.

I looked back at him over my left shoulder. The buggy wheels were throwing grit on his britches, spatting like a hard rain at the buckskin vest he wore. The Beatty boys were all big for the buckskin. It made them look like gunmen, or outlaws. Which I guess, when you think about it, is what they were.

Well, they weren't ever big-time outlaws. Not like John Wesley Hardin or Sam Bass. The Beatty gang was small-time, McDade-size outlaws. At least back then they were. Mostly they just pestered Mr. Nash, who owned the rock saloon.

They'd get drunk and shoot up the walls, or ride their horses in over the board gallery and through the summer doors. The saloon was built of field-stone and couldn't hardly be hurt none. They left a few bullet holes in the mortar, hoof prints in the pine floor. They scuttled a few poker games, I expect. No *real* damage though. Mr. Nash didn't complain. The Beatty gang were his best customers.

Marion quit running alongside the buggy. "Don't judge me by them over there," he shouted, waving towards Az and Charlie Goodman and Thad McLemore. When his arm moved out, I caught a glimpse of the blue steel end of a pistol inside his vest.

My shoulders raised in a shrug as Nathan drove us off towards the farm. How else was I supposed to know him? Or judge him, or whatever he meant? I wondered why he said that to me, and what matter it made to him what I thought. I was just a girl he used to know in school. Nothing else.

But those words of his kept coming to me—as I'd be scrubbing Papa's work shirts, or Dane's, out back in the soak box; or as I'd be feeding the chickens or gathering the eggs they laid under the porch. For days after that trip to town I thought about Marion and his hair, and about how he'd said for me not to judge him. And then me and Nathan got the garden ground started for the fall crop of vegetables, hoeing and planting seeds, and watering in. Pretty soon, Marion Beatty slipped out of my mind.

2

*P*apa tried to give us God. When I was little, just after Mama died, he'd tote us up to Sunday school, all slick-shined and bathed up with lye soap. But some of the church ladies started in trying to pair him up with different widows near about, and seeing as how Papa had already lost two wives, he didn't have it in his mind to take on a third. When I was ten he started sending us to church with Mrs. Kennedy.

Papa came from Mississippi the year after the war of the rebellion ended. While he'd been off fighting, his home had been burned, his people buried. He brought a young bride, Edna, to Texas. And right off, she gave birth to a baby girl, Pauline, before Papa even got their house built good. They lived at Blue Branch, across the Knobs in Lee County, fourteen miles northeast of McDade. In '66, yellow fever nearly killed out the whole town.

That's all I know about it. That they were named Edna and Pauline and that they were here before us. And this I know from Mrs. Kennedy. Papa didn't ever mention that other family, dead and buried in the graveyard over at Blue Branch.

Mrs. Kennedy was the nearest thing we had to relations in McDade, but she wasn't really kin. She'd been a friend to the Hutchinsons, my mama's family, before the last ones moved off down near Columbus. Mrs. Kennedy was a widow woman herself, and barren I guess, for she didn't have any children. She was older than Papa by about ten years, which put her at somewhere around forty-seven years of age.

On Sundays she'd come by an hour after breakfast to pick us up for church in her wagon. She had a colored boy named Eppie she hired to handle the team. He also worked at her ranch, odd jobs, and taking care of her cattle. We didn't have many coloreds around here anymore, and what ones there were stayed off to themselves, so we weren't used to them coming into town. Mrs. Kennedy made Eppie attend church services, and nobody ever said anything, though he *was* the only colored in the pews. I reckon he felt funny about it.

On the wagon ride Dane liked to sit up front with Eppie, and they'd talk about carp fishing in Willow Creek or squirrel hunting. Man stuff. Nathan rode in the back with me and Dellie and Mrs. Kennedy, though he grumbled about it. There wasn't room but for two up front.

Most Sundays I had to rush to get breakfast done and dishes rinsed, so I didn't have time to fix Dellie up like she wanted for church. I usually spent the ride combing her hair, putting in plaits so's her wild strands of blond would lay neat down her back. Weren't any of the rest of us blessed with Dellie's golden hair. Neither Papa nor

Mama had been. I figured Dellie's hair had to be a fluke of nature.

They were building a new church house and so, after Brother Parkins's sermon in the old building, the congregation moved outside on the grass, where the womenfolk spread down blankets and pulled out picnic baskets. The men brought out their hammers and nails, and unloaded new pine lumber off Mr. Westbrook's cart. Papa had learned not to expect us home before supper. One Sunday, the end of September, talk in the churchyard turned to the Beattys. How it came about was some of the boys, Nathan being one of them, started playing shoot-out with willow sticks, running around the old church building, making gun noises, stalking up on each other, and falling dead in the grass. I knew I'd have to check him for ticks before we could get back in Mrs. Kennedy's wagon. And folks were watching them, even some of the men who should have been too busy hammering in nails to notice kids' games.

Mrs. Bishop, along with her sleeping baby of six months, was sharing a blanket with me and Mrs. Kennedy that day, and she said, "Heard the Beattys are up to no good again."

Mrs. Kennedy was sweating, trying not to show it but dabbing at her brow now and then with a lace handkerchief. "It's this hot weather," she said. "It'll make good folks feel mean, and mean ones meaner."

Mention of the Beattys caught Mrs. McCraney's attention, and Mrs. Griffin's, whose own son, Willie, was sometimes seen in Beatty company. Both ladies moved over to our blanket and sat down.

"You're talking about that poor store clerk over in Paige," Mrs. McCraney said. "The one they robbed and shot through the head."

"In the mouth is the way I heard it," Mrs. Bishop said. "And at such close range it left powder burns on his cheeks."

The other three women gasped. Mrs. Bishop just patted her baby on his back where he laid, face-down, on Mrs. Kennedy's blanket. Drool had puddled beneath his little mouth.

"They don't know for sure Beattys done it." Mrs. Griffin looked pale. "Do they?"

Mrs. Bishop shook her head. "No, but the sheriff's posse tracked them nearly to McDade before they gave it up."

I nudged Dellie towards some children her age playing on the rope swings some of the men had hung from a sycamore tree. She didn't need to be listening to murder stories, but she whined and rolled against my back and wouldn't budge.

Dellie was a shy one, and never left my skirts. I worried for her when school started up in two weeks. It would be her first year. "Go on now and play," I said low to her.

"The way I heard it, there wasn't but fifteen dollars in the cash drawer," Mrs. McCraney said.

"Cold-blooded killers." Mrs. Kennedy took off her bonnet and mopped out the brim with her hankie. "What is this town coming to?"

All the women shook their heads in agreement. I looked out at the boys playing around the church house. Nathan was doing a quick draw, like he had a sidearm strapped on his hip. His knee-britches were all dusted up, stockings slouched down around his ankles.

"Seems a shame we have to harbor criminal types around here," Mrs. McCraney said.

"What we need is a town marshal." Mrs. Kennedy pinched at her collar, whipping it back and forth to force air down to her bosom. Hammering from the men echoed all over the churchyard. "Someone who won't put up with their shenanigans. Sheriff Jenkins has his hands full over in Bastrop."

"The Beattys don't ever do anything in McDade, though," I said and the way they all looked at me, you'd have thought I swore an oath against God.

"What about the Brenham stage?" Mrs. Bishop said. "They been held up so many times, they won't hardly run through here no more."

"And all the drinking and gambling." Mrs. McCraney put her hand on her chest like it took her weak to even thing of it. "Poor Sam Billingsley has himself a devil of a time trying to run a decent store right down from that saloon."

Mrs. Griffin was looking more and more uncomfortable. Her son, Willie, could nearly always be found at the rock saloon himself. She shouted, "Timmy Griffin, you get down from that tree this minute," at her youngest boy, who'd climbed a low-branching mesquite tree and was shooting his willow stick at Nathan. She stood up from the blanket and went in their direction.

I stood up then, too. I didn't want the ladies

thinking I had no control on my own brother.
Dellie dogged my heels across the churchyard. I
caught up with Nathan just as he was heading
away from me. I snatched ahold of the back of his
shirt.

"Stop this roughhousing, Nathan," I said.

He was laughing, red-faced, sweating like mad.
He tried to wring free of me and go after Bubby
Matson, who was running wild as an Indian down
the side of the old church building.

I knew they were just having fun, but I looked
across and saw Mrs. Griffin stripping a switch for
Timmy. I said, "If you don't mind me I'm gonna
tell Papa when we get home."

Dellie clung to my waist tighter at the mention
of Papa and the possibility of a whipping. She
hated for anyone to get it. She watched Mrs. Griffin, fear in her eyes.

Nathan was breathing hard. "You do and I'll tell
him you were talking with that bad man in town."

I let go of his shirt. I'd almost forgotten about
seeing Marion Beatty that day. Leastwise, I told
myself I had. Truth was, I'd been thinking about
him hard ever since Mrs. Bishop brought the subject up a while ago. I wondered if there was something on my face that showed it and caused
Nathan to make his threat. It wasn't an idle threat,
either. Papa would strap me good for speaking to
the likes of those Beattys.

"Ain't any harm in talking," I said lamely, but
Nathan was already halfway across the churchyard, whooping it up with Bubby Matson.

"What man, Sissy?" Dellie said, yanking on my

skirt. Mrs. Griffin was holding Timmy by one arm, switching his bottom good.

"Never mind," I said, taking her hand. I headed towards the new building, where Dane was up on a ladder near Eppie.

"Did Nathan mean that one what swung me up onto the buggy that day? Is that the one he means, Sissy? Was that a bad man?"

"Hush now." I marched to the foot of Dane's ladder. "Come down from there and take care of your brother," I said.

Dane squinted down at me and then out at where Nathan and Bubby were running. Dane needed glasses but there wasn't money for it. He looked tired.

"You can't catch him yourself?" he said.

"I've got Dellie."

He sighed, but he backed down the ladder and went across the yard after Nathan. I headed towards the women. Mrs. Bishop had moved her baby over to Mrs. McCraney's spot, and Mrs. Kennedy was folding away our blankets. The heat was getting to her, and I knew we'd be leaving soon.

Before I reached her, Daniel O'Barr came up beside me. He was huffing, dripping with sweat, even in his shirtsleeves, like all the men were down to by then. A line of wet ran the same pattern as his galluses, up from his waist, over his shoulders, then down in back, crossing under both his shoulderblades.

"Hi," he said, his face red from the sun. He had a handful of nails gripped in his palm, which he carefully turned over and over to keep from looking at me. "I was wondering about the fair next weekend. If I could escort you to it."

It was the church fair he meant, that folks were putting on to raise money to pay Mr. Westbrook for his lumber. I hadn't even talked with Papa about it yet, since you had to bring something to sell and I couldn't think of anything we could spare. There were two jars of pickles left from last spring in the cupboard. One dills and one bread-and-butters. It was about all I could come up with.

Daniel noticed I was taking my time in answering him. He adjusted his hat and waited, chewed on his lip, which was already bit down to raw meat.

He wasn't much to look at. Too frail for my taste. But he had good manners, and Mrs. Kennedy swore he was as smart as a hawk. He kind of looked like a hawk, pointed chin and nose, tiny little blue eyeballs, bloodshot with his sweat. He was three years older than me. Eighteen and already a man. About the same age I figured Marion Beatty to be, though there wasn't much comparison.

I pushed my lips together and looked at Daniel square. "If my papa says it's all right, I'll go with you."

That seemed to get him all excited. He jumped around in front of me, walking backwards. "You want me to ask him for you? I'd be glad to do it."

"I'll do it. Just come by my house on Wednesday and I'll tell you yes or no."

Daniel followed me and Dellie over to Mrs. Kennedy. And he made a big fuss, carrying the picnic baskets and blankets to the wagon for her, even though we had Dane and Eppie to do it. On the way home I picked four ticks off Nathan and flicked them over the side of the wagon before Mrs. Kennedy could see.

Papa wasn't yet easy at the idea of me keeping company with menfolk. He thought I was too young, even though my own mama hadn't been but a year past my age when she gave birth to me. So I knew what his reaction would be if I asked him straight about the church fair and going with Daniel O'Barr. He'd have given me a flat-out no and no use in arguing. That's why I planned out my story in my mind. For the good of the church was what I'd say. To take my pickles and help raise money to pay back Mr. Westbrook for his lumber. Papa was big on paying back debts.

I waited till Tuesday evening when he came in from the fields in a good humor for having done a full day's work. I set out a big spread for supper. Fresh beans from the garden, squash with tomatoes, bread, and a thick roast off the hog we still had left from last year's slaughter. Papa's eyes lit up when he saw all the food, though he didn't smile. His lighting-up eyes was the closest he ever came to a smile.

Dane and Nathan were hungry too, from working with Papa, raking hay into stacks to store for winter. It was the third cut of hay we'd gotten this year and Papa was pleased about it. The boys tied on their bibs and commenced to taking up their forks, when Papa said, "We'll say grace first."

Which surprised us all since grace was usually saved for Sundays.

It was probably just the big supper made him think of it, but I took it as a good omen. My excuse of wanting to help out the church would work better if Papa was in a praying mood. We all bowed our heads and said together, "Our Father, we thank Thee for this food. Amen." And then the knives and forks started clanking.

Dellie needed me to cut up her meat, and so while I did that, I brought up the subject on my mind. "They're having a church fair up town next Saturday." I made my voice casual-like, as if I was just making table talk.

Dane took it up. "Next Saturday? I thought it were this Saturday."

"This Saturday coming up," I said. "They asked for donations and things to sell. Canned goods and whatnot. I thought of those jars of pickles we hadn't eaten yet. The ones I put up last spring."

Dane said, "Brother Parkins hoped I could be a contestant in the greased pig scramble they're having."

I frowned at him. He was ruining my plans, asking his own permission to go while I was still working up to mine. It never paid to throw too much at Papa too quick.

"We're already late getting oats planted." Papa looked from me to Dane. "I'll be needing both your help this Saturday."

I pushed Dellie's plate back in front of her. "I think Miz Kennedy was counting on me to work one of the food tents. They're doing shifts—"

"Well, I'm counting on you to work with me Saturday," Papa said in a tone that meant there wasn't any use in discussing it anymore. I was so mad at Dane I could've thrown my butter knife at him where he sat across the table from me.

We ate the rest of the meal without talking. Papa must have known me and Dane were disappointed from the long faces we wore the rest of the evening till bedtime.

That night, I laid in bed next to Dellie and stared out the window on my side, at the sky and the spangled stars up there. At times like that one, a black mood would creep up on me and I couldn't find sleep no way. Times when this farm seemed like a burden on my neck that I couldn't shake off, like as if I was one of the plow mules harnessed to work, to the never-endingness of it, and to the seclusion. It wasn't that the church fair was really so important to me, but it become so lying in that dark bed with Dellie's little legs tangled around me, her even breath hot where it hit my back through my nightdress. It was Papa saying no, and in the saying, taking away the control from me for my own life's desires; it was him making the choices for me that soured up my stomach and brought me down so low. I flipped and flopped around that bed most all the night long.

Daniel came by midmorning, after I'd done my early chores and set to fixing the noon meal. Nathan and Dane were in the fields with Papa, and I was teaching Dellie how to make a cook fire, how much dry kindling to put in, how much green, and how to stack it right and then stoke it so it stayed burning slow. She wasn't learning fast, and I tried to have patience like Mama had with me, but it was taking a toll on my already dark mood. When I heard him rap on the front door, I let go a sigh, for I knew it was him and that now I had to tell him Papa said no to the fair.

I untied my apron and pushed at my hair, which had already gone to frizzle in the heat. Then I went to the door and stepped out on the porch, knowing better than to ask a man in when Papa wasn't inside the house.

Daniel looked clean and neat, like he'd just had himself a bath and a fresh shave. He was wearing a tweed trouser and an overjacket, a bowler on his head. Sunday clothes. He had a black-eyed Susan pushed into the buttonhole on his lapel, one I figured he'd picked on his way here, for it was already starting to wilt up like a wildflower will if it ain't put to water right away. When he saw me, he took off his hat and cradled it upside-down in the crook of his arm. He smiled big and said, "I came to call like you said do. It's Wednesday."

Dressed as he was, I felt self-conscious of my plain house dress, of the hole patched in the skirt, and of my hair scraggling out around my face. I shut the door on Dellie, who'd followed me and stood staring wide-eyed at Daniel.

"I can't go with you to the fair Saturday," I said. "Papa has work planned for us that day."

There was no mistaking the unhappy look that came on his face then. He waved away a fly that was buzzing at his hair oil. "Would it help for me to speak with him myself? Missus Kennedy agreed to chaperone us so that worry wouldn't be on his mind."

"It won't do any good. When Papa gets his head set one way, it ain't any use to pester him about it."

Daniel took a step back, and peered out towards the fields. I looked too and saw the boys raking hay in one and Papa in the other, behind the mule and plow, getting the sod turned up for planting. Knuck, Dane's coondog, was out there with them. Knuck, short for Knucklehead, for the hound knot on his noggin and because he was stupid, even for a dog. He was out there now pouncing on the boys' rakes like a barn cat would get after a rat.

"It'd be worth a try, though," Daniel said, still looking. "Worst he can say is no again."

Since I hadn't had the chance to even mention to Papa Daniel taking me, I wasn't too keen on the idea of him strolling out there interrupting Papa's work. I moved back nearer to the door and wished Daniel would too so's his figure wouldn't call Papa's attention to the porch.

"It'd be best not to disturb him while he's working," I said, but Daniel had already stepped off the porch and stuck his hat back on his head. He went out towards the fields in his fancy clothes.

Dellie came out the door then. "Where's he going, Sissy?"

I turned her around by her shoulders. "Get back inside the house," I said and went in with her.

The cook fire had burned down to nothing, but I couldn't concentrate on it. I kept watching out

the window, watching Daniel pull Papa off the
plow and them talk. I saw Papa point out over the
rows he'd made and Daniel point with him. They
walked a few feet and Daniel pulled off his jacket,
hung it over his arm. He had guts. I had to give
him that. Weren't too many around here who'd
venture a conversation with Papa so bold-like.
When I saw Papa look towards the house, I hurried back to the stove and got busy with dinner
again.

They came in to eat later, and Daniel wasn't
with them. His horse wasn't out front anymore either. Papa didn't say anything about it to me. He
sat down at the table and ate fast like he always
did when it was planting season. I kept quiet and
so did the boys. Dellie talked a little bit about
helping me make the fire. When Papa let out a
belch, then pushed back his chair, Dane and Nathan both rose, too.

It wasn't till after I had the dishes done, while
Dellie stood up on her chair drying what I'd
washed, that I happened to look outside the window again. What I saw gave me a start. There in
the furrows Papa had plowed was Daniel, alongside of Eppie, both of them in work britches and
boots, with their shirts rolled up past their elbows,
planting the oat field. Doing my Saturday work.

3

When Daniel came to pick me up that Saturday, he was driving a shiny black carriage. It had leather seats and lanterns with stars cut into the glass. The big spoked wheels turned smooth and hardly jostled me and Mrs. Kennedy, going over the rough-out road into town.

The O'Barrs had a little more money than most of us in these parts, though there weren't any of us that were rich. Times were hard for everybody, what with the price of beef and grain and cotton down so low. But the O'Barrs had been here longer than most, since the Thirties when Texas was still wild and part of Mexico. And Mr. O'Barr had more land than the rest of us, enough to run a few hundred head of cattle. Most everybody else was plain farmers, with only a milkcow or two. The O'Barrs were just about our only ranchers—besides Mrs. Kennedy, of course. But she was old and didn't run more than thirty head these days, so nobody thought of her much as a real big-time rancher. The O'Barrs were the closest thing we had. Sorry to say, though, that didn't make Daniel one bit more interesting.

He was a gentleman, helped me out of the carriage when we got to the fair, carried my jars of pickles for me, but he wasn't interesting at all. I got to feeling bad because I didn't like him that much and had only used him as a way to get to the fair, and after all the work he'd done with Papa to get to take me, so I wove my arm under his as we walked and let him escort me proper. Mrs. Kennedy went ahead of us.

They had tents thrown up on the ground across from the row of buildings that made up our town section. Between the road and the railroad tracks was a strip of land like a park almost, except the grass was natural, not planted the way I'd heard they did in big city parks. There was one huge oak there, and the rest was open space. The tree spread its branches out wide, over half of the grassy space, and that's where all the food tents sat, there in the shade from that tree.

The tree itself had a history to it. A band of horse thieves had once been hung there, from the lower branches, folks said. Back in the Sixties when McDade was still called Tie Town, before the railroad came through and changed things.

Daniel and me took the pickles to the tent where Mrs. McCraney stood. She was hosting the canned and baked goods. We were expecting folks from all over the county to come, and so the ladies had outdone themselves in their kitchens all week. I admired a coffee cake I recognized as one of Mrs. Bishop's, and right away, Daniel bought it for me. It made me feel funny how he fussed over me.

Mrs. Kennedy got busy in the lemonade tent,

and shooed me and Daniel out to the amusements in the open part of the fair. She said I could take my shift later, if things got busier and she needed me.

We walked along, Daniel and me, sharing chunks of Mrs. Bishop's coffee cake. It was a cooler day than we'd been having, like fall was in the air and signaling its approach.

We went past the quilting booth, and several of the ladies there called out to us. Daniel mostly. He was popular with the older ladies. In a couple of weeks he was going off to the university in Austin, and they wanted to talk about that. We didn't have many college boys in McDade.

Daniel paid for a turn at the fishing pond, and when I dropped the line over the partition, there was a tug of somebody putting on the prize. We laughed and tried to think of who it could be behind the curtain. When I raised the pole, on the end of the line was a pack of hairpins. I felt pretty sure the "fish" was Mr. Billingsley back there, and that he'd seen who was fishing the line. I tucked the hairpins into my pocket and called out a thank-you in case it was him.

Out on the grass, children and some of the men had a bowling game going, and there were horseshoes, and sack races, a hay bank stacked around an area for the pig scramble Dane wanted to compete in. He was coming in later with Eppie on Mrs. Kennedy's wagon, after they'd taken some of our corn to the gristmill for grinding. Papa had agreed to it since the oats were all planted. He wasn't happy about it, though. It meant he'd have

Nathan and Dellie to look after all evening by his lone self.

We watched a puppet show until the pig scramble began, which Eppie and Dane both made it in time for. Eppie got his pig over the hay bank first, and he did it quick, even with lard smeared all over his arms. Dane ended up fourth, for the pig he caught kept slipping away, till he got a grip on its hind feet and could drag it that way to the hay bales. Both him and Eppie laughed hard when the whole thing was over, rolling around on their backs in the grass, holding onto their bellies, having good fun. Eppie won two bits for coming in first, which was a lot of money for him.

Daniel and me strolled over to the sack races then, and watched the folks play that. There were twelve in each race, and most of the time, the youngest ones won. They were giving away different prizes according to the age of the winner. I saw one girl about twelve win a stuffed doll that Dellie would have loved.

Some of the boys from church came over and started pestering Daniel to enter the race. They needed one more, they said, to make another heat, and when he tried to resist, they hauled him by both arms to the entrance rope. Before the struggle was over with, he had taken off his jacket and pitched it to the ground. His balance wasn't any good and he staggered, trying to get his skinny legs into the feed sack. The crowd around was getting great sport out of the sight, and I was laughing too, right with everybody else.

I almost didn't feel the tap on my shoulder. It

was more a sense of having somebody standing too close to me that I felt. That sense, more than the actual tap, was what caused me to turn around.

It was Marion Beatty standing behind me. He tried to dodge out of my sight and tap my other shoulder as light as he had the first one. He was wearing his vest, and a gray hat with silver metalwork around the crown. I noticed the lump in the side of his vest, up high, nearly under his left arm.

"You caught me," he said, and just kind of smiled, sideways, only half of his mouth bending upwards. "Hello again." He took his hat off his head and held it to his chest. I'd just as soon he hadn't flashed that hair at me.

I knew I should have turned back to watch Daniel race, but my eyes wouldn't do what I willed them to. They stayed on Marion's face. Something in me wouldn't believe that anybody as bad as he was supposed to be could have a smile that nice.

"*You* come to church fairs?" I said and felt stupid as soon as I said it.

"I've been following you close to an hour now. Waiting till you were alone."

A chill went over my arm. "Why?"

"Cause I'm good at it. You didn't even know I was there, did you?" The smile spread to both sides of his face.

I shook my head and looked at the folks around us. They were all intent on the race. Not a one seemed to notice us standing there. I rubbed my arm but the goose pimples wouldn't go away.

"You wanna walk with me a while?" he said.

"I can't. I came here with somebody else—"

"I know. I saw you with him. Did you know he's losing?" He nodded towards where the race was happening.

I turned in time to see Daniel fall forward on his face into the grass. The crowd whooped with laughter. He was way behind the others, and he wiggled and rolled to get back upright, looking like a calf that had been thrown for branding. I got embarrassed for him and couldn't watch anymore.

"They got watermelon over there," Marion said, pointing towards the row of food tents. "Brought in a whole wagonload from Bastrop. You like watermelon? I know I could sure use some."

"Course I like it," I said. "Everybody does."

"Why don't I get you some then?" He wasn't smiling so big now, but his eyes still were, with little dots of yellow and copper speckled in them.

I looked at him a second more. Maybe two seconds. And then I went with him. I knew it was a terrible thing to do, to walk off from Daniel in the middle of his race, knowing he'd come out looking for me to be there. But I let Marion take ahold of my hand and lead me away from that sack race crowd. And once we got away and were walking towards where there was a wagon piled high with big, green melons, he didn't give me back my hand and I didn't ask for it.

He was taller than I remembered him being, lean and strong-boned. And with his hat back on his head and pulled low to shade his eyes, he looked more like a man than any others close to my age. I knew it was dangerous feelings I was having just then.

"Where're your brothers?" I asked without any clear reason as to why I was asking. Just so it wasn't so silent between us, I guess.

"They had other things to do." His hand gripped mine tighter. Or maybe I just imagined it did, my mind was whirling so. I kept looking to see if folks had noticed us together yet. Nobody seemed to. "Is that your fella?" he asked. "That one back there wearing the tow sack?"

"We go to church together."

"Does that mean he is or he ain't?"

"Ain't," I said like a fool. He laughed. It seemed to make him happy, me acting a fool. I let his hand go. His sweat stayed with me, though. I didn't rub it off.

"Ho there, young man," somebody behind us said in a Yankee clip. Marion turned and so did I. It was a photographer, in eastern garb, standing with his camera box and lantern bar. "Yes, you," the Yankee said to Marion. "Fifty cents for a photograph of you and your young lady. Preserve the memory of this day for posterity." He sounded like a panhandler.

I laughed and started to walk on, but Marion took me by the arm and turned me towards the box. He put his hand on my shoulder, and we stood there like that till the lantern in the man's hand exploded, blinding me for a moment. Before the stars cleared from my eyes, Marion had already gone up to the photographer and given him some money.

"One week from Monday at the rail depot," the man said as we walked away.

"He doesn't go to our church. That's for sure," I said, embarrassed about being called Marion's young lady, like there was more to it than a friendly stroll.

Marion was back to just smiling. He walked beside me slow, the spurs on his boots chattering with each of his steps. He kept his hand on the small part of my back. I couldn't seem to get away from him touching me. It made me feel awkward and shy, and terrible aware that his hand was back there where anybody could see it.

We came to the watermelon tent, and Mrs. Kennedy was behind the counter. Both her and me took in our breath when we saw each other. Her doubly when her eyes fell on Marion. "Why, Lily . . ." She said, then cut off her words.

"Miz Kennedy!" I said. "I thought you were selling lemonade."

Marion asked for two slices of melon and she went to cutting them quick, keeping her face turned away from me. I leaned on the counter, giddy with shame.

"Daniel's running in the sack race," I said. "He's over there running it now. Miz Kennedy?" I wanted her to look at me. She wouldn't. She kept carving up watermelon, slicing it into two small wedges, waving off flies with the knife. When she finished she gave both wedges to Marion, ignoring me. He handed me mine, then paid her. I didn't notice what they cost.

I could feel Mrs. Kennedy's eyes on my back as

we moved away from the tent. I wanted to run. I turned back towards the sack races.

"Slow down," Marion said. "You don't have to be in such a hurry, do you?"

I stopped; turned. He almost ran into me and had to jig to hold onto his melon. The juice from mine was already dripping, sticky, down my wrist. I held it away from me, my taste for it gone.

"I can't know you, Marion," I said.

He cocked his head at me. "What do you mean, can't? You already do."

"I mean *that* way."

"What way?" he said, and I blushed deep and hot. He took my chin with one finger and made me look at him again. He grinned. "You're just about the prettiest thing I've ever seen, Lily DeLony."

I stepped out of his reach. "There was a store clerk held up in Paige the other day," I said. "Held up with guns and shot through the head."

"I heard about it."

I tried to bore him through with one look. I don't think it worked. He kept grinning. "Well . . . ?" I said.

"Well what?"

"Well, was it you? Were you in on that holdup?" I couldn't believe myself, that I was talking like that to a Beatty. Talking to one in the first place. How come him to seem so friendly, so downright regular?

"Me?" He took a bite of melon. It made a shine just above his lip and on his cheeks. His tongue came out and licked some off. He got the rest of it with his shirtsleeve. "Is that what you think? About me?"

I nodded at his vest. "You're toting a gun."

"That don't mean I'm a killer. Maybe I have it in case of snakes. You never know about snakes. Besides . . . everybody carries a pistol around here."

"Not people I know. Not to church fairs."

He seemed to notice then. He looked around at several of the men that walked past, then he spit out a black seed. "All right," he said after a minute. "If I got rid of it would you like me better?"

"I like you just fine. That ain't it." I glanced back at the watermelon tent. Mrs. Kennedy had her hands palm down on the counter, and she was leaned way out, watching us. Marion saw her, too.

"I wouldn't of took you for a girl that cared about gossip," he said, and he sounded serious, and like his feelings were hurt. He wasn't smiling anymore.

"I don't."

"No?" He glanced Mrs. Kennedy's way.

"It's just . . . you're a Beatty. Folks are scared of you."

"What about you, Lily? Are you scared of me, too?"

"No," I lied, but I was scared. Only not the way he meant. Or maybe it was the way he meant. I knew I was shaking, and it wasn't from thinking he might shoot me. "I gotta get back," I said, backing away from him. "Thanks for the watermelon." And then I turned around and almost ran back to the sack race. I dropped my melon wedge uneaten into one of the trash barrels.

* * *

Daniel was already gone when I got there. I didn't see him any place around where the races were going on. I finally thought to look by the carriage and found him there, waiting on me to show up. He said he figured it was where I would come. The knee of his trouser was torn out, and he had a strawberry graze on his cheekbone, but I knew it wasn't either of those things causing his face to be so long.

"I checked the lemonade stand first, but you weren't there," he said.

"I suddenly ain't feeling too well," I said to him. "You'd better take me home now."

He seemed to get worried over my health then, and helped me into the carriage. "I'll come back for Missus Kennedy later," he said and started the team forward.

We went up the long road past the church buildings, new and old, then turned left, headed towards the farm. I glanced back one time and, I'm certain, saw Marion crossing the road on his paint horse, the sunstruck silver on his hatband flashing. I'm sure it was him in the quick glimpse I got before the trees overtook us, and we were out of town.

4

On the way into church the next morning, Mrs. Kennedy hardly spoke to me. She sat at our pew, though, as was usual, but it wasn't till after services, when we were out in the churchyard, after the picnic lunch was eaten and the men had started in hammering, that she mentioned yesterday at the fair to me.

She said, "It isn't my place to say it, Lily, but I've been worrying for you all night. And now I'm going to have to tell you, for your own good ..." She reached to adjust the ribbon on my bonnet. "You stay as far away from that Marion Beatty as you can get yourself, hear? You probably already know it and me warning you is just plain ... well ... silly."

"He came up to me," I said, feeling a rush of relief that she wasn't mad at me over it, or disappointed in me. "I didn't invite him, Miz Kennedy."

"I knew that was how it happened, and it's why I didn't speak to your papa about it. The more I thought it over, the more I knew you'd just got yourself in a ticklish situation you couldn't get out of. Were you afraid, dear?"

I blinked at her. "He was friendly enough to me."

"Oh, I don't doubt that. His papa was a charmer too, in his younger days. That's what makes a man like that so dangerous. They don't seem like they'd harm a flea, but you have to watch them. Especially that Marion. You know his poor mother died giving birth to him, and it might've done damage to his brain. It's said she had a devil of a time bringing him into the world." She patted my hand. "I don't want to frighten you, dear. I just thought it was something we should discuss."

"Yes ma'am," I said. "I don't have plans to ever see him again." I said it plain out, and then spent the rest of the afternoon thinking about him.

Brain damage. I didn't expect Mrs. Kennedy had ever spoken with Marion Beatty face to face. If she had, she would have known he wasn't brain damaged. His eyes were as clear and sparkly as rain water. I'd seen brain damage. Old Lucien Previne that stood out by the schoolyard waving at the wagons that passed by, he was brain damaged. He had a muddy look in his eyes when you peered at them, like there wasn't a soul inside him. And nobody thought of him as dangerous.

Daniel caught up to me later, as we were going to Mrs. Kennedy's wagon. It irritated me some how he waited till the last instant to speak to me on Sundays, made me suspect it was his mama prompting him to come. And when I looked down the line of wagons to the O'Barrs' carriage, sure enough, Mrs. O'Barr was standing there watching us.

He said he was glad to see me feeling better. And he said, "If you'd be so inclined, I'd like to pay you a call this Thursday." His eyes shifted everywhere but on me.

Mrs. Kennedy smiled down at us from where she sat beside Dellie in the wagon. What I didn't like was him asking me in front of everybody. I heard Dane and Nathan snickering. Eppie didn't make a sound but I saw him grinning, too.

"I'm leaving for Austin next Saturday, you know," Daniel said when I didn't answer right off. "I'd like to come say good-bye and pay you folks a visit before I go."

When he put it like that, and with everybody listening, I had to agree to it. Mrs. Kennedy was pleased, and she patted my knee as he walked away towards his mama and his carriage.

"Lily's got a feller," Nathan said in a singsongy voice. I swatted my Bible at him and hit him on the arm.

"He is such a polite young man," Mrs. Kennedy said. "Comes from such well-bred people, and it does show on him. He'll make someone a fine husband some day." And her saying that sent new laughter around the wagon again.

On Thursday evening when he came calling, Papa and Dane weren't yet in from the fields. Nathan was doing his barn chores, filling up the feed troughs and raking out the stalls. I sent Dellie for the jug of buttermilk I'd been cooling down in the well shaft, and I kept Daniel out on the front porch. He took the cane rocker Papa liked to sit in,

and after Dellie brought out the glasses of buttermilk, she sat down with me on the swing.

Mostly, we just sipped from the glasses, neither
of us with much of anything to say. I caught myself thinking how it was too bad Daniel didn't
have a little half-smile, or shimmering bronze hair
that winked at you in the sun, or soft brown eyes
or a voice that could turn a body's insides to
mush. He asked me could he write to me from
Austin. I didn't see what harm it could do, good
either, but I said yes anyway.

The conversation didn't liven up any till Papa
and Dane came in from the fields. After they
washed up, they joined us on the front porch, and
then Daniel seemed to speak easier. They talked
about the high yield of small grains that year, and
of Daniel's plan to come back to run his papa's
ranch. When I rose to go inside and start supper, I
didn't think any of them missed me being out
there.

"Fine young man," Papa said at the table that
evening after Daniel had left. It was the highest
compliment I ever heard him pay a stranger. And
it was, I knew, his way of giving me his blessing if
Daniel was who I chose as a man for myself.

On Saturday, after I knew Daniel O'Barr was already gone off to Austin, I wished like anything
that I could have felt sad.

In the meanwhile, strange things were happening to my head. I started picturing Marion Beatty's
face all the time. When I was ironing the clothes or
milking Bethel, his smile would pop up out of no-

where and cause me to scorch a collar or pull too hard on an udder. I felt dizzy then, like I'd climbed too high up a tree or got myself out of bed too quick. I relived every second with him at the fair that day, his hand holding onto mine or resting on my back. The watermelon shining on his lips. The jingling sound of his spurs as he walked beside me. The way his voice went low when he said what he did—that thing about me being the prettiest thing he'd ever seen. Just remembering it could make me blush.

I started thinking up reasons to go into town, just in case he might be there somewhere. I spent one whole afternoon in Mr. Billingsley's store, buying shoes for Nathan and Dellie to start school in. I kept looking out the windows, as far in the direction of the rock saloon as I could see, and telling the kids to keep trying on another pair. When we were done, I made Nathan ride out that way, by the saloon, which I usually avoided since there was hard drinking and gambling went on inside there. Marion Beatty wasn't anywhere to be seen.

The next week, I took Nathan and Dellie in to Miss Huddleton for their first afternoon of school. Nathan went without a fuss since it wasn't new to him and was a way for him to get out of farm work. But Dellie cried and clung to me, telling me she'd be good and help me more around the house if I just wouldn't leave her. It like to broke my heart, peeling her fingers off my arm, even though I knew that by that afternoon, Miss Huddleton would win her over. Dellie was shy but she was also smart, and learning to read and make her figures would soon be fun for her, I knew.

When I left the schoolhouse, I drove the buggy right down through the middle of town. Marion still was nowhere around. Not only had he seemed to disappear, but the whole Beatty bunch was gone, too. During all those weeks, those three to the end of October, folks didn't have anything to gossip about.

Then in November, during a week of Indian summer, word came of a man robbed out on the Bastrop road, pistol-whipped and left unconscious till another traveler happened by. Folks said it sounded like Beatty trouble, though the descriptions the man gave could have been anybody around these parts. And then the Austin stage was hit for a thousand dollars, the driver shot and killed. And some cattle were taken from a ranch over near the Yegua Creek. Too close. Only about seven miles, as the crow flies, from McDade. Everybody said the Beattys were responsible. It made me feel cold inside to hear it.

I laid awake nights, Dellie curled against me, and stared at the moon outside my window, and I wondered. I couldn't imagine Marion Beatty robbing people, pointing his gun in their face, especially not squeezing the trigger. I couldn't see him hurting anybody or being mean. And then I tried not to think of him at all. But his face would come to me so easy. The sideways grin, the way he tilted his head like a young pup, the shock of funny-colored hair that liked to inch out from underneath his hat. It caused me considerable despair.

* * *

I stopped expecting to see him every time I went into town, stopped getting myself gussied up just for shopping in Billingsley's store. Then it came time to start thinking of winter, though it wasn't due in our part of Texas for a few more weeks. Papa sold off some of his hay and sent me with the money for paraffin and lamp oil, for shells for the shotgun he'd use for hunting when the deer started their rut.

Mr. Billingsley took my list from me and went to gathering up my supplies. I got a skein of green wool yarn for knitting Dellie a new sweater. She was growing so fast she couldn't wear last year's anymore. I thought she might like a new one for Christmas. Mr. Milton, the store clerk, helped me load up the wagon, which I had brought since I knew there'd be too much for the buggy to hold.

It was after Mr. Milton went back to his customers, and after I'd climbed up behind the mule team, that Jack Beatty came up to me on the street. I recognized him right away, with his beady eyes and dirt-colored hair. He had Bird Hasley with him, and both of them were wearing their sidearms. Jack had on a two-gun belt, and Bird a single, long-barreled Colt's. They both had handkerchiefs tied loose around their necks, bandannas that in one pull could become face masks for robbing stages or innocent citizens.

Bird Hasley was part Comanche and just the dark sight of him sent fear up my spine. But it was nothing compared to my fear of Jack, who everybody knew was the leader of the Beatty gang. He put his hand on the sideboard of my wagon and looked at the mules.

"Are you Lily DeLony?" he said in a voice so deep it rumbled in my chest.

"Yes," I answered, terrified that he knew my name. My own voice sounded like a bird's chirp.

"I gotta message for you." He shifted and gave Bird Hasley a sidewards grin, almost an exact copy of Marion's, except on Jack it seemed mean and purely evil. "I reckon you know who I am," he said. Bird snickered, and the grin kept playing on Jack's face. "Seems I got me a kid brother what's pining his fool heart out for you. He seen you come into town a while ago, and said tell you he'd be waiting for you over at the graveyard if you cared to meet him." Then Jack let go of my wagon and backed away, raising his arms out in a shrug. "I can't talk sense into the lad. I said I'd deliver the message." Both him and Bird laughed out then.

I noticed Mr. Milton at the store window, frowning at the men beside my wagon. It gave me courage to see Mr. Milton there, looking out for me. I lifted my shoulders and my chin, holding the reins at the ready in case I had to run.

"Tell your brother," I said, "that I'd be obliged to him if he wouldn't send any more messages to me."

Bird stopped laughing and stepped towards my wagon. He wore his hair in a pigtail, and he looked so mangy I nearly gasped out loud to have him come so close. His teeth were black from tobacco. He said, "You don't have to be so goddamned holy about it."

Still smiling, Jack pulled at Bird's arm. "No, now, wait a minute, Hasley. Let her be. Sounds to me like she's maybe got good sense. It won't hurt the kid none to sit over there in the sunshine with all them spooks planted around him. Maybe sweat the love bug outta his system." Then he tipped his hat at me, and for that one second, he didn't seem quite so horrifying.

When Bird stepped back enough so's I could go, I popped the reins on the mules. I hadn't known my heart was racing so hard until I got down the road a ways. It was the half-breed that had scared me. Not Jack so much, really. Not after he took my side and kept that Indian from abusing me. Not after he got to talking and kind of laughing all the way through what he had to say, like he saw I was afraid of them.

Now that I was away and safe, I started to thinking more clear about the things Jack did say. The part about Marion pining his heart out for me. I wondered if it was the truth. And I thought about him waiting for me over at the cemetery, and how he might just keep waiting all day for me to come. It seemed rude not to at least go tell him myself to stop pestering me, and stop following me, and to never again send his brother or one of his friends to talk to me in public.

Instead of turning left towards home I veered right, and made a big circle around town—up the lane in front of the church, past Brother Parkins's house, and the Billingsley's place, past Mrs. Griffin's cottage, to the league-line furrows that ran all the way out across the Bastrop road. And to the graveyard. I don't think anybody saw me from that distance, as I crossed over the lower end of town.

5

The wagon barely fit through the iron gates at the cemetery. A roadrunner clacked his beak at me and startled the mules. I had to whip them hard to get them on the move again. And then I saw Marion, standing underneath a post oak with its leaves turning brown. He just stared at me and held onto his horse, and he had his hat off since he was among the dead. I thought it was respectful of him. My own mama's tombstone was about sixty feet behind him.

I brought the team up short right there where we were, blocking the gate from the inside, and got down off the wagon. Careful not to step on any graves, I marched towards him, firing my mind up with the scolding I planned to give him about sending me messages. When I got near enough so's I could see him good, I stopped in my tracks, my words fizzling in my head.

His left eye was traced under with black as if somebody had taken a piece of coal and drawn on him. His right cheekbone was puffed out and bruised dark in the center, turning to green at the edge. His ear was swollen up and there was a scabbing-over cut down his jaw. Even still, he stood there smiling at me, holding onto his paint horse.

"What happened to you?" I gasped out.

He shook his head one time and kept smiling. "I didn't think you'd come."

I stepped up nearer to him. The wounds on his face looked ugly and sore. My fingers rose to the place under his eye. He winced away from me before I could touch him.

"Are you in trouble?" I said.

His hand wrapped around my wrist. "Listen to me, Lily. I been thinking about all you said to me that day at your fair. And I want you to know something. I ain't no part of all that stuff you been hearing. It ain't me doing any of it." He took a breath. I couldn't stop looking at the bruises on his face. He turned my wrist over and punched around on my palm with his thumb. "Maybe it ain't in me to do it the right way. But I'd like to court you proper. If you'd let me."

"Who gave you that shiner?" I said.

He dropped my hand and turned away from me. Then he let go of his horse too, and sat down under the tree, leaning his back against the trunk. The horse whinnied but stayed where she was, only moving a foot or two away.

He set his hat on the ground beside him. "Ain't you been hearing a word I said?"

"I wanna know who walloped you. How'd that happen?"

He picked a blade of grass and stripped it down the middle. "Az," he said and stuck the blade into his mouth. "He done it. But I got him pretty good, too."

I knelt on my skirt, sort of in front of him but over to one side so's not to seem forward. "Az? Why would he beat you?"

"He don't need a reason." He grinned again with the grass clamped in his teeth. "We've been scrapping long as I can remember. It don't mean much."

It unsettled me to think of two brothers fighting that hard. Me and Dane had our times, Dane and Nathan too, but we hadn't any of us ever scarred each other. Looking at the welts on Marion's face, the fights we had in my family seemed plumb gentle.

He must have seen me thinking and known how it seemed to me. He said, "Looky here," and he stuck the blade of grass in his mouth some way, and he made it whistle.

He kept on doing it, his cheeks puffed out like a bullfrog, till I had to laugh. I plucked my own blade to try but nothing would come out of mine. He tried to arrange the grass the right way in my hand, and then against my lips. I got some of my spit on him. He didn't seem to mind.

"You ain't puckering right," he said, laughing at me.

"It's this grass blade. I need another piece." I found one about four inches long beside my knee.

He took the blade from me, tore it down the middle, and handed it back. "Think it'd be all right for me to call on you some Sunday?"

"You mean at my house?" I couldn't keep down the surprise in my voice.

"I know where you live. I think I could get there blind."

The blade of grass flittered out of my hand. "I go to church on Sundays."

"Some other day, then. You tell me which would be good."

I drew my knees up under my skirt and hugged them to me. "There ain't any day that'd be good. My papa'd take one look at you and load up his shotgun."

"Cause I'm a Beatty," he said without emotion. I nodded. He hung his head and I felt a catch in my chest. "So there ain't no way?" he said. "Is that what you're telling me?"

"I guess it is."

He studied me then, so hard I wished I could see whatever it was he saw. After a few seconds, he smiled at me again, and smiled like that till I did it back at him. It was like some secret message passing between us.

"I got something for you." He reached into the breast pocket of his vest. I noticed there wasn't a gun tucked up in there. He took out a square of parchment board and gave it to me. "Remember this?"

I opened the flap cover and there was the photograph from the church fair. A flush spread over me, and I shut the flap closed without looking at it good.

He laughed and pulled the photograph out of

my hands, opened it again. "No. You gotta look at it." He held it up in front of my face. "See us?"

In the picture, Marion stood closer to me than I remembered. He had his left leg crossed over his right at the ankle, jaunty-like. The spur on the heel of his boot jutted out to one side from underneath the hem of his britches. He had his hand on my shoulder, his hat pushed back a little so's his face showed up good. His expression wasn't a smile exactly, not a frown, either, but halfway in between, kind of dreamy-eyed. The cleft in his chin came clear and the wide, sharp angle of his jaw. It was something to behold and I found myself leaning forward, staring.

"See how you're smiling?" He put the photograph in my hand. "Wonder why you were doing that?"

I studied the picture a few more seconds, not the likeness of myself as much, though he was right about me smiling. I looked like a jack o'lantern. I closed up the cover and raised my face at him. "The sun was shining too bright in my eyes."

"That ain't it. You was smiling. Clear as day."

I shoved the picture at him. "Here."

He held up his hands like I was drawing a weapon on him. "It ain't mine."

Then he pushed himself up, swiped his hat off the ground, and held out his hand to me. I took it and he pulled me to my feet. I held the photograph against my bosom.

"This here's Mollie," he said, moving to his horse. He stroked her nose. "She's got the most heart of any mare in Texas." He laughed and kept rubbing her. "Got me outta many a jam, she has."

When he lifted me by the waist, I wasn't expecting it, and I didn't throw my leg over the saddle in time. I didn't hurt myself, but I was too surprised to speak. It shocked me that he could lift me that way, so easy like I didn't weigh but a pound or two. I moved my leg over just as he mounted up behind me. So close I could feel him all the way up my spine.

"I gotta get home now," I said, nervous then.

"Not yet." He reached around me and gathered the reins in his hands. "I got somewhere I wanna take you."

"I got that wagon loaded down, and those mules hitched up. My papa'll be expecting me home."

He nudged me back against him, said real close to my ear, "We'll hobble them." His breath gave me a tremble.

Mollie was as surefooted a horse as I'd ever seen, but then Marion handled her well, too. It was clear he loved to ride, the way we galloped free through open spaces. But he brought her down to a trot when we got into the woods. We crossed over Mr. March's land, and through the Petersons' back field, skirting around the town. Marion didn't pay much attention to fences, but I felt it was for me he avoided the town. So folks I knew wouldn't see us together. He came out on the road where our farm was, but down about a half-mile, on the other side of Mr. Grossner's place, so we were safe from Papa's eyes, too.

I was so busy enjoying myself, the ride and being near Marion, that I hardly realized we were headed for the three pointed hills folks called the Knobs, and the Beatty place beneath them. It wasn't until we turned off the road and in through a rusted gate, that I felt myself stiffen with alarm.

The road going in was worn down to dirt, but not in ruts like a wagon or a buggy would make. This was more a horse trail, and one not used all the time, because weeds had grown up and were now beaten down again from hooves going back and forth. We passed a plow rusting away and a low stock shelter barely visible in the field of Johnson grass and millet that had come up volunteer. Old man Beatty had been a farmer once, and this was all the evidence that was left.

Further down the trail, we passed the barn, from which a pack of cur dogs came running, barking and growling at us. The house was old and a ramshackle, with paint chipping off, mostly the underneath wood showing through. There wasn't any porch or awning. Glass was busted out of several windows, and boards put up in their place. A stinking pile of ash from a trash fire lay in the dirt in front of the door.

Marion pulled Mollie around the side of the house, where an old washtub stood full of water. As the mare dipped her head for a drink, he slipped down from the saddle and left me sitting up there. He bent to pet and talk to the curs that swarmed around his feet. Some of them looked half-coyote or wolf. A black one was hopping on three legs. Another one had an eye missing. They were all matted with dirt and sandspurs.

He straightened back up and grinned at me. "This's where I live. In case you ever get a hankering to see me sometime. Now get on down here and meet these dogs. You need to let them get your scent so's they'll know you next time."

I wasn't too anxious to step into that pack of curs. One in particular looked like it could eat me up if it had a mind to. But Marion was holding them back, keeping them tame, and so, being extra careful, I slid myself off the saddle.

As soon as my boot hit the ground, the toothy one snarled at me and tried to lunge. I went back up on one stirrup, but Marion had grabbed the dog by the back of its neck.

"This here's Mama," he said. "We call her that cause most of these others is her babies. Just put your hand out to her real slow. Let her get a whiff of you and she'll be all right."

I wanted to believe him, but Mama didn't look any more eager to meet me than I was her. She kept curling her lip at me, showing me her two long fangs. Marion kicked at the other dogs, trying to keep them back. Then he looked up at me perched on the one stirrup and laughed.

"Come on, Lily. If she takes to you, the rest will."

"And if she doesn't?" I said, my voice pitched high. They were barking all around me.

"I won't let her bite you. I'll choke her first. I promise you, I won't let her hurt you."

I took in a deep breath. I couldn't feel any blood in my face, but I stepped down onto the ground. Mama twitched, and a couple of the others poked their noses out real far in my direction. But for the most part, the barking got quieter.

"That's it," Marion said. "Just put your hand out now. Don't be afraid. She'll smell the fear on you if you're afraid. Don't let her get the best of you."

"I am afraid," I said, but I put my hand out, expecting her to bite it. The tip of her wet nose touched the back of my knuckles, and then the hair on her back laid down.

"See," Marion said. "She knows you're friendly." He let up on the dog's neck and she darted away. She wasn't happy about me yet, but at least she wasn't snarling. "It's Az that's made them mean. He teases them rough. He thinks it ain't no use in having dogs if they ain't fierce."

"I have a dog. I ain't usually scared of them," I said. There was still a few of them sniffing around my legs. I didn't want to move, at least not too fast. Mollie had drank her fill and turned her head to look at us. I thought about climbing back on her, but I didn't want Marion to think I wasn't game. He saw my distress and kicked at the ones still smelling me.

They took off for the house, barking and raising sand again at something over there. I was glad it wasn't me.

"Get outta here, you goddamned dogs," I heard somebody say, and then Haywood walked out from around the corner of the house. I knew it was

him because he'd gone to Miss Huddleton's school
for a while, too.

He wasn't wearing a belt or galluses on his
britches, and they were hanging clear down his
hips. No boots either. I never saw anybody walk
outside in just their socks before. Already there
were twigs and leaves and dirt stuck to them. He
had a day or two's growth of beard on his chin,
which looked like the only place where his face
hair would grow. The dogs ran out in front of him,
then on around the backside of the house in the direction of the red dirt and cedar of the Knobs.

"What's got them goddamned dogs so riled
up?" Haywood said when they were gone. Then
he saw me. He didn't smile.

"You remember Lily DeLony?" Marion said.

"Yeah. She growed up, didn't she?" Haywood
said, but he didn't act too interested in me.

He walked to the tub of water Mollie had drank
from and dipped some up onto his face. He
seemed sleepy and I suspected we'd woke him
from a nap. That too, along with his bootless feet,
seemed strange to me. Folks in my family didn't
take naps in the middle of the day. Not unless they
were sick, and Haywood didn't look sick.

"Does Jack know you got her here?" he said,
wiping his face on his sleeve.

"No. But it ain't none of his business. I'm getting
ready to take her back." Marion put his hands on
his hips, then crossed his arms, fidgeting like he
was nervous all of a sudden. "I wanted her to see
where we lived. In case she ever wanted to visit
me sometime."

That brought a smile to Haywood, and also an unpleasant grunt. He gave me a cool look. "You're dreaming, Shot. She ain't ever gonna come back here again."

Marion glanced at me then. I felt like I was being put on the spot. "I might," I said, even though I doubted it too. But Marion smiled big at Haywood, like he'd just won some kind of a bet.

"See," he said. "She might."

6

*B*y the time Marion got me back to the wagon, the sun was on the downward swing in the sky. He helped me unhobble the mules and I checked to make sure the photograph of us at the fair was still where I left it in the box under the seat. Then I started on my way home, whipping the mules into a hurry. I passed Nathan and Dellie on the road, walking home from the schoolhouse, and stopped to let them onto the wagon. I knew when I saw them more time had gotten away from me than I'd thought.

Dellie chattered about all the things she was learning, and though it did me good to know she was happy with school now, I couldn't listen to her. My mind was a mile ahead, thinking up the story I would give Papa for being so late. As I turned the wagon in through our gate, my hands were shaking mightily.

Neither Papa nor Dane was there. Not in the fields nor up around the house. Old Joe, our only horse, was gone from the barn, and so was the saddle we used on him. Knuck, our coondog, pranced around us as Nathan helped me unhitch the team. Dellie started carrying in what store supplies she could handle alone.

"Wonder where Papa is," Nathan said, and it wasn't like him to worry. I wondered the same thing, but I didn't speak. It wasn't usual for Papa to leave the farm untended. I prayed they weren't out looking for me.

Nathan helped me get the heavy things in from the wagon. The coal oil gave us trouble, but hauling it together, we got the drum into the barn. I noticed then that Papa's Sharps was gone from the shelf where he usually kept it. The shotgun was still there, useless without the shells he'd sent me to town for. I put the new box on the shelf beside the shotgun, and wondered why it was Papa had gone off toting his army rifle. I snuck the photograph of me and Marion into the house and locked it inside my Bible.

I set about fixing supper and sent Nathan out to double-check the fields. I knew it was no use, but it gave him something to do besides stir around underfoot. I had the fire going when he came back in and said there wasn't any sign of Papa or Dane anywhere.

By dark, they still hadn't come home, and I had started getting bad worried by then. I paced from window to window, letting out big breaths of air to calm myself. I fed Dellie and Nathan and got them on into bed. Then I did my best to keep the men's supper warm, wrapping the plates in towels, and when they didn't come still, scraping the food back into pans and burying them in the fireplace ash.

If they'd only just ride by the house one time, I kept thinking, they'd see I was safe and at home. I made sure to keep a lamp in the window, so's the light would show out on the road. And I swore to myself I'd never cause Papa this much trouble again, that I'd take whatever whipping I had coming to me, and that I'd never, ever let Marion Beatty get my mind so tangled I lost track of my duties. A couple of times, I thought I saw a torchlight go by on the road.

Around midnight, Knuck took to barking, and then I heard the barn door open on its squalling hinges. I looked out and saw Papa and Dane putting up old Joe, and another horse I didn't recognize. Dane held the lantern, and when I stepped out on the porch, knowing my time had come, he squinted at me and his face looked all twisted up.

"They got Eppie," he said, his voice cracking like it did now that it wanted to change deeper.

Papa glanced to see who Dane was talking to. I avoided Papa's eyes and came down the porch steps. The night had turned nippy and I rubbed at my arms.

"What?" I said. "Who got him?"

"Them Beattys." Dane spit out the words in hatred.

"Now son . . ." Papa stepped away from the shelf where he'd just laid down his rifle. I hoped that he'd seen I'd gotten the shells for the shotgun. He fuzzled Dane's head. "Could of been Ku Kluxers."

"Miz Kennedy says it's Beattys." Dane looked ready to bawl. "We couldn't find him nowhere."

"You mean Eppie's lost?" I went closer to the barn. I was awful sorry for Eppie, but for myself, I felt only relief. They hadn't been out hunting for me after all. Hadn't even known I'd come home late.

"Disappeared," Papa said. "Ava Kennedy put the alarm out this afternoon and we've been searching for him since."

"The whole town. She lent me one of her horses," Dane said. "But we ain't found him yet."

They came inside then, and while I set their supper out, they gave me the whole story. According to Mrs. Kennedy, Eppie had been just fine at lunch. He'd taken his plate to eat out back on her porch like always. Then he headed out to work the cattle. He'd been cutting calves from the herd, getting them ready to sell off to a Bastrop butcher Mrs. Kennedy did business with regular. Eppie'd been riding his favorite cowpony, Red, and that was the last time Mrs. Kennedy saw him.

She'd gone out herself a couple of hours later, to find out how come Eppie was taking so long to round up the calves. And that's when she found Red, laid over dead in the pasture, a hole shot clean through his left eye and out behind his right ear. And Eppie nowhere to be found.

She thought it was the Beattys that did it, but I knew different. It was a horrible tale all right, and I understood her worry for Eppie. But inside myself, I felt giddy with gladness. For it was proof to me that Marion wasn't lying about his innocence in all those crimes. He wasn't a murdering scoundrel like folks said. He'd been showing me his dogs when Eppie was taken. And Haywood had been there too, napping in the middle of the afternoon. And I'd seen with my own eyes, Jack Beatty up town just after lunch, so I figured if folks could be wrongly accusing the Beattys of this crime, they could be wrong about some of the others, too.

When they finished eating their supper, Papa looked at Dane and said, "We gotta get some sleep." They planned to meet the other men in town tomorrow at dawn and resume the hunt for Eppie. I left the supper dishes stacked on the sideboard so as not to disturb their rest, and went off to bed myself.

Eppie didn't turn up during the night, but when the men met in town to start the search again, they found Billingsley's store broken into and ransacked. No money was missing but the safe had five holes bored into it with a drill all around the lock, and done in a way that seemed the person drilling had known about safe-cracking. Why the robbers had stopped their work was the cause of a lot of arguing, but the general feeling was that they'd been scared off somehow, and most probably when they'd seen the torchlights of the men looking for Eppie the night before.

The break-in at Billingsley's store caused a bigger stir even than Eppie's disappearance. Some of the men rode straight away to Bastrop, seeking Sheriff Jenkins. The search for Eppie tapered off, and after a day or two, stopped all the way.

Half the folks figured Eppie just decided to move on and, being a colored, hadn't thought to tell Mrs. Kennedy of his intention. Half of the other half thought he'd been Ku Kluxed. And the rest, Mrs. Kennedy and Dane included, still held the Beattys accountable. Fact is, Dane believed that taking Eppie was part of the Beattys' plan all along, to get folks to looking one way while they cracked the safe at Billingsley's store. But if that was so, how come Eppie hadn't turned up yet, and why was the safe left uncracked? The whole thing had the town in an uproar.

For my own part, I stayed out of it as much as I could. I didn't give my opinion, but I didn't see Marion anymore—except to look at his picture—while the uproar was going on. I heard, though, that Sheriff Jenkins and a deputy had gone out to the Beatty place to ask questions, and that he'd also visited the McLemores down in the bottom. But no arrests were made at either place.

As Thanksgiving neared, folks got busy planning their dinners, some preparing for visiting kinfolk to come. School let out and wouldn't start back again till January, when all the holidays were over.

I went to town and took Dellie with me for spices I needed, and canned mincemeat for the pies I planned to make. I got to see for myself, and up close, the safe with the five bore holes in it. Mr. Billingsley had it moved out front of the counter, either because so many asked to see it, or to keep the public temper fired up.

As I was paying Mr. Milton for my purchases, Dellie poked her finger into one of the safe holes and got it stuck. She cried while we pried her loose, using cooking lard for grease. She ended up with only a little scratch under her nail, but otherwise there wasn't any harm done.

"You have a letter here somewhere," Mr. Milton said, wiping the lard off his fingers with a rag. He bent to look under the counter where they kept the mail box.

"Me?" I said, patting Dellie's back. She was still sniffling a little from the fuss she'd put up.

Mr. Milton picked out an envelope and turned it over like he was checking its condition. "I couldn't help but notice," he said, a smile twitching his chin whiskers. "It came from Austin. Master O'Barr, I believe."

I snatched the letter from his hand, embarrassed that somebody else besides me had to see it. "Thank you," I said and tucked the envelope into my skirt pocket.

I gave Dellie half the packages to carry, though she whined that her finger hurt too much to do so. She stopped her whining, though, when Mr. Milton brought out a twist of licorice for her from a jar behind the counter. He wouldn't let me pay for it, which was a good thing since I didn't have any money for extras today. I eyed the piece of candy as Dellie chewed. The smell of it made my mouth water.

When we left the store, I saw Marion Beatty coming out of the rock saloon with Robert Stevens, who lived out near the county line, and with Jeff Fitzpatrick, who I knew by name only. It was said Jeff had been a cowpuncher before coming to McDade, and he still had the look of it on him—

leathered face, dusty, striped pants tucked down into scuffed boots. Willie Griffin was with them and he looked staggering drunk. Marion's black eye and the bruises had all healed. I didn't think he saw me, and I pretended I didn't him, either.

I got Dellie in the buggy quick, and climbed in after her. We rode out of town going the other way, away from the farm, so's I wouldn't have to drive right by the four of them. Then I took the league-line road and circled back. My heart was hammering like a pigeon in a wolf's mouth.

The new church building was finished enough for services to be held there, and we planned that for the Sunday after Thanksgiving. There were still a few things left inside to do, like paint and some finish work. But the men labored on Saturday, getting the pews moved over from the old church house and toting over Brother Parkins's special pulpit.

Seeing Marion in town so sudden-like had distracted me so much I forgot all about Daniel's letter until Sunday morning when I put my good skirt back on again, and found the envelope in the pocket. I read it quick as I plaited Dellie's hair. It said mostly about the studies he had and how they were holding classrooms in the old capitol building since they weren't through constructing the new university yet. He said he'd just about decided to go into law when he graduated, though he hadn't told his papa of this decision yet. And he said he'd be coming home at Christmas and hoped he could see me then. I just barely had time to fold up the pages and tuck them into my drawer before Dane hollered that Mrs. Kennedy was outside waiting.

We were planning a dedication on the church-yard after Brother Parkins's sermon, and all the ladies were bringing a dish for a potluck supper. I took the extra mincemeat pie I'd made at Thanksgiving, and Mrs. Kennedy brought stewed cranberries. We were looking forward to all the good food there'd be. But we never got to the dedication part that day. As soon as Dane drove the wagon up the lane, we knew something terrible had happened.

The undertaker's hearse was parked with its rear to the church doors. Dr. Vermillion's cart was there, and the sheriff. Folks were milling all around the new front steps, murmuring low and shaking their heads. Some of the women were crying and praying, and looking pale.

Dane jumped down first and ran. Then I followed, after making Dellie and Nathan sit tight in the wagon with Mrs. Kennedy. There wasn't anything to see, but I heard Mr. Milton talking, in low and horrible tones, to some of the other newly arrived.

Brother Parkins had come over to the church early that morning, from his house next door. To light up the stoves before folks came to worship. We'd had our first cold snap blow through the night before, and he didn't want anyone to catch a chill inside the new building. When he got there he found the dead and beaten body of Eppie, stretched out on the altar like an offering from some vile heathen. He'd been stripped naked and had a cross carved into his chest with a buck knife, from gut to gullet and armpit to armpit.

It was the most gruesome story I'd heard since the Notch Cutters gang was broken up back in '77. Dane flew into a fit and beat his fists on the back of the hearse, shouting for somebody to let him in with Eppie. It took Mr. Milton and a sheriff's deputy to pull Dane back and carry him to the wagon, where Mrs. Kennedy had already fainted dead away. I never knew who told her about it, but both Dellie and even Nathan sat back there like good angels and kept her head from bouncing as I drove the wagon to the farm.

Papa came running out of the barn when he heard us home so soon. He carried Mrs. Kennedy inside the house and put her in his bed for me to tend. Then he took Dane outside with him. "To work off some of that steam," he said, and put his arm around Dane's shoulders. It was the most affection I ever remembered Papa showing to any of us. He knew Dane was aching for Eppie and needed his mind onto something else.

To me, the killing of Eppie, the way it was done with that cross carved into his breast, clearly pointed to the Klan as the culprits. Around here, they mostly worked on Mexicans and Indians that tried to get too close in with white folks. But they worked in secret and in that awful way, with crosses as if they were doing God's work. There wasn't any doubt in me who murdered Eppie.

And so it came as a surprise to me when Mr. Milton and Mr. Bishop and Brother Parkins himself showed up at our door around supper time. And they asked for a word with Papa outside, and of course, Dane went out there with them.

Mrs. Kennedy was awake by then, but she wouldn't eat supper. Not even her own stewed cranberries, which I had rewarmed and set out in her same good china bowl. She sat at the table sipping on tea sweetened with honey from Mr. Grossner's hives. I left her there and went to the window to hear the menfolk talk.

Mr. Milton did the speaking, rubbing at his goatee, saying, "The sheriff's hands are tied unless we catch them in the act. We know all this. You can't convict on hearsay evidence. We've had this problem before."

Papa just stood there, nodding, not really going along, I didn't think, with anything the other men said. I was pretty sure he tended towards the Klan as the murderers, same as me.

"My guess is," said Brother Parkins, "that it's the McLemores instigating the trouble. Seems strange to me that no sooner do they come into town than those Beatty boys become unmanageable."

"The McLemores *are* Beattys." Mr. Bishop's voice rose out, and he kind of stomped his foot as he spoke. Or maybe I just noticed it since his boots were so spit-shined and his feet so small. "They're all kin to each other. And until they're all run out of town, we'll never any of us have peace of mind."

Dellie tugged at me. "What're they saying, Sissy?" she said, and I hadn't seen she was even there until then. Nathan stood at the other window, peering out through the curtains.

"Y'all get back to your supper," I said in a whisper, and gave Dellie a little push towards the table. She went but Nathan kept peeking, ignoring me, till I pinched his ear. He yelped and I saw Papa look back at the window. I ducked away with Nathan, afraid Papa'd notice me standing there, spying.

It seemed like an hour before they came inside. Their supper had gotten cold. Any appetite I'd had crawled away while I was waiting for them to get back. They walked in the door, Papa first and next Dane, and both of them had on grim faces.

"What'd they have to say?" I asked, following them to the table.

Papa acted like I hadn't spoken. He said, "Dane, you eat your supper, then see Miz Kennedy home."

"Thank you, Josh. You've been too kind." Mrs. Kennedy smiled at Papa. She wasn't in her right mind yet. Her eyes were all red and swollen up. But I was too curious about the conversation that had happened outside to worry over her just then.

"What was that all about out there, Papa?" I said again and sat down, but I didn't touch my plate of food.

"Man talk," he said, and tucked his bib into his shirt.

7

Dane unwrapped the chaw of tobacco I'd stolen out of Papa's pouch. I'd done the dishes quick, and after the others went on to bed, waited on the porch for Dane to get back from taking Mrs. Kennedy home. The tobacco was for bribery.

"What'd they say out there? Those men that came by here?" I asked, as Dane sniffed the pinch, then fingered it into his jaw. He chewed.

"It's them Beattys. Folks are tired of buckling under to them." His mouth was so stretched I could barely make out his words. I knew then I shouldn't have given him the chaw till I got my story out of him.

"Buckling under?"

He nodded. Brown juice dribbled down his chin. He wiped it with the back of his hand. "Mister Bishop says folks in this town gotta get tough."

"What'd he mean?"

Dane shrugged and kept working the wad in his mouth, softening it, sucking the juice. "That's what they're having the meeting for."

"Meeting? What meeting?"

"Town meeting at the new church house. Tomorrow at sundown. They'll be discussing what steps to take against them murdering cowards."

I pulled my nightdress taut over my knees and sat there hugging myself, staring up at the starry sky. I was trembling but it wasn't from the cold. My shawl was wrapped tight around my shoulders. "Will you be going to it?"

"If Papa lets me. I wanna get them Beattys as much as anybody." He was talking too loud.

"Shhhhh . . ." I said, glancing back at the door. If Papa was to wake up, there'd be a whipping in store over the tobacco in Dane's mouth. For both of us. "Will you tell me what's decided? If you do get to go to that meeting?"

"What's it to you?" He spat a glob that sailed over the porch steps and landed shining in the grass. "You weren't even friends with Eppie."

"I liked Eppie just fine. I just don't think the Beattys did it."

Dane gave me a harsh look, then he got up and brushed off his britches. "What do you know? You're just a female. Stick to cooking."

After he went inside I sat out there awhile and watched the leaves falling off the trees all around the house.

There'd been another time when we'd had a band of vigilantes form, to bust up the gang of cutthroats everybody called the Notch Cutters. I hadn't been more than six years old then, but I recalled hearing how those Cutters had been caught red-handed cattle thieving from a rancher over in Williamson County, on the other side of the Knobs; and how they were killed for it and wrapped in

the hides of the stolen beeves, then left to the buz-
zards in the cedar brakes outside town. The
thought of something that evil happening to Marion made my flesh crawl.

I wondered should I try to tell him of the
meeting? And if I decided yes, how could I get
word to him before tomorrow night without Papa
knowing, or Dane? My mind went back on that
day at the graveyard and to Marion whistling on
that blade of grass, and to us riding fast and free
on Mollie. My heart filled up all over again thinking of it. How strange I'd felt with him pressed so
near behind me, all giddy and happy. Like somebody in love.

Later, lying in bed with Dellie snoring soft beside me, I couldn't close my eyes for anything. The
moon was high and bright. A Comanche moon,
Papa called it, lit up the room so I could see Dane
and Nathan in the other bed, still and quiet. I had
to get word of the meeting to Marion. So he could
get out of town quick, before they ran him out. Or
worse.

It was nearing midnight, maybe later, when I
crept out of bed and gathered up some clothes.
Nathan stirred as I pulled open the chifforobe but
I froze in place like a squirrel till his breath went
long again. I stowed Dane's britches and my boots
under my arm and tiptoed barefoot into the front
room. Floorboards creaked under my weight, even
as I tried to step lightly, staring at the opening to
Papa's room. I held my breath until I was all the
way outside and off the back porch. Then I

stopped to get dressed. I was glad for the Comanche moon and the light it gave.

I swept off my feet and pulled on the boots. Knuck heard me and came on the run, whining for a pat. I tried to keep him quiet. I'd come too far to let a hound dog give me away. The barn door squeaked when I opened it.

I threw the saddle on Joe's back. He nickered low one time and I grabbed his nose to shut him up. I led him to the gate, tried to open it without clanking the rails. They clanked together anyway. I decided then that if somebody was to hear me and come out of the house, I'd ride off as fast as I could make old Joe run. Nobody appeared. I couldn't keep Knuck from following us though. He circled out in front of the horse as if he knew someplace inside his dog head which way we were going.

The road was white and ghostly in the still night. I'd never been out this late alone and I got the jitters. Knuck barked at a horned owl that sat on Mr. Grossner's fence post till the bird flapped off into a line of trees. Bull bats swooped us a few times and they upset the dog, too. No matter how hard I scolded, Knuck wouldn't shut up. I heeled Joe hard in the flank, thinking I could outrun the hound. Knuck kept up with us for a half mile or more before he gave out and stood tuckered in the road behind us. He stared after us a while, then turned back towards the farm.

I kept Joe at a run until we were out of sight of Knuck, then slowed down some. I couldn't risk tiring out the horse too much, or Papa would know in the morning that Joe'd been taken out during the night. I walked him the last mile to the Beatty place, getting more nervous and less sure I was doing the right thing.

Outside their land, I stopped old Joe and sat there in the saddle trying to figure how to bring Marion out without the others coming too. I didn't have a plan for that, and I realized then I should have thought this thing out better. Likely as not, I'd get myself shot riding up cold like this in the middle of the night. But I'd come this far, and there wasn't anything to do but head on inside their fence and take my chance.

As soon as I turned in the gate, the pack of dogs came flying down the road at me, howling and snarling. Mama had forgotten me, and she bared her teeth and snapped at Joe's legs. I talked steady and low to calm the horse and keep him from throwing me into the middle of the brood. Joe didn't want to go any further, though, and I had to heel him hard to get him to move. That was just what I shouldn't have done, and I realized it as soon as my heels dug in. He reared up on his hind legs and let out a cry. I hung onto his mane with all the strength in my arms. He reared again and I felt myself slipping.

The *blook* of a rifle sounded from somewhere. My direction sense was twisted, with me busy trying to stay mounted. But I flew off old Joe's back, anyway. I heard a scream and hardly knew it as my own voice till I hit the ground. The air left my lungs, cutting off any scream that might have still been coming out of my throat. I didn't have energy left to roll away from Joe's bucking, but he ran off so it didn't matter none. The pack of dogs took out after him. I was about to haul myself up and chase them down, when a heavy boot anchored onto my shoulder and the cold end of a rifle shoved against my nose.

"Don't move," a deep voice said.

The breath whooshed all at once into my chest and whistled in and out of my mouth. The figure above me was shadowy. I didn't recognize the voice or the shape. There wasn't a hat on his head but the moonlight gave no clue to the hair color.

"Who're you?" the voice said.

"Lily DeLony," I stammered.

I wanted that rifle barrel out of my face. It lifted an inch or two. Not enough for me to get away, and I still had the boot heel planted in my armpit. Off in the distance, I heard Joe baying and the dogs after him.

"What you here for?" the man said.

"To speak to Marion Beatty." I don't know what made me say his whole name like that. I'd have been better off to have called him just plain Marion. Aroused less suspicion that way. Like I knew him good enough for first names. The rifle returned to the side of my nose.

"What for?" The voice was gruffer.

I heard people running up to us. Sounded like two more, or maybe three. They had a lantern. I caught the flicker of light from the corner of my eye. One said, "What you got there, Henry?"

"A girl. In boy's pants," the one with the rifle answered. His boot lifted off my arm. I hadn't known till then that he was hurting me, and I'd wrenched my back in the fall off Joe. The barrel of the rifle didn't move from my face. "Says she come to talk to Shot."

Boots scraped the ground around my head. The one holding up the lantern swung it high over me and I saw his face then. It was Haywood. Azberry and Charlie Goodman stood with him.

"That's his girl," Haywood said. He reached a hand down to me and the rifle moved aside.

"I'll be goddamned." Azberry laughed, showing his teeth. "You mean Shot's got hisself a split-tail."

I took Haywood's hand and stood up. I felt anger blush on me as I swept dirt off my sleeves. In different circumstances I'd have belted Azberry's mouth for using such filthy talk.

"Jack ain't gonna like this," Henry said. "Strangers showing up here." He was Henry Pfeiffer. I'd known it as soon as I heard his name. I was lucky he hadn't shot me. Rumor was he'd shot a man's lip off one time. Somebody he'd been in a card game with.

"Jack's off getting his own piece of tail," Az said. He scratched at his chin and looked at me. I didn't like the way he did it, running his eyes down to my feet. "Ain't much to her, is there?"

Haywood shifted the lantern to his other hand and peered hard at me. "What you come here for, girl?"

"I need to tell something to Marion. To all of you." I wet my lips, my mouth as dry as a prairie. Joe was still bawling, way off now. "Think you could sic your dogs off my horse?"

"Go get them, Az. Help him, Henry." Haywood

kept his attention on me. Az reached out and gave him a shove.

"You ain't giving the orders, shithog. I'll take the girl. You go get her horse." Az put his palm on Haywood's chest and moved him aside like he was made of nothing. Then Az turned to me. "Let's hear it. What you come to tell us?"

My heart thumped. I couldn't recall ever having seen Azberry Beatty this close up before. He was rough-looking and smelled bad, and he had scar pits all over his face that even his beard couldn't hide.

"Is Marion here?" I said, my voice weak.

Az grinned again. "He's in bed sucking on his thumb like a good little babe. Talk to us now. Tell us what you come to say." He stepped in nearer to me.

I swallowed. I wished like anything I hadn't come and prayed those dogs weren't tearing up old Joe. I didn't want to help Az by telling him about the town meeting, but there didn't seem to be anything else for me to do. I took a step back from him.

"Folks in town are planning a meeting tomorrow night. They're talking against you all," I said.

"That so?" Az closed the space between us again. "How do you know about it?"

"Some men came to my house to tell my papa to be there. I was worried for Marion."

Az hawed at that and turned to Charlie Goodman. "She was worried for Marion," he said, mocking me. Charlie laughed. So did Henry Pfeiffer. Az looked back at Haywood. "Go tell the little bastard his split-tail's out here panting after him."

Haywood handed the lantern to Charlie and backed away. Then he turned towards the house. I didn't want him to go. I knew nothing at all about him, but I felt less safe after he left.

"You done good coming to tell us that," Az said to me and looked me over again. He walked behind me. I kept my eyes forward. "There sure ain't much to you, is there?"

"Az—" Henry said. "Maybe we oughta go find her horse. He was bucking her pretty good when I come up. Charlie can stay with her."

"I might like to buck her myself," Az said from behind me. He got back around to my front, and his eyes were the coldest I'd ever seen. I shivered. He stared me down. "If she had a little more meat on her bones."

"Where is this meeting?" Charlie Goodman said. He didn't sound any friendlier.

I pretended I wasn't scared, tried to sound angry when I answered. "At the church."

"New or old?" This came from Henry.

"New, I guess."

They talked about that for a minute, the three of them. And I was glad their attention was on something besides me. It seemed like it took forever before Haywood brought Marion out. He came running to me, and I don't know what happened inside me. In my right mind, I'd never have gone to him the way I did. Not in front of the others. But relief at seeing him swelled up so big inside me I thought I'd pop. I raced towards him, and when he put out his arms, I went into them.

He pulled me in hard. His coat smelled woolly and the lint from it tickled my nose, but I felt better right away. Protected.

"Aww, now ain't that sweet." It was Azberry's voice.

"Leave them be, Az," Haywood said.

Marion loosened up his hold on me enough to peer into my face. He was smiling. "Well, it ain't how I expected. But I'm glad you came to visit me."

"I've got something to tell you," I whispered.

"Let's go find her horse," Henry said.

"Good idea before I puke up my guts at all this mush," Az said. "Leave Shot to his skinny poontang."

I felt Marion stiffen. "Shut your mouth, Az."

"Who's gonna make me?" Az came closer to us, gave Marion's shoulder a shove so he bumped into me, off-balance. "You don't want me to whup your ass right here in front of this here little girl, do you? Cause you know I can. And you know I will. In a second. Any way you want it."

They stood there glaring at each other, and I was afraid that because I was here Marion would act in a way he shouldn't. He was taller than his brother, but also much more slight of build. Az had powerful shoulders and broad, coarse hands. I remembered the bruises and cuts on Marion's face from before.

Charlie Goodman hooked his arm around

Azberry's neck. "Come on, Az. Let's go get that horse."

When they were gone, I stepped away from Marion, remembering myself finally, and feeling shy then without the lantern light. He picked straw out of my hair, and by the light of the moon, I saw the smile come back on his face. The top to his long johns showed underneath his coat. I'd woke him from his sleep.

"They're having a meeting at the church tomorrow night," I said.

His finger touched my lip. "Haywood's already told me about it. You care for me, don't you, Lily?"

I almost couldn't stand being so close to him again—the way the moonlight was catching his eyes and making them sparkle. A big choke came to my throat that I couldn't swallow.

His lips pressed my brow, almost right between my eyes. I watched his Adam's apple bob up his neck. Then he bent his head and rested his forehead against mine, looking at me, our noses almost touching. My knees felt like the hinges had given out, and I remembered getting thrown off Joe and that I'd be sore for it tomorrow.

"I don't really know you very well," I said. "Just what folks say about you is all. And ain't any of it too good."

"I'll tell you something about me." He lifted his head from mine and put his fingers in my hair. "Simon. That's my middle name. Marion Simon. Ain't that the worst thing you ever heard?"

Then his lips brushed mine and it was awkward and clumsy, and it didn't last but about two seconds. He seemed embarrassed by it. I know I was. Nobody besides my mama had ever dared to kiss me. We didn't either of us know what to say. But then we didn't need to. Two rifle shots rang out before we could get back to talking again.

8

Marion whirled around, away from me, in the direction of the shots. Then we heard the dogs yelping, and somebody's voice, though I couldn't make out what was said. It was just voices coming to us on the wind. Marion took my arm and started walking me towards the house.

"What's wrong?" I said. "What's going on?"

I stumbled on a rut but he kept me from falling, kept me moving forward and at a quicker pace than was natural for me. The voices were getting closer to us, and I thought I spied the lantern light far across the field.

We got to the barn and Marion pulled me inside. It was warmer in there and I was glad for it, but I wished he would talk to me again. He seemed nervous and he was making me so.

"Soon as they get your horse back, I'll see you home," he said, lighting a lantern that hung on a hook by the barn door. "You shouldn't be out on the road this late alone." He sounded suddenly grim and I longed for the happiness I'd felt from him a few minutes before.

"What's wrong?" I said, watching him get the

saddle onto Mollie. He shook his head, then peered at me over the top of her as he yanked in the cinch, looking at me like he was trying to decide how much to say.

"Az just shot my dog," he answered finally.

"How do you know?"

"I heard it." He gave the saddle a tug to check if it was on good. "He's been threatening to do it. It's cause of you. He's trying to rile me up. Make me look bad in your eyes."

"He's just horrible mean."

It slipped out of my mouth before I thought how I was speaking of Marion's brother and that he might take offense. He didn't seem to. He led Mollie to the barn door and grabbed up the lantern.

"He wouldn't be showing off so bad if Jack was here. Come on. They'll be bringing your horse soon."

I followed him and Mollie out into the night. We both looked towards the field. The group was coming, all clumped together. Haywood had old Joe in tow. Az was carrying Henry's rifle over his shoulder and a dead dog by its back heels. None of the other dogs were along.

"Where's Jack?" I said, not really caring, just to deaden the sickening sight of Az swinging that dog carcass like it was a coon he'd just hunted down.

"Over in Rockdale getting married."

That surprised me enough to take my eyes away from the group coming at us. Jack Beatty married? Somehow matrimony didn't fit with the man I saw in town that day with Bird Hasley. I couldn't imagine who'd marry him.

Marion stood there waiting for the others to get within speaking range. Azberry walked up first and plopped the dead dog on the ground between him and where Marion stood holding onto Mollie.

"That goddamned mutt like to bit my leg off." Az was grinning.

Marion didn't say a thing. Just stared hard at Az. I looked down at the corpse. I couldn't stop myself. It was Mama laying there in the dirt. I hadn't liked her, but I felt bad seeing her dead like that, her dark tongue lolling out of her mouth. The bullet hole at the base of her neck just looked like a round dirt spot on her, hardly any blood, nothing enough to kill her.

Haywood came towards me, leading Joe. "I caught your horse. He's pretty spooked. Better ride him easy."

I took Joe by his bridle and pulled him across the space between where Marion and Az stared at each other back and forth. Joe stepped neat over the dog and didn't hit her with his hooves. When we were up beside Mollie, I climbed on Joe's back. He twitched a little, but he let me get in the saddle and set my boots right in the stirrups.

Marion saw me moving to go then, and snapped back from the trance he'd been in, staring down Azberry. Haywood took the lantern as Marion mounted Mollie, then we rode down the trail, headed towards the gate and the road to home.

With Marion beside me, I wasn't nervous about the darkness. Old Joe was tired after running from the dogs, so we went slow. Marion stayed quiet at first, and I thought he must be grieving for his dog. We'd gone most of a mile before he spoke, and then when he did, it wasn't at all what I expected to hear.

"How come you looked past me in town the other day?" he said.

He took me off guard. I didn't think he'd seen me outside Billingsley's store, and I was glad it was night so he couldn't see me now, turning red.

"There's been so many things going on lately," I said. "So much talk. So much killing and thieving. I guess I let it color my mind some."

"It ain't any of it me, Lily. I told you that before. I ain't even any good with a gun." He laughed then like it was plain silly to even mention. "It's how come them to all call me Shot. Cause I ain't one. They gave me that come-by name as a josh. Do you believe all this I'm saying to you? It's important to me that you do."

I looked at him. He had his head cocked in my direction, his hair shining. "I wanna believe you," I said.

"Then do. Why would I lie to you?"

"I don't know. It's just . . . They found Eppie today. Miz Kennedy's boy. Killed dead in a terrible way. And folks are saying it's you, Beattys, that did it."

"That's a bald lie."

"It's why I came to tell you of the meeting. I think you should get outta town for a while."

"But I ain't done nothing. Besides getting born

to the wrong family. They can't hold a man to count for something he ain't got control on."

He rode along quiet for a minute or so, keeping tight hold on Mollie so she wouldn't run out ahead of old Joe. The moon reflected a pair of eyes off in a clump of brush. A coon or a jackrabbit. Our horses' hooves seemed to hit the ground right together.

"If I was to go ... leave town?" he said, slow and thoughtful-like. "Would you come with me?"

The question jolted me. It seemed senseless, and I couldn't believe he even asked it. "No. I couldn't," I said, then searched quick for an excuse I could give. "There wouldn't be anybody to look after Dellie. My little sister."

He seemed to ponder that. His head turned my way. "If it weren't for that, would you?"

"I'd think about it," I said, just so's he'd quit talking about it.

"Well, in that case, I ain't going nowhere without you," he said, and I knew then I'd given him the wrong answer.

At the edge of Mr. Grossner's place, I pulled Joe to a halt. As Marion reined in his mare, she nudged her nose at Joe and snorted. There didn't seem to be anything more for me to say. I felt I'd wasted a trip in the night, for it was clear he wouldn't heed my warning.

I looked off down the road where the moonlight touched the roof of my house, and the barn, and the smokehouse between the two. "I can go on in alone from here," I said.

"I'll wait here till you're inside safe."

"It'd be better if you didn't."

He reached across and took the rein from my hand. His other arm slid around my waist and he lifted me, pulling me towards him, out of my saddle and swung me sideways onto his horse. It still seemed impossible to me that he could do that so easy. Swing me one-handed and keep check on Joe at the same time. I wanted to tell him to stop picking me up like that, like I was a bag of duck down or something, but it never got out of my mouth.

He kissed me. This time it was more and different than the last. More tender yet stronger, less timid, like he was staking a claim on my heart. His horse jostled us a little, and my arms went around his neck to hold on. He took it as something else, a sign from me that I was agreeable to this kiss, and he squeezed me even tighter, keeping Joe's reins in one hand. I stopped being able to breathe after a while, and then his mouth moved off mine. His lips slipped down my chin to my throat. Goose pimples broke out all over me.

"I gotta get inside," I whispered. I didn't want to leave, but didn't want to be any later getting inside the house, either. Papa rose at four-thirty, which wasn't all that long from now. I had to brush briers off Joe, and hide Dane's torn britches before I could get into bed myself. And aside from all that, Marion kept kissing on me like he couldn't get enough of it. It was making me a mite shaky.

"Meet me somewhere tomorrow night," he whispered near my ear.

"I can't."

"Yes you can. You got out tonight."

"It's too big a risk."

"I'd risk anything for you, Lily."

But I'd meant risky for me, not him. Papa would whip me good if he caught me sneaking out like this—to meet any man, but especially Marion Beatty. Yet I heard myself say, "Where?"

"Here." He raised his head and looked all around us. His breath came shallow. "See that big oak tree yonder. I'll wait over there. When I see you come out, I'll signal you. Come afoot. It'll be easier. Mollie can carry us both."

"That tree's on Mister Grossner's land. He doesn't like trespassing."

"I can take care of myself, Lily," he said, smiling.

I let him kiss me one more time, but I cut it short and slid down from his horse. Since I was already on the ground, I led Joe by hand to the gate. I told Marion to head on, that I'd be fine from there, but he didn't go. He sat, kind of leaned over Mollie's neck, and watched me take Joe in through the farm gate. He was still there the last I looked, just before I took Joe to the barn and unsaddled him.

Knuck was either off hunting somewhere or else sound asleep. He didn't make a ruckus. I was grateful for that. I brushed down Joe quick. It was hard to see inside the dark barn. I'd have to hope Papa didn't go anywhere in the morning and that I'd have another chance at the job in the daylight.

In the barn, I changed back into my nightdress. I rolled Dane's britches around my boots on my way to the back porch, and eased in the door. I stuffed the bundle behind the stove until I could get the boots cleaned off and a needle and thread after the pants. I tiptoed past Papa's room and into my own. Nathan and Dane were still snoring like they had been.

As I slipped into the covers beside Dellie, I wondered how long I'd been gone. And I wondered if Marion was still out there in the night. I thought about his kisses and I touched my own lips, all around, with both my hands, trying to feel them the way he had. Were they soft? Warm like his were?

If a kiss was such a wicked thing, if it could lead you down the path of sin and degradation like Brother Parkins preached, if this were so, then why had God given it such a heart-stretching sweetness? If it were true, and one kiss could ruin a body's soul, then mine was ruined sure; for right then, I took my pillow in a hug. And I pressed my lips against it, closed my eyes, and I conjured forth his face in my mind.

9

*I*n the morning, I woke up to rain, and it vexed
me for I couldn't light up the cook stove with
my boots and Dane's britches jammed in behind
there. Yet the rain kept everybody inside and underfoot. I sat on my kitchen stool, pretending I
wasn't good awake yet, which wasn't far from the
truth after being out so late, and I counted out the
bundles of kindling inside the wood bin. I had
plenty but it was a way to get Dane outside, sending him after more from the dry box in the barn.
Papa was another matter. But after worrying the
windows for a spell, and giving me confused
glances like he wondered what was keeping me
from breakfast, he paid a visit to the privy.

While they were both gone I hurried to gather
the bundle out from behind the stove. The boots
were in worse shape than they seemed in the dark
last night, caked with dirt and scratched deep into
the leather. Dane's britches, too. There was three
tears on the legs, one at the knee that was so big it
would take a patch to close.

I raced to the bedroom before Nathan could notice what I had huddled in my arms. He sat by the

fireplace, rubbing morning sand from his eyes, and he wasn't paying me any mind. But after I was in the other room, bent down stuffing the bundle underneath the bed where Dellie was sleeping, she raised her head.

"What're you doing, Sissy?" she said, and startled me. My stomach jumped up to my neck. "What're you putting under there?" She leaned her head over the edge to look but I yanked the quilt down to cover up the opening.

"Nothing. You lay down there till I tell you to get up."

"I'm ready now," she said.

"Well, the house ain't warm enough yet. You get back under the covers."

She reached her arm out to pull the quilt up enough so's she could see underneath the bed, and I spatted her hand, hard. It sounded like the fat popping off bacon. Her mouth rounded into an *O*, then her chin took to quivering, and big tears spurted out her eyes. She was loud about it, and I sat down on the bed to take her up in my arms. She wasn't having any of me, though, and edged to the far side against the window, bawling deep from her throat.

I heard the back door bang shut, and then Papa came in the room. His shirt and hat were wet from rain. At the sight of him, Dellie quieted down some, but she was still snubbing.

"What's got into her?" Papa said to me. He took off his hat and gave it a shake. I could see from his expression he'd thought something bad had happened in here.

I stood up to face him. "She wanted to get outta bed but I told her no since the chill ain't off the air yet. I don't want her to take a cold."

"Nuh-uh." Dellie scrambled away from the window. "Sissy's hiding something under the bed."

My chest went to heaving. By then, even Dane was back in the house, and standing next to Nathan at the bedroom door behind Papa to see what the racket was about.

"Is that so, Lily?" Papa said. He looked at me for the truth and I gave him a lie.

"Yes sir, but it's only womanly things that I didn't wanna leave laying about."

The tops of Papa's ears turned bright pink. "I see." He cleared his voice. "Hush up that bellering, Dellie, and do as your sister says." And he turned quickly from the room, shoving Dane and Nathan away from the door, even closing it after him as if there was something tainted in there with me and Dellie.

I didn't mean to be indelicate with him but it was the only way I knew to stop his questions. Matters of a womanly nature caused him great embarrassment. It'd been one of the hardships of having only a papa to raise me.

When my monthly cycles had started four years ago, I'd thought I had some dread, unspeakable disease—thought, in fact, that I was dying. I never said a word to Papa, but for five months I burned the bloody rags I used in a fire out near the creek bed. I stopped riding old Joe, thinking that was the cause. And time would pass with no blood forthcoming so's I'd think I'd cured it, only for it to start up again and worry me to distraction. And not just blood, but terrible, doubling-over cramps in the stomach that seemed to get worse each time the bleeding began. I prayed to God to see me through it, and to let me live long enough to raise Dellie to take my place in the household.

It was Mrs. Kennedy who finally told me, after she noticed a spot on my skirt one day. It was on a Sunday after church and I'd been fighting the pain all through Brother Parkins's sermon. She leaned to me and whispered, "You've had an accident, dear," and the way she said it, so calm-like, gave me courage. I said, "Oh, Miz Kennedy, something awful is happening to me."

She must have seen the horror on my face because she put her arm on my shoulder and walked me to a private spot away from everybody else, and she told me of the facts of womanhood, and of the curse laid on us by God Himself for Eve's sins. None of the Bible teaching part concerned me, though. I was too relieved to know I wasn't dying.

And though I knew it caused Papa embarrassment, I thought sometimes of all those months of worry, of him not telling me and me unwilling to ask. And it seemed to me he should have done something for me, at least said to me, "There's things you need to speak with Miz Kennedy about," for surely he knew my time had come.

"I'm sorry I smacked you," I said to Dellie, and her pout seemed to lighten. "But it's some things I need to have private. When you get a little bigger you'll see what I mean."

"Please let me get up, Sissy. I need to go pee bad." She looked at me with her face wrinkled up, eyes still red from crying. I felt guilty then for scolding her.

I leaned again under the bed and dragged out the chamber pot. I gave the bundle of boots and britches a shove deeper into the corner. "All right then. Keep that quilt tucked around yourself though. It's cold in here." And I stood there with her till she was through, in case she took it in her mind to sneak another look underneath the bed.

I cooked up breakfast, and shortly after, the rain stopped so the men could get outside. Monday was washday, and I decided to take a chance that the sunshine would last. I set Dellie about stripping the beds, while I put the patch in Dane's britches and sewed up the tears. The boots would have to wait for later.

We carried the baskets down to the creek, and dumped the clothes into the soak box Papa had built there, just under the water line. With the rain, the creek had turned muddier than I liked for washing, but I put in soap and left the clothes there while I got a fire going under the kettle out beside the barn.

Dane came and helped haul water. Papa had him chopping stumps in the newest cotton field, now that the old plant stalks were cleaned out and the morning rain had softened the ground. I knew the water hauling would be a nice break for Dane, and it was why I called him in to help me.

He'd already ripped the pair of britches he'd put

on that morning, so I didn't figure he'd notice the patch in the ones out in the soak box. I saw old Joe and our best draft mule, Ernest Lee, out in the new field with Papa, plowing up the most stubborn stumps. He'd given Nathan the plow lines to handle, and seeing them all out there, I remembered that I hadn't had a chance to curry the horse again this morning. But I guessed it was too late for that now. I hoped he didn't have infectious dog bites on him.

When I got the clothes in the kettle to boil, I set Dellie there with the turning fork, and I used the time to take a shoe cloth to my boots. The scuffs wouldn't buff out, but it gave me a minute to think and remember last night with Marion. Chores took my mind away from him, and I longed for quietude and a chance to dwell on the things he said, feelings he gave to me. A thought flashed through my mind of running away with him like he said, of getting off this farm. But then the thought moved on as quick as it came.

We got the clothes hung out just before time to fix dinner. The afternoon we spent boiling down some of the hog meat in the smokehouse that had gone rancid, for soap. Dellie was beginning to be good help to me, and I let her build the fire for supper.

It wasn't until after we ate, when Papa and Dane began to wash up for town, that I remembered the meeting full-force. When they were gone, I sat down at the fireplace and read Bible verse to Dellie and Nathan, sneaking peeks at the fair picture I kept tucked at the back, trying to keep my nerves calm, wondering what was going on in town. Waiting till time, after everybody was home and in bed, to go out to Mr. Grossner's tree.

The Beatty gang busted up the town meeting. They rode in on their horses into the new church building and shot off their pistols. The bullets shattered out windows and pocked the ceiling. They smashed Brother Parkins's walnut pulpit that he'd had made special three years ago by a German craftsman in Bastrop. And they tore up the place till everybody ran outside and back to their homes and farms. I felt responsible.

Dane told me everything when they got home. He came in right behind Papa, whose face was still white from the experience. Papa wouldn't discuss it. He went straight to bed without a comment. I pulled Dane out to the front porch where we could talk, and it was clear he wanted to talk.

"Them Beattys were on a rampage," he said, struggling to keep control of his voice. "Bullets flew off everything. Rebounded, some of them, and hit other things. It's a miracle no one was killed."

"Which Beattys was it?" I whispered, shaking with the knowing of what I had caused.

"All of them. Ten or eleven of them. Or more. I didn't have a chance to count them. I was busy dodging bullets."

"Which ones did the shooting?"

"They all did. We talked with Mister Milton out on the road after they left. He says we have to take the law into our own hands now. He says no two-bit town marshal's gonna do the trick. And Sheriff Jenkins is got too much ground to cover. Mister Milton says the citizens of McDade'd have to band together to bring this gang of outlaws to justice."

"Outlaws . . ." The word felt strange in my mouth. I gazed at the road, towards Mr. Grossner's place. I could barely make out the big oak tree on the hill.

"They're outlaws all right. If you could of seen them. Rags tied over their faces. Guns a foot long. Just their eyes showing. Mean eyes ever one."

"What kind of horses did they ride?"

He looked at me and shook his head like I was a dunce. "Plain horses."

"Black or brown?" I said, took in a deep breath. "Any paints?"

"Who cares about the horses?"

I stiffened my chin. "Well, didn't you notice *any* of the horses? The colors of any of them?"

He stood up and slapped at his legs like he had the itch. "There were all them colors. Blacks, browns, roans, paints. They were shooting, Lily. I didn't think to check the horses." He let out his air, and sounded like he wanted to swear at me. Then he stomped inside so loud I felt sure he'd wake Papa or one of the little ones.

I rested my face in my hands, elbows planted on my knees. My head felt too heavy to hold up. Paints. He said there'd been paints. "Maybe somebody else was riding his horse," I whispered to myself. "Could of been anybody."

I didn't go inside. I sat out there till all the lamps, save one in the front room, were shut off. I listened to the house get heavy with stillness, and I sat there shivering at the coldness in the air and inside my heart.

It was such confusion I felt. I always expected I'd meet somebody new at church someday, or maybe just marry Daniel O'Barr when the proper time came. I didn't count on Marion, or that any man would ever make me feel so weak-headed and sick in the stomach. I wished to God he wasn't a Beatty, yet knew the wishing was pure foolishness. The Lord knew it too, and I asked Him to show me the right way to go, and told Him I'd trust in Him that He would. And it was almost at that exact moment that I heard a horse whinny up the road. It seemed to me like a sign.

Knuck came tearing around the house, barking. I stepped off the porch and called out to him. He passed me by and headed for the gate, where he stood and kept up his noise. I got there quick, told him it was all right, and scratched on his head till he brought his barking down to a whine. And I looked out over the road towards Mr. Grossner's place.

The moon and shadows played tricks with my eyes and I wasn't sure I saw a thing. Back at the house the light was on still but there wasn't any movement within. I peered again into the darkness and still wasn't sure. Knuck's ears stayed cocked.

Then it came—a two-note whistle that fluttered to me on the breeze. It was him. Over by that tree like he'd said. But I looked and still couldn't see. With one more backward glance at the house, I eased open the gate and stepped through. Knuck went too. He barked twice more until I shushed him with my voice held low. A shadow by the tree moved down to the road.

Knuck ran out ahead of me, and by the time I caught up, Marion was already in a squat, petting the dog, shaking his ears in the rough-play Knuck liked.

"This a blue-tick?" Marion said, and his voice flowed over me like honey.

"Coondog," I said.

He laughed. "There's all kinds of different coondogs, Lily. Black and tans, red-bones. This one looks like a blue-tick to me." Knuck plopped a thick paw on Marion's knee. "Hey there, fella." He slapped easy at Knuck's jaw, bringing on a playful growl.

"You came early," I said.

He looked up at me, then stood. Knuck pranced around us, wanting more attention. "It's not too early, is it? Your folks still up?" He looked toward the house, where the lamp glowed inside one window.

"No. But they're alive at least." I tossed back my head.

"What do you mean?"

"You know what I mean. Your brothers and their friends busted up that meeting. Papa was there, and my brother, Dane. They could of been hurt."

"Nobody got hurt."

A sinking feeling came upon my chest. "You were there, too. Weren't you?"

"All we did was ride in and ride out."

"Shooting guns."

"Not *at* anybody, Lily. We were just breaking up the meeting. I wasn't gonna let nobody hurt your pa."

"You don't even know Papa."

"Course I do. I know everything about you. I was looking out for him. And your brother." He put his hands on my shoulders. "Don't be sore at me. It wasn't my idea, but the meeting did get canceled. If that ain't what you wanted, how come you to go to all that trouble to tell us about it?"

"*You*. It was just *you* I wanted to know about it. So's you could get outta town."

"Lily . . ." His hands squeezed me. "It's my kinfolk. I'd of had to tell them anyway."

I looked away from him then. He was too close, and his hands were warm on my shoulders. "Well, I didn't mean for you to tear up the church house. It took too much work to get it built."

"It ain't tore up." His hand passed over my forehead and down my back, petting my hair. At our feet, Knuck whined. "Lily. Look at me. It ain't tore up."

I tried to keep from looking. I tried my best, but my eyes went to him anyway, just as if my brain wasn't telling them no the whole time. And he sounded so sweet and so sorry and hurt by my accusing him of wrongdoing. When my eyes moved onto his face, it was all the encouragement he needed to tell him it was all right to pull me up against him and cover me around with his arms.

"You're freezing," he whispered, then he pulled off his jumper and hung it around my shoulders before he took me back close to him. He started walking me. "Let's get over here off the road."

"I gotta get inside," I said, but he pulled me on anyway, across the ditch and up to Mr. Grossner's fence. He stepped on the bottom wire and yanked up on the top two, making a hole for me to duck through. Knuck scooted under the fence and ran up over the rise.

I didn't stoop over, but stood there looking at how easy Marion found it to trespass through somebody's fence. I pulled his jumper tighter on my shoulders. "You said you weren't any part of all that. You told me so yourself last night."

"I ain't. Not usually. It's just cause of Jack's not being here. Lily . . ." He let up on the wires. "I can't stand by and let a mob make threats against me and my kin. They were talking about night raids. Calling out names."

"Was yours one of them called out?"

"They said Beattys. And McLemores. Goodman. Stevens. They called the roll. Now come on over here, Lily. Come up by this tree and talk to me a while. It's all I've been looking forward to all day."

I ducked through the fence and let him take me up to the tree where Mollie was standing. I figured she must have jumped the fence, like she did so easy that day we both rode her. Knuck took off after something in the woods. I couldn't see what. A varmint of some kind. His hound dog bark echoed in the night.

"I can't stay but a minute," I said. "I left a lamp on inside . . ."

His lips cut off my words, kissing me softly,

once. Then twice. His arms folded around me, pinning mine against my ribs. My hands couldn't go anywhere except up onto his back. He wasn't wearing a gun. Dots came up behind my eyes and I felt like I might faint away. Then the kiss got too long and too forceful, and he was holding me so close a gnat's hair wouldn't fit between us.

I wrenched my face away from him. His mouth slid over my jaw and under my hair. "Stop it, Marion," I said, but he didn't hear it. I tensed up and tried to twist free. "Stop it!"

He let me go. "What's the matter?"

I took off his jumper and gave it back to him. Then I started for the road. It was mostly grass and easy to walk in the dark. I heard him following me. Mollie grunted and I heard her following, too.

"What'd I do?" he said. He tried to catch my arm, but I swung it clear and picked up my pace. "Hold up, Lily! Tell me why you're mad!"

"I just gotta get in." I kept going.

At the fence he stopped me. "I'm sorry. Whatever I done, I'm sorry," he said.

"I can't meet you out here anymore. It ain't right." I waited for him to duck under the wires. He did it quick, then lifted up the fence for me to pass through.

"Then let me come meet your pa and we'll do it proper. I know I can win him over, once he gets to know me."

"No!" I stood before him and hugged my arms, chilly without his warmth. "Don't you understand yet? My papa was at that meeting. He's against you. The whole town is. They want you locked up. All of you. You need to get outta McDade before something bad happens. Go someplace else."

"This's where I live. It's my home. I was born here and raised here the same as you." He sounded forlorn, and I wanted to hold him again. I didn't dare.

"I ain't saying go forever," I said, softer now. "Just for a time, till their tempers die down."

"If I done that, I'd have to take you with me."

"I couldn't go."

Mollie nuzzled up behind him. He slung his jumper over his shoulder and looked at me, his eyes shining in the darkness. "How could you live without me now? I couldn't without you."

There was no way for me to keep from loving him. I saw that, standing there in the night. And it was as if God was sending down a message to me like I'd asked Him to, only I hadn't expected it to come so sudden and blinding.

I put my hand on his face and he pressed it there, turned my wrist to his lips. He said, "I don't wanna excite you, Lily. But the lamp inside your house just went out."

I picked up my skirts and ran. Knuck darted through the gate when I opened it, like he'd been waiting for me to get there. He raced out ahead of me as if this was a game and great sport. My heart beat hard. I didn't even turn to see if Marion was still there.

The minute I stepped inside the house, I smelled the lamp. I struck a match and saw that the oil had run out and the wick burned down to smoke up the bottom. No one was stirring, so my breathing eased, but I held open the door to try to let out some of the smell. While I was doing that, I heard Papa's bed squeak, then he came on the run out his door, holding a candle.

"What's burning?" he said when he saw me, his face drawn tight in the candle flame.

My heart took up its quick beat again. "This lamp burned out is all."

He moved to the stove and grabbed a pot holder. "We need to get it down from there so's it don't start a fire." And that he did, setting the blackened lamp on the fireplace hearth. I kept holding open the door, and hoped he wouldn't notice I wasn't dressed for bed. But Papa didn't miss much. He turned from the lamp and narrowed on me.

"Where you been?"

"I—" My eyes searched the room, landed on the chair and my Bible there on the wood table. It was unlatched and I could see the edge of the photograph sticking out. "I fell asleep reading."

"That's carelessness, Lily."

"Yes sir."

"You could of burned us all up."

"I know. I'm sorry." I hung my head, my face as hot as his candle flame. I hated being scolded like a child.

"Get yourself to bed," he said and watched until I went. I took the Bible into the bedroom with me, and hid it in my drawer.

I used the light coming from his candle in the front room to find my gown in the chest, changed out of my clothes, and crawled over Dellie to my side by the window. The boys had the one that faced the road and I wished mine were over there so's I could see if Marion had gone. I tried to close my eyes but they wouldn't stay that way, and Papa didn't go back to bed soon.

I stared at the soft glow coming through the door and let myself think about running off with Marion. Let my mind really play with the idea of leaving the farm. This bed. That kitchen out there. The thought of it didn't make me sad.

10

*F*olks were too disturbed by the damage done
to the church to plan another indignation
meeting right away. Instead, the Sunday sermon
from Brother Parkins became a kind of coded message to the congregation to rise against the evil
around us. He preached on the meek inheriting the
earth, and then on the strength of the backbone
over the wishbone. And this made all the more
powerful with the reminders of the intrusion all
around us—the absence of the walnut pulpit, the
black tar paper stretched over the shot-out windows, bullet holes in the ceiling joists. You could
sit in that church and feel the anger of the men
who had worked to build it growing with each
word Brother Parkins uttered.

And Brother Parkins had the gift of preaching.
Even without his carved wood pulpit to stand behind. He cut a stern figure in a deep black suit,
like he was in mourning for a lost loved one instead of pieces of his building. He reminded us
time and again of Eppie but worked it into his sermon so's it wasn't too obvious that he was reminding us. Whenever this occurred, I could feel

Dane tense up, and count on some tears from Mrs. Kennedy when everybody bowed their heads and prayed for the demons in our town to be banished to hell. It was only me, I think, who sat there with my eyes open, feeling out of place. Even Dellie's hand in my lap, laced tight through my fingers, began to seem like a doll's hand to me, and unreal.

After I told Marion that I couldn't meet him anymore under Mr. Grossner's tree, I didn't see him for over a week. It was an awful week for me. I found myself staring at his picture during the daytime, and lying awake nights, waiting to hear Knuck barking down by the gate. On the third and fourth nights I even stayed dressed and walked down there when the rest went to bed. But no two-note whistle came to my ears.

I remembered the question he'd asked me about how I was going to live without him. My heart took to yearning for him so, I knew he was right. There wasn't any way, now that I'd felt the warmth of him, that I could live content without him.

Then on Tuesday, Mrs. Griffin pulled in our gate with little Timmy in the buggy beside her. She came to invite me to a knitting party she was having next day at her house. "For us ladies to finish up on our holiday gifts," she said. "I do hope you can come, Lily."

I knew Papa would let me since I'd already caught him making gifts himself, a wagon for Nathan that he had hidden high up in the hayloft, and a stick horse for Dellie that he'd asked me to trim with yarn.

I gave Mrs. Griffin some tea and we sat on the porch, for the weather had played a trick on us, and warmed up enough to take in fresh air. Nathan was glad for the company of Timmy, and they ran and played around the yard. Papa and Dane had taken Mrs. Kennedy a wagonload of hay for her cattle, and Dellie sat with me and Mrs. Griffin on the porch. We didn't lack for conversation. She told me who all was invited to the knitting party, mostly the ladies from church, and of the coat scarf she'd just finished for her boy Willie. She asked after Daniel O'Barr, not knowing I wasn't keeping up with my correspondence with him. The Beattys weren't even mentioned.

Then just as they were leaving to run down to Mrs. Bishop's, the last on the guest list, Timmy put a note into my hand. He did it like he was trying to be secret about it, but his mama saw it and laughed.

"He's already admirous of the ladies," she said as if to excuse his brashness. "He's been copying down poems from a book of mine. Passing them around to female folks. I don't mind much since it's helping him practice his lettering." She laughed again and it seemed like she, too, was being secretive.

Later, after she'd gone and I read the note that had been crumpled up in the pocket of Timmy's knickers, I wondered did Mrs. Griffin know what the words had said? When I thought of it, it seemed like she might have, from the peculiar way she'd been acting. The note read:

Deer Lily,
I will com to git you tonite after tin. Pleese wait fore
me outside your gait. It is the only way I no to see
you. Do not be cross with me fore sending this note.
                                        I am yours,
                                        Marion

I took the paper to the privy and read it through
twice in the light from the moon cut on the door.
It was the sign-off, the *I am yours*, that moved me
most. I pressed the note to my nose, seeking some
scent of him. There was nothing but the smell of
paper and ink. But it was a letter from him. My
first. And I folded it smooth and tucked it inside
my dress, next to my bosom. I left it there all afternoon where I could feel it.

Papa didn't go to bed till nearly ten himself, and
I worried that he wasn't good asleep when I went
out the front door. But I stayed on the porch a
minute and he didn't come after me, so I eased
across the yard towards the gate. There was a
southeasterly wind that night that helped to muf-
fle my footsteps, and I got to the road without stirring Knuck. It was so warm, I even heard a
mosquito buzz by my ear.

I waited for two or three minutes only before I
heard the hooves of a horse coming at me from the
wrong direction. From town way. So I hid behind
a cedar tree. It was dark of the moon, and I was
fearful of snakes since it had warmed enough to
bring them out of their dens. I crouched there to
wait out the rider, hoping Marion wouldn't come

just then and be caught. The cedar got my nose to itching and I pinched it hard to keep from sneezing.

The horse got up even with my gate and I couldn't make out anything past a shape. But the rider didn't go any further and after another minute of hiding, it dawned on me that it must be Marion after all. I stepped out from behind the cedar and at almost the same instant, let go of the sneeze.

I heard a quick movement, then the horse shifting. "Lily!?" Marion's voice said, and I went to him. He didn't come off the saddle but reached a hand down to pull me up. "Why were you hiding in there? I nearly jumped outta my skin."

"Well, how come you were in town?" I settled against him, sideways so's I could see his face and rest my head on his shoulder. The smell of him came to me—a smell of earth and sagebrush, and something sweet besides, like new leather shoes.

"I ain't been in town. You'll see," he said and gave me a squeeze. He started Mollie up the road the same way he'd come from. "You got my letter. I was afraid you wouldn't."

"How'd you do that?" I said, smiling, happy to be on that saddle with him.

"Willie Griffin. He said he could get it to you. But he was pretty liquored up at the time, so I worried."

"His little brother brought it to me." I took the folded paper out of my bosom and held it up. "I've still got it right here."

He hooked his arm, the one not holding the bridle reins, around my neck and lifted my chin to kiss me. I guess he trusted Mollie enough to stay on the road, for he took his time with the kiss. But he also took care not to scare me with it again.

Then he said, "Swing around here so's you're astraddle. I got somewhere I wanna take you and they're waiting on us." He helped me get straight. My feet rested on top of the toes of his boots.

I leaned backwards against him and he spurred Mollie to a lope. I worried some about where we were going. It seemed too many folks were knowing about us now. But the gladness in me was more than the worry, and I let myself enjoy the ride, being next to him.

We went through town and on past, towards Paint Creek. And then we came to a house set off the road inside a group of trees. There was a white fence around it and lamps burning through the windows. Marion got off Mollie and reached for me.

"Who lives here?" I said, wary. His hands took me around my waist.

"Jack does now. With Estelle." He lifted me down. "He said it's all right if we come here." He held my hand and took me to the door.

Estelle was Jack's new bride, and she wasn't anything like I expected. She had dark hair that flowed straight down her back and she was pretty in the face. But she wasn't a dance hall girl or a saloon floozy like I might have thought Jack would pick. She came from Rockdale, the daughter of a cotton ginner, and she was clearly adoring of Jack.

He looked different to me too, and it wasn't just

that he was washed up and unarmed. He sat in a rocking chair, his boots pulled off, and in his shirtsleeves and galluses. And he smoked hand-rolled cigarettes and smiled at me and Marion when we came in, and at his pretty wife. It just seemed to me then that he wasn't so fearsome as I'd thought before. He said hello to me and called me by my name.

When we went inside the house, Estelle moved to greet us. She said, "So this is Lily," and she hugged my neck like I was her kin. Then she hugged Marion, too.

That whole night was a revelation to me. We sat, the four of us, and talked about cotton farming mostly. Jack had paid a year's rent on that place to Mr. Wilson, who'd just moved off to La Grange. And Jack planned to raise cotton on the six acres that came with the house. He asked me questions about my papa's crops, and he listened to the answers I gave, and his eyes seemed to have lost the hardness I remembered in them that time in town.

We didn't split up, women and men, as was usual in a situation like that. Marion and I sat on a slat bench together and he kept his arm placed around me. And Estelle had the stool, with Jack's feet in her lap, and he kept reaching for her hair, dibbling it through his fingers while he talked, which he did in a deep, lazy voice. It could have put me to sleep. Marion smoked some of Jack's cigarettes, listening too, and it was suddenly clear to me that he looked up to this brother that was five years older than him.

After we'd been there over an hour, Estelle took

me back to their bedroom to show me the lace curtains she'd hung on the windows, and some of her wedding gifts: a blue star quilt that was already spread down on the bed, and a wall sampler with the words "In Wedded Bliss, December 2, 1883," embroidered in gold thread.

I said, "It was nice of you to let us come so late at night. I hope we ain't keeping you from your sleep."

"Oh, you're not. We'd be up anyway. I'm having a time trying to change Jack's days around. He doesn't liven up until the sun goes down." She laughed. "I guess every one of them's got owl's blood in their veins."

She was talking about the Beatty boys. And talking of them with affection in her voice. I'd never heard them spoken of in such a tone before.

"So you know Haywood and Az, too?" I said.

"Why, sure I do. Jack's got to have his brothers all around him. That's why we came to live in McDade. He feels responsible for them since he's the oldest. I've been lonesome for my home, though. But now that I know you, I think it'll be just fine here."

She was smiling so wide I felt bad, and embarrassed. I don't know why I did what I did next, but I opened my mouth, and the words just came out on their own. I said, "There's a knitting party in town tomorrow. Hazel Griffin's putting it on. I could take you as my guest if you'd be interested to go. I could come for you in my buggy."

Her eyes fairly danced. They were green eyes

and full of light. "Wouldn't it be too far for you to come?"

"I could just leave earlier, is all. It won't be any trouble."

A darkness came onto Jack's face again when Estelle told him of my invitation. I was already regretting speaking and Jack's look sent a chill through me. He took ahold of Estelle's white hand without getting up from his chair, and said, "That ain't a good idea. The hostess of the party's the one who needs to invite you."

Marion sat forward. "It's Willie's ma, Jack. I think it'll be all right."

Jack glanced around Estelle at Marion. "But what about them other biddies?"

Marion gave me a quick look. He seemed nervous about it. "If Lily takes her, I think it'll be all right."

Jack saw how much Estelle wanted to go and he studied on her a while. Then his eyes met mine again and it felt almost like a warning. "All right then. You can go if you want to so bad," he said to Estelle, and she bent to kiss his cheek.

"Can you do that?" Marion asked me later, when we were back on Mollie headed home. "Take her to that party?"

"I said I would." But I was feeling doubtful myself now that we were away from the peace inside their house. "Maybe I oughta check with Miz Griffin first."

"It's too late now, Lily. I gave Jack my word that you weren't just getting Estelle's hopes up. He's trusting me. And you. She don't know about the reputation he's got in town. And he don't want her to know. She comes from a good family."

"Then why did he bring her here?"

"Well, because ... he got that deal on Wilson's land, and he's planning on being a farmer now. Soon as he can raise up enough money—" He cut this last part off like it slipped out before he could stop it.

"How's he gonna do that, Marion?" I said. "Raise the money?"

"He doesn't know yet. He's still thinking on it."

11

The only good part about taking Estelle to Mrs. Griffin's party was I got to see Marion that next morning. He'd stayed the night at Jack and Estelle's and so he was outside waiting for me when I rode up on the buggy. I'd had a hard time convincing Papa to let me take the buggy alone to town, but since it was only a mile he thought I'd be driving, he gave in.

I had my knitting needles with me and the sweater I was still making for Dellie. It'd been close to two months since I started on it, but there wasn't ever time to knit. I hadn't thought to bring baked goods, and wouldn't have yet, had Estelle not come out with a batch of tea cake cookies stacked in a Christmas tin. Marion said she'd been up since dawn baking them.

It made me feel a little jealous the way he sounded so admiring of her. And she was dressed just right too, in fine white batiste cotton like a christening gown. Her hair was rolled up into one of those fancy knots I could never make. My own hair was pulled through the back of my bonnet and loose down my back. I'd combed it good, but

I knew it was a mess by then from the long drive. It made me feel sick to look at the lacy gloves on her hands, and dowdy beside her, in my linen skirt and velvet jacket, the nap of which was worn down bare in spots. I had on Dane's brown skin gloves that were scarred black from the reins rubbing and my hands were swallowed in them. I thought about pulling them off right quick and tucking them under my legs, just driving the buggy barehanded and taking what blisters popped up.

Jack came out and helped Estelle onto the seat. He looked more like himself with his boots and vest on, but he wasn't in as good a humor as he had been last night. A deep line creased his forehead between his eyes, and he stood out in front of the house with Marion and watched us go. Estelle waved at them, then turned back to face forward with me.

"Jack's such a worry wart," she said with a laugh. "He said for me to be sure and tell these ladies my maiden name so they'll know I've come from a decent, respectable family. Now, why would he say that, Lily?"

"He said to use your maiden name?" I'd been thinking of how to introduce her around and this seemed like a good idea to me. "What *is* your maiden name?"

"Odom. But I don't think he meant that, do you?"

I cracked the reins to pick up our speed. I didn't want to be late and have to walk in with all the ladies already there. I figured I could sneak Estelle by better if we were sitting there already when the rest came in. "Why don't we just say you're a good friend of mine from Rockdale and your name's Estelle? No last name's even needed that way at all."

"Well, I am proud of my family but I'm also proud to be Missus Jack Beatty. It took him long enough to ask. I don't see any reason to hide it."

"He asked your papa for your hand?" I hoped the surprise didn't show in my voice.

"He most certainly did, and he was really gentlemanly about it. And when Father asked how he would support me, Jack said any way he could."

I glanced at her and she was smiling sweet with the memory of it. And I wondered how somebody could marry Jack Beatty and not know what they'd got.

We rode on towards town. After the frost we'd had, the post oaks were all losing their leaves fast now, and they fell like rain around us. The mule's hooves crunched along steady, while Estelle told me all about her wedding. The more I heard, the more surprised I got.

They'd had a church ceremony, Methodist since that was how she'd been raised. She'd worn taffeta, and Jack a wool suit. I couldn't picture him in a suit somehow. And he'd been disappointed, she said, that his brothers hadn't been able to come. But Robert Stevens had been there to stand up for him, and I tried to picture Robert in a suit too and couldn't see that either.

She showed me her ring, which I'd noticed last night but not seen up close. It was delicate gold, shaped into ivy leaves and stems, twining round and round her finger and glinting in the sunshine. It must have cost Jack big money.

We got to Mrs. Griffin's and there was only a couple of wagons out front. Estelle got down from the buggy and waited for me to dig out the halter weight. She seemed fidgety but excited. My own stomach was boiling as I hauled out the heavy disk to tie onto the mule so's he'd be there when we returned.

About then, Mrs. Bishop and Mrs. McCraney pulled up. Tom Bishop was driving the team, and the silver brads on his boots flashed as he got down to help the ladies from their seats. He tipped his hat at me and Estelle, and said, "Need a hand, there, Lily?" when he saw me struggling to get the mule weighted down. I waved him on and finished quick as Mrs. Bishop and Mrs. McCraney came up to us.

"You've brought a friend, Lily?" Mrs. Bishop said to me, and I jumped to Estelle's side. She was holding her cookie tin and my knitting bag and she smiled at the two ladies.

"Yes. This is Estelle. She's new in town. Came from Rockdale," I said. "The Odom family. Do you know them?"

Mrs. Bishop took Estelle's gloved hand. "Why no, I don't believe I do. Welcome to McDade, Estelle."

To my misfortune, Estelle wasn't a bit shy. She started right in to talking about how she found McDade to be a pretty place. And when Mrs. McCraney asked which part of the county she'd moved to, Estelle looked at me and said, "Lily? Where do I live?"

"East," I said over my shoulder, then thought I should have lied. I hurried along, hoping Estelle would follow. She tagged behind between the two other ladies.

"Well, we do hope you'll visit our church this Sunday," Mrs. Bishop said. "We're doing a bit of rebuilding, but I'm sure you'd enjoy Brother Parkins's sermons."

"He gives a powerful message." Mrs. McCraney stepped up to Mrs. Griffin's door and knocked. "I always say when Brother Parkins gets through with us, we know we've been preached at."

"They're nice," Estelle whispered to me. She looked rosy. I noticed she was still holding my knitting bag, and I took it out of her hands as Mrs. Griffin came to the door.

"This was such a wonderful idea, Hazel," Mrs. Bishop said as she entered the house. Mrs. Griffin was smiling and saying hello, and then she saw Estelle and her face went white. She held the door for us anyway and shook Estelle's hand when I introduced them. Then she kept me back while the rest went on in.

"Lily?" Mrs. Griffin said under her breath. "What have you done? I know who that girl is. Willie pointed her out to me last week up town."

I went red. "I'm sorry, Miz Griffin. I should of asked you first. But she's lonely and she doesn't know anybody."

"Yes, you should of asked me." Mrs. Griffin's face was as stern as she could make it, but it was too round and kindly to look mean. She pitched her voice down to a whisper. "Did Marion put you up to it?"

I swallowed and shook my head. It was the first time anybody outside of Beattys had spoken his name to me like that—like it was a sure fact I knew him, and well enough to talk of him out in public. I realized then that she had known who wrote the note little Timmy gave me, and that she more than likely knew what it said and maybe read it even. I wondered how come she hadn't told anybody. Then figured it was because of Willie being their friend.

She reached for my shoulder. "Come on in. We'll just have to make the best of it, won't we?"

The ladies were all seated around Mrs. Griffin's parlor. She had nice, upholstered furniture, lots of flowery pictures on the wall. Her husband had been a railroad man and had made good money before he fell onto the track at a switchyard in San Antonio. Folks said he'd been a drinker and had a wild streak in him. If it was so, he'd passed that trait on down to Willie.

I took the chair beside Estelle and noticed how friendly she talked with everybody. Mrs. Milton and Mrs. Billingsley were already there, and Estelle was in conversation with them, talking about her papa's store in Rockdale, since both these ladies had husbands in the mercantile trade. They all seemed to like her already and I relaxed some. Maybe, I thought, I could get by without anybody knowing who she really was.

More ladies came then and most brought food.

Mrs. Griffin laid out everything on the dining room table with little cups for tea or coffee and glass plates. We filed around in a line, filling up the plates with cookies and strudel, marzipan and fudge. We'd had a bumper crop of pecans in McDade this year, and nearly everything on the table was loaded with nuts. I felt guilty again for not thinking to fix something to bring.

Mrs. Kennedy came while we were dishing up. She brought a fancy coconut cake with pink frosting. Mrs. Griffin took a knife to it and cut it into perfect two-inch squares. I was watching her do that, and envying how neat she did it, not getting crumbs all over the place like I would have. And I wasn't paying attention to the fact that Mrs. Kennedy had started talking to Estelle on the opposite side of the table. I didn't notice, that is, until I heard Mrs. Kennedy say, "Estelle what? Do you have a last name, dear?"

The knife in Mrs. Griffin's hand sliced crooked, and she looked up at me in horror, and I looked back at her. Estelle said, "It's Beatty. Estelle Beatty. I'm Mrs. Jack Beatty."

The whole room fell quiet, save one gasp from Mrs. Slater. The mantel clock above Mrs. Griffin's fireplace seemed to tick louder. I felt the eyes of Mrs. Bishop and Mrs. McCraney hard on me. Estelle's hand, the one with the twining ivy ring, fluttered to her chest. She looked around, befuddled.

Mrs. Billingsley cleared her throat and set Mrs. Griffin's glass plate down on the table. "Lovely party, Hazel," she said and went to pick up her knitting bag in the parlor. Mrs. Milton followed her, and we heard the front door close. One by one, the other ladies did the same. Some said the food was nice. Some gave excuses for why they were leaving so soon, things like children at home untended or suppers to get started. No one was especially rude, but it wasn't long before it was just me and Estelle and Mrs. Griffin.

"What did I say?" Estelle asked us, looking after the last of the ladies.

"You didn't say anything wrong," Mrs. Griffin said, and I was glad it was her that answered. I wouldn't have known what to say. "Let's go in the parlor and sit down."

We followed Mrs. Griffin, and Estelle plopped down on the brocade sofa like she'd lost her balance. I took the chair by the fireplace, for it was the only one not covered with cloth and I felt easier there. I wanted to crawl under the rug.

Mrs. Griffin sat in a white wicker chair where she could see us both, and she looked at us, one to the other. "You girls have to face it that some folks ain't so accepting. And you might as well know now that your menfolk are gonna cause you embarrassment time and again without even knowing they're giving you grief."

I felt odd, her including me in this talk. I'd expected her to be angry that I'd broken up her party, but she seemed more sad than angry.

"When Horace was still alive," she said, "I used to hear things from people. Gossip most of it and untrue. But it made it hard for me to make friends."

"You mean, it's Jack?" Estelle sat up suddenly. "It's Jack they don't like?"

Mrs. Griffin's smile was soft. "We'll just say, he's not that popular around here." She looked at me then. "Lily, you ain't in any better boat, now that it's out, and you know it'll be out within the hour."

"For what? What did she do?" Estelle said.

"For associating with the Beattys." Mrs. Griffin kept her eyes on me as she said this.

Estelle stood. "Is that true, Lily?"

When I nodded, she headed for the door. She was outside before either me or Mrs. Griffin could stop her. Both of us just sat there a second or two more, staring at the pattern in the rug under our feet.

"She'll learn," Mrs. Griffin said. "Or else she'll have to find herself a new husband."

"I'm awful sorry, Miz Griffin. I felt bad for her being so homesick and all. I don't know what took ahold of me to invite her. It didn't do anybody no good."

"I understand, Lily." She walked me to the door.

Estelle was sitting prim in the buggy, her hands, and their gloves, folded in her lap, eyes straight ahead. And she stayed in that pose till we were all the way out of town. Then she crumpled. It made me feel worse, seeing her cry, like I could cry too if I didn't watch myself. She didn't have a handkerchief and I gave her one of mine. She blew her nose.

"I'm sorry, Estelle. It's my fault. I knew it was a bad idea to take you there and I did it anyway."

"What have they got against him, Lily? What has he ever done to any of them?"

"Ask Jack that," I said, and then I thought about Jack and how I'd have him angry with me now, too. It wasn't a comforting thought.

By the time we pulled up to their house, she wasn't crying anymore, but her face was pale and her eyes were swollen. I didn't think I should go in with her. She got down from the buggy on her own and thanked me, for what I don't know. I sent the mule down the road and had gone twenty or thirty yards before I heard Marion running up behind me.

"Lily, wait!" he said, and I pulled to a halt. I let him come but I didn't want to face him neither. He jumped up on the seat beside me and leaned his head down till I didn't have any choice but to look at him. "What happened?" he said.

I lifted one shoulder. "It wasn't all right after all. I gave them credit for having better manners than they do. They found out who she was, and they didn't want any part of her. It wasn't very Christian-like."

He put his arms around me, both of them, and drew me close. My head rested on his collarbone. He held me there like that but I didn't cry. I never would have believed he'd be so forgiving of me for letting him and Jack down. I clung to him and I wouldn't have cared if the whole town had paraded by and saw us. Fact is, I was tired of hiding him and felt it didn't matter to me anymore what people thought.

He rode with me a while, driving the mule for

me, till it got so's we were getting too far for him to walk back. He kept smiling at me, leaning down to touch his head to mine, just as if it hadn't been the worst day in my memory, next to when my mama died.

When he pulled the mule to a stop, he got down from the seat, held onto my hand, and said, "Don't you fret none, Lily. It ain't you're fault now. And it ain't only them ladies either. Jack knew. He knew when he brought her here. Just like you said."

I pulled his hand to my lips and kissed the back of it and rubbed it against my cheek. At that moment I felt I could go anywhere with him and spend the rest of my days just looking at his face.

Then he slapped the mule on its rump and stood there waving at me, smiling, till I was on down a ways, before he turned around and headed back to Jack's house afoot.

12

I got home midday, not two hours after I left Mrs. Griffin's. Papa was sitting on the front porch when I turned in the gate. The buggy wheels scattered the chickens that were scraping for bugs or something green to eat in the fallen leaves on the ground.

Dane ran out to me, Knuck hard on his heels, and reached for the driving reins. "Papa says for me to put up the buggy. He wants a word with you."

I glanced at Papa, then gave the reins to Dane and climbed down. I knew from the way Dane was acting, and from seeing Papa on the porch and still good sunshine left, that I had trouble coming to me. The walk across the yard seemed to take forever, with Papa's eyes hard on me. As soon as my foot hit the bottom step, his voice halted me.

"The Bishops rode by here more than two hours ago. Said the gathering in town was over. Where you been all this time?"

My mouth got dry. I stared at the toe of his boot. The seam at the sole was worn loose and his sock poked through. "Giving somebody a ride home."

"Who?"

"Somebody you don't know."

"I asked you who." He leaned forward as he said it, his hands gripping his knees like he might spring at me.

"Estelle Beatty," I mumbled, lowering my head. I felt dizzy. My neck burned.

"Speak up, girl. And don't roll them eyeballs at me. I'll knock them outta your head."

"Estelle Beatty," I said out loud.

Papa glared at me while I stood there quiet and still, sweating under my arms, though it wasn't warm enough out for sweat. I thought I heard somebody rustling inside the front windows but didn't turn to see who was there.

After a moment, Papa took out his pocketknife and opened the blade. Then he brought out his tobacco and cut off a corner. He did it automatic, without looking. His brows knit together as he chewed, and he ran the tip of the knife under the nail on his thumb, scraping out dirt and wiping it onto his knee. I stayed statue-like in front of him, hoping if I was still enough he'd forget I was there. Of course, he didn't.

"Ava Kennedy come by here, too. A little while ago. She come to tell me things about my own daughter I would of never believed. She said she seen you keeping company with one of them Beatty boys, and now you're telling me you was taking their sister home in my buggy."

"Not their sister. She's the wife to one of them."

His head jerked up. "You know them intimate, do you?"

"She's new here. She don't have any friends at all."

He folded his knife and stood up. He wasn't a big man, but he seemed so to me then. He was trying to control his temper, but I shrank from him anyway. "I forbid you to be friends with them people, Lily. I can't allow it. Do you understand me?"

I looked to the side of the porch at where a mockingbird was squawking up in the magnolia tree. Marion's face came to me like he had been just a little while before, smiling sweet, his hair curling down his forehead. Papa couldn't keep me away from him. There was no way. My eyes welled up and I bit at the insides of my cheeks.

"Everybody in town is gonna be watching you now. If you don't think I'll find out, you better think again," Papa said. "Are you hearing me on this?"

I tried to keep the tear from leaking past my eyelid. It dropped out anyway and dripped down my face. I didn't brush it off. To brush it off would have been to admit it was there, hanging on my cheek. I wouldn't do that with Papa staring at me. The sight of it seemed to make him angrier. Air whistled in his nose.

"You've been seeing one of those boys, hadn't you? Just like Ava said. You seen him today, didn't you?"

"No." My voice came out sharp. I didn't intend it to sound so.

"Don't you lie to me."

I looked at him straight in his eyes. "Miz Kennedy's the one who's the liar."

His hand came up sudden and popped me so loud I staggered. It wasn't the pain of it, though he hit hard enough to leave finger marks that I saw later when I looked in the chifforobe mirror—it wasn't the pain but the surprise of it that knocked me back. He'd whipped me before but never struck my face. He seemed shocked by it himself and looked down at his own hand.

"That's for lying to me," he said, his voice low. "And for getting fresh. Don't ask to go into town, Lily. Don't ask to go nowhere. You'll stay here on this farm till I say different." And he walked off the porch and around the side of the house towards the barn.

The rocker where he'd been sitting thumped back and forth on its runners. I watched it till it quit, then I slumped onto the swing and crossed my arms over my stomach. I felt cold inside, angry and sad, but the tears had dried up in my eyes.

The front door squeaked open, and Dellie's head poked around the frame. "Sissy? Are you all right?"

"Leave me alone," I snapped at her, and didn't even look her way.

I never expected Papa to keep me from church too. But when Sunday rolled around—slow, so slow—he walked Dane and Nathan and Dellie out to Mrs. Kennedy's wagon and told her I wouldn't be going. He gave me extra chores to do, gave me a hoe and sent me out to cultivate the rows of oats that were coming up in the fields. I turned over the topsoil and chopped out weeds, and resentment built inside me until I thought I would scream. Was Marion wondering what had become of me? Had he heard yet of my imprisonment on this farm? The days crept by like years.

I couldn't get the interest up to do anything about Christmas. It was only a week away and Dellie's sweater was still half-finished in my knitting bag. I had nothing at all for Papa and the boys and couldn't think of anything they'd want from me.

On Tuesday, as a norther was blowing in, the men went out after a Christmas tree. We cut one down every year and brought it into the house to decorate with strands of popcorn and paper cut-outs. It was Dellie Papa did it for, but I wasn't up to the work he'd need from me.

While they were gone, and while Dellie was busy with scissors and red tissue paper left from last year, I went to the bedroom to write Marion a letter. I used the good stationery Mrs. Kennedy had given me two years ago upon graduating from Miss Huddleton's school. There'd only been two sheets used so far: one to send off for a fashion catalogue that I never ordered from and that Dellie ended up cutting to pieces for paper dolls. The second sheet had gone for stoppering a hole in Papa's chin where he'd whacked it open one day while shaving. He'd bled like a stuck pig, all over the back porch steps, where he'd set his pan of water. I pulled out two more sheets of the stationery.

In the letter I wrote, I told Marion that Papa had me tied down real tight and that I hadn't been free to see him in case he'd tried. I said how I missed

him and thought of him every minute of each day.
I said if he could think of a way to send me a letter
I would appreciate it. And then I asked after
Estelle and Jack, and if I'd caused them much trouble. And I signed it "With love, Lily." It took me a
lot of courage to write out the word *love* like that
so bold.

Then I wrote Mrs. Griffin. I thank her for invit-
ing me to her party and I apologized again for
causing her embarrassment. And I asked if she
could have Willie deliver my letter to Marion. I
folded his up inside hers, pushed them both into
an envelope, and sealed it shut with a glob of wax
off the candle piece beside the bed. I wrote "Mrs.
Hazel Griffin" on the outside, and I tucked it
under my pillow. When I went back out to the
front room, my step was lighter.

"Let's make some cookies," I said to Dellie, and
her eyes lit up like new moons.

By the time the men got back, we had three
batches out of the oven, and the house smelled like
gingerbread. Papa almost smiled when he walked
in, and Nathan pulled us outside to see the tree
they'd cut.

"I'll be needing some thread for the decorating,"
I said to Papa. "Could you send Dane in to
Billingsley's?"

Papa gave Dane the money and I went to get the
envelope. I put it into Dane's hand right out in the
open so nobody would get suspicious, though I
got a little breathless myself as I did it.

"Deliver this to Miz Griffin," I said. "It's a
thank-you note."

* * *

On Thursday, Timmy Griffin drove his mama up to our gate. The wind was blowing hard that morning, and a bank of new clouds had built in the north sky. Papa and Dane were out in the barn, getting the animals battened down for this storm that was coming in hard on the tail of the last one. Nathan was the one that saw the Griffins, and he ran out without his coat on to open the gate.

I had Dellie at the table making shapes from a pasty dough of flour, salt, and water that we'd paint after it dried out, then hang on the tree Dane and Papa had stood in the corner. I left her there and went to the porch, wrapping on my shawl. When I saw who had come, my pulse quickened. Mrs. Griffin carried a box in her hands.

"Morning, Lily," she said, coming up the steps. She gave me one look in the eyes, then no more. "I brought a fruit cake to y'all. Do y'all like fruit cake?"

"Oh, yes ma'am, we sure do." I took the box from her hands and started to pull up on the top.

"Don't open it *now*," she said quick and under her breath. Then she made a smile. "I just gave it a brush with butter before we came. It probably ain't set good yet."

I took the box to the kitchen cupboard, and Mrs. Griffin went to look over Dellie's shoulder and admire the shapes of dough—the stars and bells and one angel that had come out kind of lopsided on the wings. She gave Dellie some hints about cutting them straighter.

Nathan and Timmy sat on the floor by the fire.

They talked in whispers and laughed, deep in
their ownselves. Timmy had brought a bag of mar-
bles and they rolled them around under the furniture, belly-crawling after them like lizards. One
careened up under the cook stove, and they went
for it with the handle end of my broom, banging
and knocking against the cast iron till Mrs. Griffin
spoke sharp to them to be quieter.

While nobody was looking, I eased open the
box. The fruit cake smell rose to me and I spied a
piece of paper tucked in between the cake and the
side of the box. I plucked it out and slipped it
deep into the pocket on my skirt.

"Would you like some coffee, Miz Griffin? I got
some, fresh ground from this morning." I turned
around. She was looking right at me. I flushed
with knowing she'd seen me get the note.

"Thanks, but I've got some more errands to run
before this cold comes in."

"Well . . ." I nodded. "We sure do appreciate the
cake."

"I'm glad for that." She came to push at the
strands of hair that was flying out from my clip,
and she peered at my face then, like she wanted to
say something else besides what she said next. "I
just hadn't ever learned how to make *one* fruitcake.
It always comes out enough to feed the whole
country. Y'all have a merry Christmas now, Lily.
You hear?"

When they were gone, I rushed out back to the
privy. The letter was stuck together with goo from
the fruit cake. I peeled it apart and held it up to
the light from the door.

Deer Lily,
I to miss you and think of you dayly. I feered you
were ill or mad with me. I am glad that is not the
case. Can you com out of the house at all? If so I
think I can find a way to be in your barn one nite.
Tell me wat to do. Put a note outside your gait. I
will find it.
Jack and Estell or well. Thank you fore asking.

Fore ever yours,
Marion

Papa came out of the barn just as I closed the
door on the privy. His voice made me jump.
"Whose wagon was that out front while ago?" He
stood wiping his knuckles with a rag.

I tried to put an innocent look in my eyes. "It
was Miz Griffin. She brought us a fruit cake."

The rag in his hand kept working. I thought he
stared at me too long, but he said, "We'll come in
and have a piece."

I nodded and went back into the house.

The fruit cake still sat where I'd left it on the
cupboard. I lifted it from the box and set it on a
plate. I had out a knife and was slicing it thin,
when Papa and Dane came in the back door. Papa
saw me with the cake and his face relaxed.

"We'll have some of this cake, Dane," he said,
"then I'll need you to chop plenty of wood. Keep
the fire going, Lily. We'll need the heat tonight."

The coming norther worried me but not for the
same reason as it did Papa. I wondered how Marion would find a note from me outside the gate
with the wind howling. I didn't know if he'd even

come out in the cold, but if he did I didn't want
him to come and find nothing. I thought on it all
afternoon. I closed myself up in the bedroom and
I stared hard at his picture.

Near sundown, I took Nathan's leather coin
pouch out of his drawer. I didn't think he'd miss it
since it didn't contain any money and rarely did. I
scribbled a note. Two words. "Tomorrow night." I
folded the paper into the bottom of the pouch and
drew the string tight, doubling in a knot. I went
out the back door with the pouch tucked under
my arm.

Dane had the ax and was chopping wood on a
tree stump. He already had a nice stack, and when
he raised his eyes at me, he looked bone-tired.
"I'm going to close up the gate," I said and walked
around the side of the house. Papa wasn't in sight.

The chickens had all taken cover beneath the
porch and the house. I could hear them clucking
under there. There wouldn't be any eggs for a few
days, not till this cold snap passed. Something
about frosty air always shut down those hens. I'd
have to do Christmas dinner without.

I got to the gate and pulled the panels together.
I acted like I was having trouble with it, in case
somebody was watching, and I stepped outside by
the road. The wind blew hard while I was there
and my shawl got hooked on the fence.

Then I saw a good nail, poking out of one of
the posts just enough to hold the pouch, and
down near the ground where the wind wouldn't
take it too easy. I bent and pulled the pouch from
under my arm, wrapped the strings around and

around the nail. I stacked a rock against it to hold it in place, but the leather of the pouch blended so well with the colors on the ground, I wondered if he'd see it down there. I thought of the words he'd written: *I will find it*. I touched my chest where I'd put the letter inside the front of my dress and felt the stickiness of the fruit cake. Then I closed the gate and headed back towards the house.

13

The next morning, it was cold out. When I went to milk Bethel, my hands nearly froze before I could get in the barn. The hinges on the door squealed loud enough to make the mules bray. I thought of Marion and how if he did come, that squeaking would give him away. After breakfast, while Dellie and Nathan were cleaning up the dishes, I went out with a cup of lard and greased the hinges and the bar bolt that locked the door. I greased up the back door to the house, too, so's it would open and close quiet.

Papa and Dane were in the shed running the grinding stone, sharpening the ax and the tools Papa would need for slaughtering the big hog we'd fattened up all year. Both of them were too busy to notice when I went to the gate.

The pouch was in the same position as I'd left it. Even the rock was still there. But the note inside was gone. It surprised me so, I nearly cried out. I tucked the empty pouch into my apron and hurried back to the house.

The days were getting shorter, but I churned butter to make this one pass quick. And while I did that, I read to Dellie to keep my mind off Marion, though his picture kept slipping out of the back pages until I felt sure she saw it there. I got through The Book of Ruth and most of Samuel before the dasher made the butter come. We spent till supper time working out the extra milk, filling up the molds.

By nightfall I was ragged with nerves. I wondered when Marion would come. I worried about Knuck barking, about Papa or one of the others not being asleep. *Tomorrow night* was all my note said, and I felt stupid for not giving a time, a way. I couldn't even be sure it was Marion who'd emptied the pouch. A stranger on the road might have seen it there and thought it held money. Anything might have happened.

Papa stayed up for some time after the rest of us went to bed. He had out his whetstone and was sharpening his small knives now, and I never realized he had so many. I laid in the bed and listened to the sound of the steady scraping from the front room. Dellie fell asleep first. Then Dane and Nathan went too, and still Papa's knives scraped— *scraped*. I thought the sound would never stop, or that I would fall asleep myself before it did.

Finally, the lamp light left the front room and got dimmer. His boots thunked around the floor for several more minutes. Then I heard his bed creak and the light went out. I kept my eyes wide open so they'd get used to the dark. I had left my dress out and easy to slip into. I listened for the door to the barn.

I waited with my face to the window, trying to

see outside. The pane was dusty and the barn door not within my sight, but I watched for some movement. An hour must have passed with me like that, staring out at the night. My vision got blurry. The wind whistled through the roof of the house and popped in the walls. I saw no sign of Marion.

Finally, I crawled over Dellie. I would go to the privy. That would be my excuse if somebody woke up. And while I was out there I would look in the barn. I pulled on my dress just in case. I took my boots in my hand, and wrapped on my shawl.

I held my breath as I eased through the house. The lard on the back door worked. No squeak. The cold blasted me in the face and sucked out my lungs. Knuck wasn't on the back porch and he didn't come running. I figured my scent was carried off in the wind. I pulled on my boots, just ripping a knot right quick to hold the laces out from under the soles so's I wouldn't trip.

I tiptoed down the path to the barn. I don't know why I tiptoed. I expected any second for Papa to walk outside after me. I got ready to veer towards the privy if he came. I pulled my shawl tighter against the wind. It blew right through the crocheted wool.

The barn door was unbarred. It moved out an inch and then in with the rhythm of the wind. The hinges slid smooth as I turned inside, not letting the door swing open too wide.

The instant I stepped in the barn, a hand closed on my arm, then dragged me to the corner, between the loft ladder and the door. It was too dark in there for me to see, but I knew his smell. His mouth found mine. And then he just held onto me.

"I didn't know if you were here," I whispered against the roughness of his coat. "I've been listening for you and watching. I didn't see you come."

"You didn't see me at the fair, either. Remember that? I told you then I was good at sneaking." He sounded like he had a smile on his face. A noise came from across the barn and I jumped. He kept ahold of me. "It's just your hound dog. He's over there. I brought him a bone."

I could hear it now, the gnawing sound of Knuck's teeth. "You thought of everything."

"So did you. You got hog fat on that door." His hands threaded through my hair. "Run off with me, Lily."

"Where?"

"I don't care. Let's just go."

I snuggled closer to him. "I can't. I want to but I can't."

"Why not? What's here for you? You can't even step past the fence."

He started kissing me again, and when he did that I almost said yes. Let's go and now. As we are and no more thinking about it. I couldn't hear anything, see nor feel anything but Marion, his arms around me, his warm mouth. This time when he quit the kiss, I didn't want him to.

"I got Mollie tied up on the road," he said. "There's a dance going on over at the old Earhart place. They gotta Christmas tree and a fiddle band. Mollie's waiting on us. Come on, Lily, go with me there. I wanna show you off to everybody."

"Your brothers are there?" I said, my breath catching.

"Them and lots of other folks. I'll get you back home safe. Your pa won't even miss you.

I wanted to. The thought of swirling in Marion's arms to music and to laughter was pure heaven in my mind. I leaned there against him, pondering on it, wondering what kind of sin I was committing just in wishing for it.

"Lily?!"

It was Papa's voice. Outside. My eyes popped open. Marion let me go, and I leaped away from him quick. And just as quick the trembles sprang on me.

"The dog," Marion said so soft I barely heard him. He backed further into the dark. *The dog*. What did he mean by that? I couldn't ask out loud. I groped towards the sound of Knuck's chewing.

"Li-*ly*?"

Papa sounded like he was coming from the direction of the privy, like he'd gone there first to check for me.

I grabbed Knuck by the head. He growled when I took away his bone. I started pulling him by his neck towards the door. Marion reached out and snatched the bone from my hand just as the door swung open. He ducked quick behind it.

"Lily?" Papa stood in the opening. The night shown in behind him.

"Yes, Papa. I came for Knuck. He got shut up in here some way and he's been howling. You didn't hear him?"

"No."

"Well, he woke me up." I was afraid to let go of the dog for fear he would run to Marion and the bone. I walked, holding him by the skin on his neck, towards Papa.

"Let him a-loose then," Papa said.

I went a couple of more steps that way, holding onto Knuck. Papa didn't move from the door, so I let the dog go and I gave him a pop on his hind-end to make sure he went. He took off running around Papa's legs. I straightened from my slouch.

"All right. He's out," I said. "Now maybe I can get some sleep."

Papa stood still for five or ten seconds, not moving to let me go by. Then all at once, he swept me aside with his arm and strode into the barn. "Come outta here, you black-hearted bastard."

I'd never heard Papa cuss like that and it shocked me, scared me. Scared Marion too, I think, because he jumped out from behind the door and darted outside. I heard him run. Papa whirled in time to see the flash of shadow and then he went deeper into the barn. I rushed outside and watched after Marion. He was already almost to the gate.

Papa burst out of the barn. He was breathing hard, making vapor all around his face, and he held his shotgun in his hands. He cocked both barrels and raised the stock to his shoulder.

"No!" I pushed at his arms. "Dear God, Papa! Don't shoot him!"

"Get back, Lily!"

I grabbed for the barrel of the gun. "Stop it, Papa! Please! Don't shoot! I love him!"

He wrestled the gun out of my grasp, then dropped it at his feet. He grabbed me by my shoulders and shook me so hard I bit my tongue. I could taste the blood.

"He's white trash! Do you hear me! He's a criminal! Do you hear me, Lily!"

He turned me around and slung me over his hooked knee, and he began to whip me with his hand. It didn't hurt me. I didn't care. At least that shotgun was on the ground and Marion was gone from here and safe.

Papa's temper played out, or he realized I wasn't hurting from his hand. Or maybe, he saw finally that I was too big for him to tan me. And that I wasn't scared anymore. And that I wouldn't cry from it like Dellie or Nathan would. Anyhow, he let me go and stepped away from me.

"Tomorrow I'll see him arrested for trespassing." His voice was stern but quivery with anger. He bent to retrieve the shotgun.

"I *asked* him to come. He wasn't trespassing. And he ain't a criminal, Papa. Not him."

"It's *my* land, Lily. And he ain't welcome on it. Tomorrow I'll ride in to the sheriff." He turned and started up the path towards the house.

I went after him. "Please, Papa. I won't see him anymore. I promise it. I won't talk to him. Don't arrest him, Papa. I give you my word."

He kept on walking. "I don't trust your word no more."

"You can on this. I swear it. I swear to God and Jesus Christ, I won't see him anymore. Papa. Please. Don't call the sheriff on him."

I grabbed at his coat as he started up the porch stairs, but he slung me off and turned around. "Get ahold of yourself, girl."

"I ain't gonna see him anymore, Papa. I ain't. Please. Don't put the sheriff on him."

He stood there above me, looking down, the shotgun resting on his shoulder. "Listen to you," he said. "He's got you lying to me. He's got you sneaking around behind my back. Acting like a hussy. You ain't my Lily. I don't know what happened to her. But she ain't you." And then he went inside the door and shut it behind him.

For a moment, I stood there on the dirt path looking towards the far end of the road, listening for the sound of hooves. Nothing was there but the wind. I thought about running after Marion, running till I found him, or just plain running. But my feet moved up the steps, and my hands reached out for the door handle. I let myself inside.

14

A rifle shot woke me. I came off the pillow and
sat up just as if I hadn't been asleep. Dane
and Nathan's bed was empty and the house was
warm. Dellie was still and quiet beside me.

I looked out the window. Daylight barely
showed. And then I saw them, Papa and Dane and
Nathan, dragging the hog behind them, out of the
pen to the live oak between the house and the
barn where Papa would hang him. Papa had his
rope looped around his shoulder, and they were
struggling, the three of them, with the hog.

When Papa shot a hog it meant he thought cold
weather was here to stay now. It also meant a
hard, grueling day's work ahead. Not just today,
but tomorrow and Monday after that.

The awfulness of last night settled on me again
as I got out of bed. I scuffled around the room getting dressed, trying hard to forget what had happened, what I'd promised Papa, and God. I put on
my coat and took the broom with me to clean the
spiders out of the smokehouse.

The hog kept Papa busy too, though, gutting
and scraping, and getting the carcass spread out to

cool overnight. He didn't go into town, or mention the sheriff or last night. But then, he didn't speak to me all day neither. I stayed in the smokehouse scrubbing the salt box.

Sunday came, and after the kids went off to church with Mrs. Kennedy, Papa and me worked on the hog alone. We didn't speak except when there wasn't any other way for us to communicate. He cut up the carcass and I trimmed the fat for lard. We worked on a board at the back of the house in the cold, separating out the sausage meat and the souse meat from the hams and ribs. Knuck sat at our feet all day, waiting for a scrap to fall.

We went in for lunch and I cooked up some of the chitlins, which we ate with corn bread and slices of the hot, late onions out of the garden. And still we didn't talk. We never had talked that much, but now the silence was full of tension and spite. It was a relief to hear Mrs. Kennedy's wagon on the road, then Nathan and Dellie came tearing around to the back of the house.

"Somebody got shot last night," Nathan said. He was short-winded from running. "Outside Mister Billingsley's store. Killed too." His eyes flashed in the telling.

Dane appeared from around the corner, walking slow. Papa looked up from the cleaver and aimed his question Dane's way. "Who was killed?"

"I don't know." Nathan answered. "But they were all talking about it at church."

Dane came up then. He gave me a look, then said to Papa, "Boze Heffington was the man's name. Deputy sheriff over in Lee County. Mister Milton and Mister Bishop said tell you they'd be over here to speak with you about it this evening."

"What happened?" Papa wiped his hands on the rag he kept tucked into his overalls.

Dane glanced at me again. "They were robbing Billingsley's store again. Got eight hundred dollars this time. Mister Billingsley had so much money in the safe on account of Christmas and business being brisk. That deputy sheriff must of caught them at it. Nobody knows for sure, except that he was here investigating a burglary that happened over in Fedor last week. He's dead now, though. They found him this morning out in the thicket west of town."

They all glanced at me like it was me who'd done it, like I was guilty. Except Dellie. Her eyes were wide on the meat laid out on the board. She didn't like the sight of blood. Not even from a dead animal. I kept trimming and sorting the cuts into piles, pretending I hadn't heard Dane's news.

"It was Beattys and McLemores that done it," Dane said, and it seemed like he was talking right to me. "Mister Ogden at the livery stables says he saw them milling around. Saw Haywood Beatty throw the dead man over his horse and ride outta town. And Mister Nash said that the lot of them were in and out of the saloon all night, acting suspicious. Sheriff's in town now. Everybody's asking to be deputized. Mister Bishop says won't nobody get arrested for it, though. He says folks over in Bastrop ain't worried about our troubles over here at this end of the county."

Papa's eyes filmed over and his mouth set into a line. "Enough talk," he said. "Go inside and get outta them Sundays. There's work to do."

Knuck followed the three of them to the porch, then came back to his spot under the table when they went inside. The cleaver in Papa's hands kept working, cutting out bone. We were down to the hams and shoulders. The meat made a sticky sound where it hit the board as Papa chopped.

I kept trimming, pushing the fat into a kettle for lard rendering. I'd done well to keep my mind free of Marion for most of two days, but now with this news, I felt stung. I wondered of the truth to it, and why Mr. Milton and Mr. Bishop wanted to speak to Papa. Was it because of me? Did they think I knew something in advance? I waited for Papa to ask me some question about it while the kids were inside the house and we were alone. He didn't say a word.

My mind was so hard on thinking all afternoon—my heart busy denying Marion could have been involved with such ugliness, and saying to myself he couldn't be held to count for his brother's deeds—that I didn't hear the horses on the road or riding through our gate till Knuck started barking.

By then, we were all helping with the hog. Dellie washed the meat cuts in a pan of water, though she didn't like touching them. Nathan had gone out to find and chop the blades of bear grass we'd need to hang the meat in the smokehouse. Dane was getting the brine souse ready and chipping up clods of saltpeter.

Mr. Milton and Mr. Bishop rode their horses right around to the back of the house where we all were, both of them still in their church clothes, watch chains dangling at their ribs. Mr. Bishop had a pistol under his coat and it bulged clear, just below his breastbone. Mr. Milton carried a saddle gun with him. A double-barreled shotgun like the one Papa was keeping in his room now. It was Mr. Bishop that dismounted first and walked up to us in his fancy tooled boots.

"Evening, Josh," Mr. Bishop said to Papa. "Killed yourself a big hog, I see."

"Yep." Papa drove the cleaver tip first into the board and left it there. "About four hundred pounds, I reckon."

Mr. Bishop nodded. "Looks like a nice one."

Mr. Milton got down off his horse and came to stand with Mr. Bishop on the other side of our cutting board. Both their horses wandered off a little ways, back towards the side of the house, and I wondered why they didn't tie them up to something, or at least hold onto them so's they wouldn't get into things they shouldn't.

"Got bad news," Mr. Milton said.

"Heard about it." Papa turned to me then, and it surprised me when he spoke my name. "Lily. Take Dellie inside the house."

I dipped my hands in the kettle. The water felt warm, though it was straight from the well. Blood swirled off my fingers. The men stood there watching me, waiting for me to get inside. I took my time wiping my hands on my apron. Dellie followed me to the back door.

I sat her down by the fire and told her to stay put and warm her feet and hands there. Then I went to the kitchen window. I stood back so's I could see them outside but they couldn't see me. Mr. Bishop did most of the talking, gesturing with his hands. I could hear the drone of his voice but not his words.

With a long-handled spoon, I reached towards the window sash but I couldn't raise it, not even an inch. I looked at Dellie over by the fire, and she was looking back at me. Her face was drawn. I myself felt miserable inside.

"Put your ear next to the door, Sissy," she said. "Right up on the wood. That's how I do it."

It wasn't what I expected from her, but it made me realize she understood more of what was happening with me than I'd thought. I wanted to hug her then, because I felt she wasn't against me the way the rest of the family was. I moved to the door like she said to me.

The wood was cold to my ear and mostly all I heard was the wind and some other humming noise I couldn't identify. Mr. Bishop was still talking. I made out the words "McDade" and "McLemore," but that was all. I covered my other ear with my hand. He said, ". . . this town a safe place for decent folks to live in again."

Papa's voice mumbled something, and Mr. Bishop answered, "It's up to us, Josh."

Mr. Milton interrupted then, but I couldn't make out what he said. Their voices moved off and when I looked out the window again, Papa was walking them around to their horses. All three of them had their heads bent in solemn conversation.

I went to sit at the fire beside Dellie. My body felt froze to the bone after all day in the weather. I stuck my hands out to warm them, the same way as she did.

"Don't be sad, Sissy," she said to me. "It's almost Christmastime."

I put my arm around her and we both of us looked over at the decorated cedar tree in the corner. "Tonight we'll put the candles on," I said, and she gave me a tight hug.

Papa made no mention of the visit by Mr. Bishop and Mr. Milton. Nor did he allow us to speak of it, or of the killing or the robbery at Billingsley's store. Nathan tried once, and Papa shushed him with a stern look.

To me the incident didn't seem real. I didn't know anybody named Heffington, and so I couldn't feel bad about him, though it was, of course, a terrible thing if there'd been a murder. I had promised I wouldn't see Marion anymore, but that didn't mean I could stop thinking of him, wondering what he knew, if anything, about the whole matter. I thought about writing him another letter, but I doubted even Mrs. Griffin would see it delivered now, after this new trouble. I wondered if he'd been thinking of me too, worrying that I was all right after Papa catching us in the barn. I wished I knew why he hadn't tried to reach me some way.

I held the photograph from the fair under a candle and studied his face hard. I tried to read something there in his expression, in the jaunty angle of that crossed foot. Something that would tell me once and for all what was inside of his head. Something that would quell the doubts growing in me. Nothing came from the staring, and when I heard somebody walk up near to me, I clapped my Bible shut and snapped the lock.

The whole family was tired from all the work that day, but we put candles in tin cups and clipped them to our Christmas tree. Even Papa helped some, with the lighting. Then we sat back and watched the candles flicker, and we sang a couple of carols. My heart wasn't in it, but Dellie was about to bust a gut with excitement for Santa Claus. And even though Nathan no longer believed, and tried to act grown-up and uncaring, I saw the twinkle in his eyes too. I'd have to think of something to give them both. After about ten minutes, we blew out the candles and went on to bed.

Monday was Christmas Eve, and Papa excused me from the finishing of the hog. All that was left was to pack the meat in salt or brine, and then there'd be no more work till time to start hanging the smaller pieces with the boiled blades of bear grass Nathan had gathered.

While the menfolk worked out in the smokehouse, Dellie and me got started with the cooking for supper that night. We'd have one of the fresh hams, corn bread dressing, sweet potatoes roasted in the ash in the fireplace, then sweetened with cinnamon and butter. I cut open a pumpkin that I'd stored these weeks in the corncrib, and dug out the meat for pies. Dellie spread the seeds on a pan and roasted them to put in with the dressing. The cooking took all day, but we'd eat the food again tomorrow after church. On Christmas Day even Papa went to church, so I knew he'd have to let me go, too.

The men came in after dark hungry from the smokehouse. They washed up, and we sat down to the feast. Papa led grace and then the boys went to passing bowls. For Dellie and Nathan, Papa kept his humor up. I tried also. He even said to me, "It's tasty, Lily." It was the first kind words he'd said to me in three days.

After supper, we lit up the Christmas tree again, and Dellie started us singing carols like we'd done last night. This time, though, we kept up the singing for near to an hour. Papa knew all the words to the songs and helped the rest of us to remember when we got stuck. We sang "Hey, Ho, Nobody Home" at least three times since it was Dellie's favorite.

It occurred to me as we were singing that I would give Dellie what was left of the stationery from Mrs. Kennedy. And for Nathan, I'd stay up late hemming a pair of pants that Dane had outgrown. I'd kept them tucked away all this time in the cedar chest, saving them for when Nathan got big enough. But I knew he'd be pleased to have them now, even with a hem, since he'd never owned a pair of long pants save for his coveralls. I could fix them quick so's he'd have them to wear to church tomorrow. For Papa and Dane, I could think of nothing to give.

Dellie and Nathan both went to bed without a fuss. Dane helped Papa carry the wagon for Nathan out of the hayloft and set it on the back porch. Dellie's stick horse we put by the Christmas tree. I thought she was too big for it, but Papa had done a fine job of carving the head and painting on its face. I glued on some yarn for a mane, green because it was the only color I had enough of. Then I sat down to put the hem in the pair of pants.

Papa disappeared outside again. Dane sat down by my chair to watch me sew and to have another piece of pumpkin pie. He'd poured himself a glass of buttermilk, and it left a skim on the mustache that had started to grow above his lip.

"I didn't get long pants till I was twelve," he said, and I knew he was trying to strike up a talk with me. We hadn't been easy with each other since Eppie was found dead, and that wasn't usual for us. Always before, we got along good. Maybe it was Christmas making him think sentimental towards me.

I gave him a smile. "These are the very same ones."

"You remember the day Papa took us to town and bought them? He got you a fine pair of button shoes and me them pants."

I laughed. "And I got sore at you for making me call you mister all that day. Just because you were wearing long pants. I'd say your name, and you wouldn't answer me for nothing till I put the mister in front of it. *Mister* DeLony."

Dane laughed, too. "Whatever happened to them button shoes?"

"My feet grew another inch."

That busted us up and it wasn't really that funny, just something to laugh about and feel good with each other. We covered our mouths to keep from waking up Nathan and Dellie.

It struck me then how Dane was growing into a man, strong and tall. Fourteen on his next birthday, come March. I wondered if he had a girl he fancied, and I started to ask him since we were feeling friendly. But just then Papa came in the back door, and he was carrying his Sharps rifle in one hand, and a thin, flat box in the other.

"I'll just go ahead and give these to you," Papa said as he came to where we were sitting by the fire. He laid the rifle across Dane's knees and the box in my lap, on top of the pants I was hemming. "The crops ain't been good this year, and there hadn't been much money," he said. "Well, you both know that. But I wanted to give you something."

Dane's face glowed as he took ahold of the rifle. "Papa . . . this . . . ?" Words seemed to fail him.

Papa looked uncomfortable and wiped at his nose with the back of his hand. The cold outside in the barn had given him the sniffles, and I was thinking he might need a dose of quinine before he went to bed to stave off chills.

Dane kept staring, openmouthed, at the rifle in his hands. "This was yours in the war, Papa."

"I want you to have it." Papa pointed at the box in my lap. "Go on and open yours, Lily."

I pushed the needle through a fold in my skirt and lifted the box. It was heavy. My fingers untied the coarse string he'd used to wrap it shut. The thing that was inside took away my breath.

It was made of pewter, or something like it, heavy and molded into the shape of a wide, opening cabbage rose. On the backside was a mirror six inches around and I could see my whole face inside it. The handle was long with delicate curves.

"That was your mama's," Papa said, his voice sounding full. "I was saving it till you was old enough to give it proper care."

"Thank you, Papa," I said, almost whispering. I felt bad for not having anything to give him, and for feeling such distaste for him of late.

There was some extra lines around his mouth that I noticed. Not a smile, but close. He said, "You're like her, Lily. If I didn't know better, there's times I could see you and think it were her." As soon as he finished speaking, he dipped his head and hit his nose with the side of his hand again. "You young'uns get on into bed here pretty quick," he said and turned for his own room.

Both Dane and I were in such a state over Papa's generosity, we just sat there a minute, focused on the doorway to his room. Dane held the rifle lovingly across his knee, his hand smoothing back and forth along the wood stock. He said, kind of lower and whispery, "Did you get anything for him?"

I shook my head. "Couldn't think of anything."

"Maybe I could drive in early to Billingsley's and get him something. Some tobacco maybe."

"How'll you pay?"

"Trade him for one of the hams out in the smokehouse," Dane said. "Think he'll be open after getting robbed?" Then he seemed to realize what he'd just said and to whom. His eyes slid off me and back onto the Sharps. "S'cuse me," he mumbled.

I set the mirror on the floor beside my chair and unpinned the needle from my skirt. "Talk about it all you want to," I said, and took back up my hemming. "It doesn't bother me none. Marion didn't have anything to do with it."

Dane leaned forward over the rifle on his knee, studying on me. "How d'you know?"

"I just know. He ain't like the rest of them, Dane. If you ever spoke with him one time, you'd see."

"I ain't gonna speak to him. You better not either, Lily. Papa ain't joking on that. George Milton and Tom Bishop are gonna see to it them Beattys is run outta town."

The needle pricked my finger. Blood came up and I stuck it into my mouth. "Who told you that?"

"Didn't nobody. I heard them talking to Papa yesterday. They're planning something."

"With Papa?"

"With the whole town."

I reached with my other hand and clutched his forearm. "What, Dane? What're they planning?"

"I don't know. They didn't ever say. But even if they had, I wouldn't tell you nothing. I'm sick of seeing you in trouble, Lily." He leaned back from me. "Dan O'Barr was in church Sunday asking after you. Said he might come by here tomorrow evening after services."

"I ain't interested in seeing him." I took another stitch.

"Well, you oughta think about it. To ease Papa's mind a little. I'm just saying for your own good, Lily."

I blinked hard at the hem I was putting in and tried to keep my chin from qivering. I nodded but didn't look at him again. After a while when I didn't say anymore, he took his rifle and went off to the bedroom.

I watched him go, then rested my head against the back of the chair, the needle in my hand idle. There were cobwebs in the corners of the ceiling that I'd missed my last time through with the broom. I sat and stared at those cobwebs up there until the weepy feeling passed away from me.

Right then, I wished with all my heart that Marion hadn't ever stopped me on the street that day last summer. Or that when he did I'd ignored him and not let him carry my store package for me. Why couldn't I have just not spoken back to him when he said my name, like any other of the town ladies would have done? Why did I have to be different? Why'd I have to be the only one to see the good in him and love him for that, looking past the bad? Inside I felt like a wound-down spring about to pop.

I laid the pants for Nathan aside, half-hemmed, and trudged myself to the bedroom, too. There'd be time in the morning before church to finish the sewing.

15

I wasn't yet asleep when the whistle-sound came from outside somewhere. It wasn't a two-note whistle exactly, but close enough for me to sit up and listen sharp for it to come again. It did. I wondered where Knuck was and why he wasn't barking, though I was thankful for it.

I crawled over to Dellie and my feet hit the cold floor. I eased into the front room and peered out the windows, first one, then the other. It was dark outside, but as I stood there, the whistle came again. One long note trailing down to nothing. The sound wasn't exactly like I remembered, but I hurried back to the bedroom for my clothes. It was then, just as I put my hand out to open the chifforobe, that I heard the creak of Papa's bed, and after, his footsteps on the floor.

Quick, I got back into bed with Dellie and pulled the covers up to my neck. My eyes closed tight and I lay still but I didn't hear him come. His footsteps kept moving at the other end of the house, then changed in tone to boot steps. My eyes opened a crack and the soft, faint light from a candle came to our door. The rustling from the other room continued.

I huddled my head in the pillow and behind Dellie's turned shoulder, but I watched and waited. Finally, he appeared at our doorway and stood there a second or two. He had on his coat and his hat. He held his shotgun pointed down towards the floor. He looked in our room, then blew the candle out. The next thing I heard plain was the back door closing.

I rolled to the window as his form passed and disappeared around the barn. I sat up, my chest aching like my ribs were bound tight. It was all a puzzlement to me, but I knew then that the whistle hadn't come from Marion.

I eased to the foot of the bed and went back into the front room. The wick on the candle at the table where Papa'd left it still glowed. At the windows, I pulled open the curtain an inch and saw him go by the side of the house, leading Joe. I heard voices, then spotted the torchlight out on the road.

The bolt on the front door clinked as I slid it back, but I didn't care none about being quiet. I stepped out in my night clothes into the cold on the porch. There were men on the road outside our fence. A lot of men. I couldn't make out faces but one held the torch high above them all. Papa went through the gate with Joe and pulled it to behind them. Then he got on the saddle and rode off with the men in the direction of town.

My head was spinning. Papa? Riding with a vigilante band? There could be no other explanation.

And on Christmas Eve. And gone after the Beattys. I felt sure of it.

I went quiet but fast, and got my clothes, brought them back to the kitchen table. I relit Papa's candle and dressed by its light. I took Dane's heavy coat. The sleeves covered my hands but it was warmer than anything I owned.

The wagon for Nathan's Christmas gift sat on the back porch and I nearly tripped on it going out. I caught a whiff of a polecat some place nearby. Papa had pinned up Knuck inside the barn to keep him quiet and from following. He must have done it when he went after me and Dane's gifts, for he'd known that he'd be riding tonight. And he'd known the dog's barking might wake the rest of us. It felt deceiving, pure and simple. And for me it took the special off the gift of the mirror that had been my mama's, made it feel, in a way, like he'd smeared her goodness making her part of this. Knuck whined to be let loose and I talked to him low to keep him quiet.

I lit the lantern outside the mule pen. Ernest Lee was the fastest of the two mules, but there was no saddle for him, nor bridle. I had to make a hackamore for him, and I'd never been much good at tying rope. Tonight my hands moved sure, though, and I felt that God was with me in this. That whatever Papa and those men were up to, it wasn't the Lord's bidding and I was right to break my promise to Him. I slipped the rope onto Ernest Lee's nose, and he took it as easy as if it was a fancy, silver-mounted head-stall. Then I led the mule out

of the barn. Off in the distance, coyotes were yo-
deling.

I used the rails on the gate to hoist myself onto
Ernest Lee's back, and I kicked him hard to get
him going. In the opposite direction from the men,
out the two miles towards the shadow of the
Knobs, and to the Beatty place. I prayed that when
I got there Marion would be there, too.

On the mule the road passed by slow. I tried to
urge him faster but it couldn't be done. He wasn't
used to a rider. Behind a plow or under harness he
would have responded better. With me on his
back, I was afraid he'd rear if I pushed him. We
went at a trot. No more. I hoped I wouldn't be too
late.

Outside the Beattys' land, there wasn't any sign
of life. No light in the house. No dog pack. I
jumped down from Ernest Lee as soon as we were
up the trail by the barn. I scared up some critter
that darted sideways in front of me. I turned my
ankle on a rabbit hole. When I got to the door, I
cried out Marion's name and beat my fist on the
frame. I knew I'd missed them.

I didn't expect the door to swing open. I almost
fell inside. A pair of strong hands caught me, and
then a lantern lit across the room. It was Haywood
holding me up, but there were men all around, lying on a bed, on a busted cot, on the floor, which
was nothing but hard-packed dirt. There was trash
and filth every place, empty whiskey bottles
turned on their side, and globs of dried tobacco.
The house smelled rancid and like the soured
sweat of men's bodies.

I recognized Charlie Goodman then, and Robert Stevens when he rolled over on the cot. All of them wore long johns, save Haywood, who still had ahold of me, and Azberry, who looked sleepy and bloodshot where he sat on a bedroll near the far wall. The pistol in his hand was pointed my way.

I stepped out of Haywood's grasp. "S'cuse me," I said, stunned by the sight before me—enough to make me forget temporarily why I'd come.

Az threw up a laugh and lowered his gun. He called, "Get in here, Shot, and take care of your woman," and then to Haywood, said, "I thought you was keeping an eye out."

"I was. How'd I know she'd come a-shouting up the road?" Haywood said, then bent to look dead-on into my face. "What's up, girl?" he asked me. His eyes were downward turned and sort of sad-seeming at the corners. His voice sounded serious and full of concern. I thought of him killing that Heffington man and wondered if he really had done it.

But Marion came into the room then, buttoning on his britches, stretching his galluses over his shoulders. His hair was frowzy about his forehead and his boots weren't on his feet. When he appeared, he took my attention from Haywood straightaway. It didn't seem to me that Marion fit in this house, with the gamy mess laying all about. I felt for him then, having to live here and like this, with this class of people.

I said, "They're coming for you. All of you. I came to tell you so's you can get away from here."

"Who's coming?" Marion walked up closer to me. The sight of him made me weak. All over again. Just as if I'd never sworn to God to be done with him. Even there, in that awful place, in that fearful situation, I wanted to burrow into his arms.

"Vigilantes," I said. "They're gathering a mob. They got fifteen or twenty already, and they were headed towards town for more. I don't know what they're planning, but I know they're after you."

All the men rose at once. Robert and Charlie began to dress. Azberry said, "Them hoodoo sonsofbitches. Just let them try to swing me from a tree."

I hadn't thought of lynching till he said that. I gasped at the image it drew to my mind.

Marion took my arm. "You're sure about all that?" he said to just me.

"Papa's with them," I answered.

He steered me towards the door. "Go on home now, Lily." The others were moving around behind him, strapping on their guns, stepping into boots, mumbling amongst themselves.

"I'm going with you," I said.

"No you ain't." His face was hard, like I'd never seen it before. I longed for the crooked smile. He opened the door and nearly swung me through it. "Go now."

I heard Azberry say, "Goddamnit, get your ass back in here, Shot."

Marion glanced at the door, then gave me a little shove away from the house. "Now get, Lily. Go home."

I took a step backwards. He seemed satisfied

by it and turned into the house. From inside, somebody—I think it was Haywood's voice— said, "We'll get to Jack's. Ain't nobody knows where he lives."

"What if it ain't far enough," another one said. Robert Stevens maybe. I didn't know their voices good enough to tell for sure who did the talking.

I turned to look behind me towards the road. No torchlights yet, but I had no doubt they'd be coming soon. Ernest Lee had wandered away from the barn where I left him, but I didn't go that way. I had it in my mind to see Marion safe and out of here.

The first ones came out from the house. Az and Charlie Goodman. I stepped out of their path but they didn't seem to see me. They went straight for the barn. And then Haywood and Robert Stevens walked out. Bird Hasley came with Marion. I hadn't seen Bird in there before, and the sight of him, so tall and Indian-like, and with that pigtail down his back, scared me.

Marion saw me and grabbed my arm. "I said to go home, Lily."

I walked with him, skipping to keep up. "I ain't going."

"You can't come with me." He stopped at the near side of the barn. Az and Charlie had already mounted their horses and were riding out. They must have been keeping their animals under saddle because enough time hadn't passed for them to have done all that cinching.

"I'll follow you then," I said. "I gotta mule here."

Haywood and Robert Stevens rode out of the barn, going at a full gallop.

"Not tonight, Lily," Marion said. "I don't want you to get hurt." He still had hold of my arm, and I didn't think he knew how much his grip was hurting me now.

"I won't be trouble. And I ain't gonna get hurt. I promise."

"Leave her." Bird Hasley came out of the barn on his horse and bringing Mollie. "You ain't got time for arguing, Shot. Leave her and come on."

Marion hesitated, then he let go of me and took Mollie from Bird. "Go home, Lily. I'll send word to you later," he said and got onto his horse.

They took out across the hill behind the house, heading away from the road towards the back end of their land. I stood there at the open barn door and watched them go. Marion didn't look back at me and I felt empty.

When the sound of their horses died, I turned to hunt down Ernest Lee. He'd moved off into a patch of dead thistle. I fetched the rope trailing after him and pulled him into the clearing. He brayed and tug-o'-warred with me, but he finally came.

I got home without meeting anybody at all on the road. Joe wasn't back at the barn yet when I turned Ernest Lee into the stall. Knuck barked to be let loose from his pen. I left him there and snuck back into the house.

I couldn't see any way I could sleep, but I got into bed with Dellie. Now that I was back home, it was easy to imagine none of it had happened, that

I hadn't left and that Marion hadn't shunned me. I prayed he was safe, and asked the Lord to forgive me for the excess of love I had in my heart for him. I knew it was a sin for me to let somebody hold such powerful sway on my soul. I prayed for God to lessen the strength of my feelings, and at the same time, I listened for Papa's return. I flopped around on that bed so much and for so long, I feared I'd wake Dellie. But somehow, amidst all that inward struggle, sleep came and overtook me.

16

When Dane shook my shoulder, there was barely enough light in the room to see. I felt I'd come out of a deep and horrible dream till my mind cleared enough to remember it wasn't a dream I'd had.

"Papa's still asleep," Dane whispered. "I'm leaving for town."

I sat up and pulled the quilt off me. "I'm going along, too."

"You can't go." He was dressed and ready. He stepped back and frowned at me. "What if Papa wakes up?"

"He won't." I pulled on the skirt I'd left out on the cedar trunk. I'd worn my chemise to bed. "He was gone most all the night."

Dellie sat up rubbing her eyes. "Did Santa Claus come?"

Dane frowned at me. "How do you know that?"

I leaned on the foot of the bed to put on my boots. "I heard him go. He had his shotgun, and he rode out with some other men."

Dane's eyes got as round as a coon's. I tied my laces and kept watching him. He wouldn't stop me from going now. He knew as well as me what that night ride meant.

Dellie's little legs kicked off the covers. "Did Santa Claus come?" she said again, cross because nobody had answered her. Nathan, over in his bed, kept snoring.

"Yes," I said. "He came, but he forgot Papa. Me and Dane's gonna go up town to buy something for him. You play quiet and don't you wake him, hear?"

We got the fire going in the fireplace and left Dellie beside it, scribbling with a pencil on a sheet of the stationery. There were four piles of taffy candy on the kitchen table that hadn't been there last night, and a five-cent piece each for all of us. From Papa, of course, but Dellie swore Santa had come.

Dane eased the door to Papa's room shut, and we didn't wake Nathan either. We took our two coins off the table. It was enough to buy a pouch of tobacco, and Dane stuck the money into his trouser pocket. I wasn't really thinking of a gift for Papa anymore. I wasn't thinking of his anger either, if he woke up and found us both gone. My thoughts were on Marion, wondering if him and the others had made it safe to Jack's house.

It took a while to get Joe hitched to the buggy. He was balky and tired after having been ridden all night. Dane said we should take one of the mules. I didn't pay him any mind, though, since Joe could get us there quicker. I kept on struggling with the hitch till it was on, and we finally got under way, but it took more time than it should

have. The sun came out good and full before we
were halfway to town.

"Reckon Mister Billingsley'll be open for business today?" Dane said as we rode. He was doing
the driving but I had a mind to take the reins from
him and give Joe a smart crack on his back to get
us moving along faster.

"I've never known him to close, save for church,"
I said. All I'd worn was my shawl and it was nippy
enough I needed more. "I expect he'll be there now
and closed later, when Brother Parkins starts his sermon."

Dane nodded and didn't say anything else. Both
of us were thinking of Papa and the mob last
night, though I guess for different reasons. Dane, I
figured, was feeling glad about it, while inside of
me, a terrible dread had begun.

When we turned off our road onto the one that
led into town, we saw Willie Griffin on his horse,
coming down the lane in front of the church
house. We got to the crossroad at the same time as
him, and he stopped like he wanted to speak.
Dane pulled up on Joe.

"Where you bound so early?" Willie said, and
his eyes were on me. He wasn't but at most
twenty, but his face looked older to me that morning, and yellow from the heavy drinking he did all
the time. He had on a gun and riding gauntlets, as
if he'd just gone a long way or expected to soon.

"We've got business in town," I said.

"I think you should turn back," he said. "It ain't
a sight for boys and ladies down there this morning."

"What do you mean?" Dane took offense at being called a boy. Willie caught it and just smiled kind of halfhearted.

"What do you know, Willie?" I said, and he knew I was asking if Marion was safe.

He gazed down the road, then back at me. "There's been three men taken during the night, bound and lynched to that big oak by the tracks. They were just pulling them down when I was there before."

"Pulling who down?" Dane stood, straining to see up the road. I could see as far as the tracks and no further. I felt suddenly sick to my stomach.

Willie Griffin spat on the ground. "Not who you think," he said to me. "They got the McLemores and Henry Pfeiffer. A mob came and took them outta the saloon last night. I wouldn't go down there if I was you."

"You're going," Dane said and sat down.

"Well, I ain't you." Willie heeled his horse on by us and started down the road. We watched him go a piece.

"Should we turn around?" Dane said to me.

I shook my head. Relief had come to me fast behind the first sick feeling. It wasn't Marion. None of the Beattys. I knew I'd saved their lives.

"Think Papa was part of that lynch mob?" Dane said, his voice dark and spooky. It made me shudder.

"Do you?"

Our eyes met but we didn't answer our question. He gave the reins a wallop and we started down the road behind Willie.

Soon as we cleared the trees, the whole town was spread before us. The bank first, then Bassist's drugstore, the barber shop, Billingsley's store, the beef market and the rock saloon, all joined in a row and connected one to the other by walls and a long gallery in front. The road we were on went directly to the town buildings, then crossed over Main Street where they faced, then ran on down between the saloon and the livery, the blacksmith shop and Mr. Westbrook's lumberyard. And across Main from all these buildings, in the meadow between the tracks and town, grew the spreading limb oak tree where three pieces of rope hung like heavy, chopped-off vines. When the wheels of the buggy hit the railroad tracks, I nearly bounced off the seat, for my attention was dead on that tree.

Willie Griffin hitched his horse to the rail at the side of the rock saloon. He glanced our way before he walked in through the doors. Men were milling around all up and down the long gallery, but there weren't any lynched bodies in sight. Old Captain Highsmith, who'd once been a cavalry officer but now was just our town drunk, sat on a bench outside the saloon. He was talking fast and hard to anybody who'd listen, waving his hands along with his words. Almost everybody wore a gun, and I didn't see one other female, young or old.

Dr. Vermillion was out front of Billingsley's, sitting with Tom Bishop on two nail kegs, a big open book spread between them. I thought at first it was a Bible and that they were reading verse, but as I stepped down from the buggy, I saw it was some kind of medical journal. Mr. Bishop raised his face at me and Dane, and gave us a curious look.

"Merry Christmas, DeLonys," he said, and I thought he sounded downright jolly.

Nothing anywhere seemed out of the usual, and I began to suspect that Willie Griffin had given us a tale. But then those ropes were hanging from that tree, and I couldn't remember ever seeing them there before.

I didn't speak back to Mr. Bishop, but Dane did and stopped to look at the big book they were reading. I heard Mr. Bishop say he had somebody at home with a fever, either his wife or his baby. He had on a new pair of boots, a Christmas gift most probably. They were made of reddish leather and shone the sun in my eyes. I went on into the store.

Mr. Milton stood behind the counter. The sight of me seemed to startle him, too. "Lily," he said. "What can I do for you on this lovely Christmas Day?"

I looked out the two front windows. The sun was shining, sure, but it didn't seem like a lovely day to me at all. If three men had hung last night, and if my papa was one of the ones who'd done it, and if all this had happened on the birthday of our Lord and Savior, I didn't see anything to call this day lovely. I didn't smile at Mr. Milton.

"I came for a twist of tobacco," I said. "Ten cents worth."

He went to the jars and dipped his hand in. He knew the kind Papa chewed and broke off the right amount. He reached for a pouch out of the different size piles beside the jars. Ten cents bought one of the largest ones.

"Was Santy Claus good to you this morning?" he said, just to make pleasant talk. He drew the pouch string closed and held out his hand for the money I owed.

I remembered then that the coins were in Dane's pocket. I turned to call to him, but before the words came out of my mouth, Jack Beatty stomped into the store. His face was as dark as storm clouds. He had on a long coat, his black hat, no vest. If he was wearing his guns, I didn't see them. I jumped away from the counter. He seemed not to notice me, anyhow. His eyes were fast on Mr. Milton. He stopped in the middle of the store.

"Milton," he said, his voice like a growl. "You goddamned sonofabitch. You been talking against my brother."

I looked at the door and saw Haywood on one side, Charlie Goodman and Bird Hasley at the other side. All three of them had guns drawn. I eased further to the back of the store, back by the yellowed lace that had been on the shelf for two years. Dane had disappeared, and so had the doctor. I didn't see Marion anywhere, either.

Even though Jack wasn't showing a gun, Mr. Milton looked scared spitless. "What do you mean by that, Jack?" he said.

"I'm talking about them three men you hung last night. I just been to the saloon and Mister Nash said the mob came in calling for Haywood, too. For the killing of that Lee County man he didn't have nothing to do with."

"I don't know anything about all this, Jack."

"You're a damned liar, Milton. And them men you strung up happened to've been two of my cousins—"

A shot sounded out on the street and Jack turned to look. The ones at the door looked too, down towards the saloon. Mr. Milton reached under the counter and brought out a pistol, and when he did that, I screamed, "Watch out!"

Jack whirled towards me but his eyes were vacant, like his thoughts were someplace else. Charlie Goodman fired and hit a glass case above Mr. Milton. Glass came clattering down behind the counter and Mr. Milton ducked. Then Jack rushed out of the store, headed in the direction where the first shot had come from. The three at the door stayed with their guns out.

"Don't come outta here, Mister Milton," Charlie Goodman said, pointing with his six-shooter. "Stand up from there now, and just ease out around this counter."

Haywood saw me and waved for me to come out of the store. He was trying to watch both directions, me and whatever was happening outside. He jumped from one foot to the other.

Mr. Milton came up from behind the counter with a shotgun in his hands. He fired and blew a big hole in the wall beside the door. The recoil of the double barrels jerked his whole body. Haywood leaped backwards and took off running the same direction Jack had gone. The globboon by the door spun like a top and fell over, spilling dried lumps of chew onto the floor. I dashed for the outside.

"Come back, Lily!" Mr. Milton hollered, but I ignored him and raced between Charlie and Bird.

Men were standing all out in front of the saloon and the beef market, watching where Jack and Az were struggling with Mr. Bishop on the street. Mr. Bishop had hold of a pistol. Jack's hand was on the barrel. And blood was gushing from Azberry's left hip.

Marion wasn't anywhere around. My eyes skimmed the faces of all the men. I saw Robert Stevens run towards the line of horses belonging to the Beattys, tied horn to horn at the end of the saloon beside Willie Griffin's. Mollie wasn't there.

Everything happened fast then. Az stumbled backwards and Jack reached to catch him. And when Jack did that, he let go of Mr. Bishop's pistol. Tom Bishop stepped back and fired once, clean and sure. The bullet hit Az right between the eyes. Blood poured out of his head. My hands flew to cover my face.

Haywood yelled, "Stop that!" and more shots were fired, from him and from the two by the door to the store. I saw grimace on Haywood's face as he reloaded his gun, stepping out onto the street.

Charlie and Bird ran then, and Mr. Milton came out of the store with his shotgun raised, both barrels cocked back. "Get outta the way, everybody!" he said, aiming from waist high. All the men along the boardwalk crouched down or ran inside of doors.

I looked towards the street as Tom Bishop

whirled on Jack and shoved the pistol against his coat. The bullet whipped Jack sideways, and as he was falling, a blast from Mr. Milton's shotgun tore through his forehead, knocking him backwards. He dropped in a heap on the ground beside Az. I screamed out and sank to my knees.

Haywood was hollering, fanning his pistol at Mr. Bishop. All the shots were wild and missed. I heard him shout, "You sonsofbitches! You killed my brothers!"

Then Willie Griffin ran from the saloon with his gun drawn, but he never even got off one round. He fell to his knees and then facedown on the street, his pistol firing straight up in the air as he collapsed.

Guns were going off all around me. Two horses hitched in front of Bassist's drugstore yanked themselves loose and ran off, dragging the rail with them. I huddled behind a gallery post, shaking and covering my ears, crying too. The smell of gunpowder choked me, and a cloud of smoke hung over the street and under the gallery awning. I clenched my eyes shut and tried not to think, nor see again the brains and gore spurting form Jack's head, the dark red hole between Azberry's eyes. The whole world felt like it was spinning. I drew my shawl up over me and hunkered there.

When the shooting stopped, Dr. Vermillion found me and helped me to my feet. My ears were ringing. I didn't see Dane anywhere. Mr. Milton and Mr. Bishop had disappeared, and so had Haywood and Bird and Charlie Goodman. Three bodies lay mangled in the street, and I knew all three of them, had just spoke to two of them a few minutes ago. I'd never seen anything so horrible before, and it froze my tongue inside my head. I watched somebody walk over to Jack Beatty and put out a fire that was burning on his coat.

"Lily! Get up here!" Dane was on the high seat in the buggy, trying to keep ahold of Joe, who was twisting and shying away from the gunsmoke and all the noise just ended. Dane's face was stark white. "Let's get outta here!"

I looked at him and he seemed like a stranger to me. They all did. Like what I had just seen changed me somehow, scarred me inside. I hated them all. Dr. Vermillion, the men poking at the bodies lying in the dust on the road, the ones lined up along the gallery. The whole town.

I kept my eyes on my boots and I walked away from Dane, right through the middle of the crowd. I didn't look at the dead bodies. Somebody said, "Good God, his brains is spilled out all over." I heard Dane call my name. No one else paid me any mind.

At the side of the saloon, I unlooped one of the horses. It was Jack's horse, I was pretty sure. And I put my foot on the stirrup, hiked up my skirt, and swung onto the saddle. I turned the horse towards the back of the buildings, away from the main street and the horror there, away from Dane and the buggy, away from the road back to the farm.

I kicked the horse's flanks, and we darted through the back lots behind the stores, around the outhouses, up past the bank, and further down, the schoolhouse. The stirrups were let out too long for my legs. I had to stand in the saddle to reach them.

The horse was a daredevil, and leaped fences and ditches with no hesitation. He ran harder and faster than I'd ever gone, and it was all I could do to hold on. I didn't have to direct him. He headed the right way, down the road to Paint Creek, going home to his stable.

At first, I thought I dreamed I heard my name over the pounding of the hooves. Like I was going insane and hearing voices inside my head. Then I saw somebody crash out of the yaupon ahead and fall into the ditch. It was Haywood, holding his left arm cocked over his chest. He wasn't wearing a coat and his shirt sleeve was matted with blood. His face looked twisted and pale. He waved me down and I pulled back hard on the reins. The horse nearly pitched me forward over his neck, but I got him stopped quick.

Haywood crawled up the bank from the ditch. He limped bad. Blood was all over his right leg, saturating his britches. I jumped down to help him, and he leaned on me till it was all I could do to keep from falling too.

"You're shot," I said.

"I couldn't get to my horse."

He took ahold of the saddle one-handed. It hurt him bad to climb up there. I could tell from the way his eyes rolled to the back of his head. He looked ready to pass out. I tried to help him by using my shoulder to push him up. But I stumbled under the burden of him, and in the end it was his own strength that got him into the saddle.

"Where's Marion?" I said, mounting in front of him.

"At Jack's. Please. Get me there, too," he said, and he was barely whispering. He laid heavy against my back.

Several times I thought he would fall off the horse before we could make it there. I rode as fast as I dared with him unsteady behind me. When I felt the wetness at the back of my shirt, I knew it was from his blood, and I feared he might die. By the time we turned in through the trees that surrounded the house, my shoulders were aching and trembling with the weight of his limp body.

I called out for Marion and called loud. He came banging through the front door and ran to the horse. The dogs were there too, somehow. They barked but didn't growl, familiar as they were, I guess, with Jack's horse and Haywood on it. I'd never been so glad to see anybody in my life as I was to see Marion then. He pulled Haywood down from the saddle, and Haywood clamped onto Marion's shoulders. They started for the house.

I ran beside them, wanting to help, not knowing how. I was afraid to touch Haywood in a way that would cause him more pain. And Marion had ahold of him good, almost carrying him across the yard.

"Where's Jack and Az?" Marion said to me.

"Shot," Haywood answered. "Both dead. They didn't make it." His eyes were barely open. "Stevens run off. And so did Goodman and Hasley. Griffin's dead, too."

"Bob's here," Marion said, and I watched his face for a reaction to Haywood's news. Maybe it was because he was too busy bearing the weight of his brother, or maybe the truth of it just hadn't set in, but Marion's face didn't change one inch. He took Haywood careful up the porch steps.

"Two men against all us. Seven of us, counting Griffin," Haywood mumbled. "And the two won the fight. It was a piss-poor showing, Shot. We could of used you."

I held open the front door for them and they bumped inside the house.

17

*F*or the first minutes after we got Haywood inside, I felt lost. I didn't know who to go to, or which one to help. It was Marion I wanted to comfort, but he seemed to need it the least. And Estelle broke up when he told her Jack was dead. He said it so plain-out, just "Jack's dead, Estelle," and nothing else to soften the blow. So I held onto her and let her cry against my shoulder.

Bob Stevens was there, and he'd been shot himself in the crossfire as he rode out of town. The bullet had passed through his lower arm clean, in and out without catching on a bone. He helped Marion as best he could with a sling tied around his neck, to get Haywood back to the bed. When Bob came out, he took Estelle from me, sitting down with her on the slat bench and talking low and soothing to her. Saying to her how brave Jack was, and loyal to the end, rushing to his brother's side when he saw Az was shot down.

Marion called me to the bedroom where Haywood was laid out, the embroidered sampler on the wall above him. "I need you to hold onto his knee, Lily. Keep him from bending it. Hold tight now. He's strong as an ox."

I did like Marion told me and kept my eyes on the gold-threaded words above us—"In Wedded Bliss, December 2, 1883"—while he dug with his pocketknife for the slug lodged in Haywood's thigh. Blood was running all over Estelle's blue star quilt. The room turned white for me, fuzzy and out of focus. I held onto Haywood's knee and it took every bit of my strength to keep it still. Silently, I begged myself not to faint.

Haywood screamed and whimpered, then yelled out at Bob Stevens, "You ran, you cowardly sonofabitch! You ran off and left me there, goddamn you!" Then his hollering wound up to a spine-chilling yell that went on for near to a minute before it tapered off into great, panting heaves of his chest.

Marion pulled forth the bloody lump of lead, bits of flesh still clinging to it. His face was pale but set hard, and although it was cool in the room, sweat streamed down his brow. I couldn't believe the pluck he had in him, digging in his brother's flesh with that knife, so careful and steady. He seemed unmindful of Haywood's white-knuckled hand on his back, clutching to a fistful of his vest.

"It's out," Marion said, whether to Haywood or to me, or just to himself, I couldn't tell.

With the flat of the knife blade, he painted on a poultice that was mixed up in a bowl on the bedside table. Mostly mud it looked like, with a little spiderweb stirred in for clotting. A swirl of blood was already there on the top of the mud. Robert Stevens's blood, I guess.

While we dressed the thigh wound, Haywood laid there moaning. For a time, even with the poultice on thick, blood soaked through the bandages quick as we tied them on. It took nine layers wrapped tight before we stopped the flow. By then, blood was everywhere—on my hands, Marion's, our clothes. The color had left Haywood's face. He looked gray and dead to me already, save for the moaning.

Bob came to the room as we worked. He leaned on the door frame and watched us a minute. The sling around his arm was made from a piece of flannel, plaid like it came from somebody's shirt or off the corner of a blanket. He reached into his pocket, brought out a thin-rolled cigar, and struck a match, one-handed, on the seam of his britches. I noticed the flame shake as he drew off it. Haywood's shrieking had jangled everybody's nerves.

"Az started the row," Bob said, like he felt the need to defend himself to Marion. Smoke came from his mouth along with the words. He waved out the match. "He picked a fight with Tom Bishop right off. Just like Jack said don't do. He went up to Bishop and told him to get outta town or he'd kill him, and that's what started it. Bishop says, 'Who's gonna make me,' and you know Az. He can't stand that kinda talk. He gave Bishop a shove, and the next thing I know, Az is shot. That's the way it all happened."

Marion raised his head from the bandaging. "I

don't care to know about it. I don't hold nothing against you, Bob. Haywood don't either. He's just half outta his skull right now."

I saw the sadness flickering in Marion then, and I remembered when my mama died, how I hadn't wanted to talk about her after that, and still didn't really like to. I thought I understood what he was feeling. Haywood's head ground against the pillow like he was going into some kind of fit.

Bob left the room again, and Marion picked up the knife. He swished it in the pail of bright pink water on the floor by the bed, and said gentle to Haywood, "Lemme see that arm."

"No, goddamn you. You ain't doctoring on me no more." Haywood licked his lips and kept his eyes shut, but his voice rose in force. "You just try it and I'll whup your ass. Bob's too for running out on me. I ain't crazy. I know what I'm saying. I'll whup the tar outta both you sonsofbitches. You shoulda been there with me, Shot. Goddamn you, you shoulda come." His voice worked up to a frenzied pitch, and I heard Estelle in the other room cry out at some of the things he said, "They shot them cold-hearted. Blowed their brains out. And cause of me. Trying to clear my name. That goddamned Fitzpatrick. That goddamned yeller-bellied, running bastard. Jack said don't trust him. Goddammit, Shot, why wasn't you there? Why didn't you come when you seen Jack hadn't took his guns?"

Half of what he said didn't make sense to me. And he didn't wait for answers from Marion, but kept raving on and on, foul language spewing from him. Marion tried to hold Haywood still, but saw it was no use. Finally Marion sat up straight on the side of the bed.

He looked at me then, and kept looking at me till I thought he was trying to tell me something I should be doing. Haywood rambled on some more, and I knelt by the bed quiet, no longer listening, wishing I could read Marion's look.

He picked up a rag from the pile beside the bed, and his hand slipped into his vest at the same time, pulling out his pistol. I hadn't seen it there, and a gasp escaped me as he drew it out. He kept his eyes on me as he wound the rag around the butt-end of his gun. Then he moved quick and sudden, striking Haywood a blow on his temple that rolled his head still. I jumped at the sound of it, a deep, cracking thump.

"I didn't hurt him none," Marion said quick, and unwrapped the pistol. "He's just knocked out is all. There's a place you can hit a person. . . ." He touched his own temple, showing me. "Probably should of done it twenty minutes ago. Give him some relief." Then he saw me staring at the gun and he set it on the bedside table, beside the poultice and fleshy piece of lead. He pointed at the pistol like it was poison. "That thing ain't even loaded."

"Were you in on it?" I said. The question just came to me sudden-like, from nowhere. "That robbery at Mister Billingsley's store Saturday night?"

He glanced at Haywood, who was sleeping sound. "No." He checked to see if I heard him, then picked up the knife, wiping both sides of the blade, back and forth, on his pants. "You didn't see me up town today, did you?"

A thought flashed through my mind, a shameful thought that I hated myself for having right then. He'd been here in this house with Estelle. Alone.

"You were here all that time?" I couldn't help asking. My voice sounded weak and whining. He didn't seem to notice it.

He bent forward and cut open Haywood's sleeve. "Willie rode out here early this morning to tell us of the lynchings. And Jack sent me to see after Marie. Wright McLemore's wife. She didn't want my help, though. She came outside with a pistol cocked on me. . . ." He winced as he peeled back the blood-soaked garment from Haywood's arm. "Buckshot," he said, taking in a breath. "Somebody was using a scatter gun."

"Mister Milton," I answered.

The tip of his knife started picking in the holes. I counted eleven of them, spaced in a kind of triangular pattern, turning Haywood's upper arm to red hash.

"What're you doing here, Lily?" Marion said. "Why ain't you at home with your family having Christmas?"

I wet a clean rag in the pail and leaned across Haywood to sponge away the blood Marion's knife had started. "I went to town to find out if you were all right," I said. "I saw the shooting and I was afraid you were there some place."

He dislodged the first ball and it came out whole and round, and easier than the bullet in the leg had. He gave it to me, and I didn't even flinch

when it dropped into my palm. I set it in the rag
on the table with the other piece of lead.

"Stop worrying about me," he said, working on
the next ball.

"I can't."

He turned his head towards me and looked at
my face, all over it—my chin and mouth, my eyes
and forehead. He seemed to take an hour with it,
though it was really only a few seconds that
passed. "We robbed that store, Lily. Me just like
the rest of them. I done it for Jack. So he'd have
some money to start up this farm. I was there. I
done it too."

Something inside me started to sink, my heart or
my lungs. Something. Like all my innards were
oozing down to my feet. "I know," I said, staring
at him. I didn't want him to hear the lie in my
voice.

He studied me a second longer, then his knife
went back to work on the buckshot. "It was just
for him. Cause of Estelle giving him trouble over
it. He trusted me with it." He glanced up at me
again. I was looking straight back at him. I think
my mouth was hanging open.

Haywood stirred and groaned. "I can't take no
more, Shot," he said, reaching for his wounded
arm.

"Hold still," Marion said sharp. "I just now got
your leg stopped up, and you're gonna waller
around and bust it open again."

"Just lemme lay here and rest my way back to
health," Haywood mumbled, and his hand fell
back on the bed.

I couldn't quit watching Marion, one second loving him, the next shrinking away. I tried to see him in Billingsley's store that way, breaking into the safe, taking money what didn't belong to him. But I couldn't make the picture of that person fit with this one before me. This one with lips white around the edges, bent about the task of saving his brother's life.

It was past noon before Marion got all the bullets picked out. By then Haywood had fallen into a fever. We piled coats and blankets on him to sweat it out of him. Marion paced around the room, and I could see he felt helpless.

Estelle gave me one of her dresses to put on, a dark blue one with tiny, cloth-bound buttons up the front. It hung too long on me and dragged the floor, but at least it wasn't covered in blood. She gave Marion one of Jack's shirts. Gray with long, thin stripes. It could have been Marion's shirt. The shoulder seams hit him just right.

She took our bloody clothes to soak in a pan of well water on the kitchen drainboard. Her face was splotched and puffy, but the washing gave her busy-work for a time. Then she went back to sitting in Jack's rocking chair, facing the door, like she expected him to walk through it.

Midafternoon, Bird Hasley and Charlie Goodman came riding up. Not from the direction of the road, but through the woods that surrounded the cleared six acres Jack had planned to farm. They came on a gallop, and it was Bob Stevens who saw them through the window. He and Marion ran out to greet them.

I went after them but stayed on the porch to listen. The dogs came up to stand by me. They seemed like ordinary pets to me now. Even the one on three legs, and the one with the missing eye.

Charlie and Bird stayed mounted. The left sleeve on Charlie's coat was empty, and he was holding his arm close in to his body. He was doing the talking when I went out.

"We tried to get their bodies and bring them back here to bury," he said. "But they got them all locked up inside the bank. Spread out right alongside of Henry and Wright and Thad. And there's men all over the place. They got the sheriff up there."

"I think they're planning a posse," Bird said. His horse dipped his nose and stamped his front hoof, anxious to run again.

"A posse?" Bob rubbed at his sling. "What for? Ain't they hurt us enough?"

"They ain't through," Charlie said. "I wouldn't be a bit surprised to hear the sheriff was a part to that mob last night himself."

Haywood's voice came from inside the house, yelling, "Is that Goodman I hear? Tell that goddamn sonofabitch to come in here. I wanna talk to him. Goodman! Get your yeller-bellied ass in here!"

"You got Haywood," Charlie said, looking at the window on the house.

Marion nodded. "He's shot up pretty good. I don't think he can ride."

"I'm shot myself," Charlie said. "Took a ball in my shoulder. He can ride." Then he yelled towards the window. "Haywood! You wanna talk to me, you get your ass out here and do it yourself."

Haywood's voice came again, even louder this time. "You ran off and left me with it! Just like your buddy Fitzpatrick done to me, you sonofabitch!"

Bird looked down at Marion. "Get him and let's go. If he's hollering like that he can ride."

Bob headed inside. He made a breeze going past me. Marion stopped on the steps where I stood, holding onto the porch post. Our eyes were almost level. A couple of the dogs nosed up to him, waiting for pats that didn't come.

"What're you fixing to do?" I said, even though I'd heard.

"I gotta get Haywood on Jack's horse."

"You're not taking Jack's horse." Estelle stood right behind us. I turned. Her face was firm. "You're not taking Haywood, either."

Haywood's voice yelled out, "Stevens, you get that jackass Goodman in here!"

"You'll kill him if you try to take him," Estelle said to Marion. "He's lost too much blood."

Bob came out the door with his hat on his head and his gun belt in his hand. He ignored us talking and went down the steps and around to where his horse was tied. Charlie and Bird eased theirs that way, too.

"They'll find him here," Marion said.

"He'll slow you down and they'll catch you, too," she said.

"Let's go!" Bird called out. His horse was standing at the ready, tail twitching. Marion glanced back.

"Estelle's right," I said. I felt I should say something. It calmed me down some just to hear my own voice.

Marion focused on me. "I wasn't in that mess today. They ain't after me."

"You robbed that safe, though," I said. I still felt dazed by it, though my mind was coming to grips with what he'd done and why. It seemed to make him pause, me saying it so outright like that.

"Come on, Shot," Bob hollered. He had himself in the saddle now. "We ain't got all day."

"I ain't going yet," Marion told them. "Ride on. I'll catch up to you." He moved past me, headed inside. Estelle went behind him.

Charlie, Bird, and Bob all started off across the field, back the same way they rode in. I watched them go, and it felt like the last time I'd see any of them again. I felt that way about Marion too. Like I was about to lose him forever. The thought set off a panic in me and I rushed inside the house.

Haywood was quivering with chills, still calling for Charlie Goodman. Marion said, "He's gone. He's shot up too. I gotta get you outta the county. They're forming a posse. Think you can ride?"

The shakes came on Haywood worse. I thought he'd been talking out of his mind, but when he peered up at Marion, his eyes seemed clear. "I don't think I can. My leg don't even wanna move. You better just go on without me."

"They ain't looking for me," Marion said. "I wasn't there today."

Haywood hacked out a laugh. "You think that'll matter to them? Wright wasn't with us the other night. Nor Henry. They didn't stop to find that out before they put a rope around their necks, did they? And you *was* with us. Old man Ogden seen you, too. You better hightail it outta here, little brother."

Estelle touched Marion's shoulder. "Go somewhere and send a wire to my father. Leon Odom. Tell him to come for me in his wagon. When he gets here, we'll take Haywood to Rockdale with us. To a doctor, where he belongs. I can hide him here until then."

From Marion's face, I knew he wasn't happy with that plan, but he didn't have a better one. And Haywood was trembling so hard, the whole bed shook. Estelle wet a rag and started bathing his forehead, like as to convince Marion that she'd take care of his brother.

Marion shrugged on his vest and picked up his gun off the table. "All right. But I'm coming right back," he said and dug his coat out of the pile on top of Haywood.

His hat was on the kitchen table, and I hurried to get it for him. He took it from me and went out the door. I followed and stopped at the steps to watch him go, with the same losing-him feeling I'd had a while before. I held onto the porch rail.

He got five steps onto the ground, the dogs all swirling around his feet, sticker burrs and dried mud balls rattling in their fur. Then he turned and looked back at where I stood above him. "Ain't you coming?" he said.

I raced inside for my shawl.

18

We rode to Sayersville, thirteen miles south-west of McDade, where the Katy rail line came through. We rode together on Mollie, since Marion hadn't wanted to leave Estelle and Haywood without a horse. Nighttime was coming on when we got there.

The telegraph office was inside a store, which we saw from the shingle hanging by the door. Marion went in alone, and I took Mollie to the trough at the end of the building. She'd worked up a thirst, and it took her a while to drink her fill.

It was the first chance I had all day to think of home and the pair of pants I'd left half-hemmed. I wondered if Papa was looking for me, if they'd gone on ahead to church, if Daniel O'Barr had come by the house afterwards. I figured Dane had known I was headed for Marion when I took off on Jack's horse. At the time, I hadn't planned to be gone this long. Hadn't planned anything at all except to see if he was safe. I knew the trouble I'd be in, but it was too late for worrying about that now.

Bad as it seemed, I'd enjoyed the ride to Sayersville behind Marion, getting to hold onto his

back and lay my face against him. It was a welcome relief from the tenseness at Estelle's house,
with everybody shot up and sick. And Marion's
spirits seemed easier away from there, too. He
came out of the telegraph office with some biscuits
and a small blue jar of cane syrup. We poked our
fingers into the biscuits and poured the syrup into
the holes we made. It was the first thing I'd eaten
all day.

It wasn't till we were headed back and nearly
there, taking the road like we were out for a Sunday ride, that we came upon the posse. They were
riding by torchlight, and it looked like twenty-five
or thirty men. Marion saw them first and wheeled
Mollie in the middle of the road. "Hang on to me,
Lily," he said, and I wound my arms tight around
him.

We took out into the woods. Limbs and briers
pulled at my clothes, and I leaned my face as near
his back as I could get. I looked behind us once
and saw they were giving chase. I wondered if
Papa was in that bunch. It wouldn't have surprised me to find he was.

I'd lived around McDade my whole life, and
knew back roads and cow trails, but that night
with Marion, I was lost from the moment we left
the roadway. It was dark all right, but it wasn't
that as much as how he rode right through thick
woods like they weren't there. And if we happened on a creek or a cutbank, he turned Mollie
loose, trusting her to keep her footing. I tried to
recognize places we passed, farmhouses or fence
lines, but pretty soon I gave up. The next time I

looked behind us, the torchlights and the riders were gone.

When we came to a bottom, Marion brought Mollie down to a walk. She was lathering and tired, her head hung low. He twisted backwards at me. "You all right?"

I nodded and laid my forehead against him, trying to catch my breath. I hadn't known I was scared until we stopped. He slid down off the saddle and took Mollie on lead.

"There's water over here," he said.

I stayed on her back while she drank from the creek. Marion walked away a few steps, looking all around us. There wasn't anything I could see but black night. Stars freckled the sky like somebody had slung whitewash up there.

"What'll we do now?" I said.

"Keep on. We can't go back. If they *are* following us, we'd take them right to Paint Creek." He pulled his canteen off the saddle, unscrewed the cap and offered it to me, shaking it first to see how much it held. It sounded nearly empty but I wasn't thirsty. He took a big swig. "Are you scared?" he said, wiping his mouth on his sleeve.

"Are you?"

"No."

"I ain't either," I said and pulled the shawl tighter around my shoulders. It was beginning to get cold, and the biscuit had made my stomach start rumbling. I watched him kneel by the creek to fill the canteen, and wondered where we'd stay the night. "I thought you said they ain't after you," I said.

"They probably ain't. They saw a rider and got worked into a dither over it." He came back and relooped the canteen on the saddle horn. "But they didn't know Mollie could fly like the wind." He stroked her nose and bent to smooch her between her nostrils. She bounced her head at him. "We might better ride the creek for a mile or two. Lose our tracks just in case." He said this to the horse, like it was her he was giving this plan to. Then he looked at me. "I expect they'll be calling off the search now that it's pitch dark. Do you want me to take you home? I can probably sneak you in some back way."

"I ain't going home," I said and heard the truth of it.

He kept rubbing Mollie's neck, but his face was turned my way. He stayed like that for a few seconds, and I knew his eyes were on me. I could almost feel them lighting up my skin. I wished I could see him better, stare into his features like I did his picture every night. To get a look at his soul. I knew he wasn't a criminal. No matter what misdeed he'd done. And I knew doing wrong, even for the right reason, didn't excuse the sin. But he wasn't an outlaw. I'd have felt that from him if it was so. Even without moonlight to see his face.

Mollie splashed through the creek, and water got on my legs. It felt like ice, and the night air made it worse. It wasn't long till from the knee down I felt frozen. We rode another hour or more, until the creek gave out and my tailbone began to ache. I wasn't used to being in a saddle for so long, and I felt the sores beginning to come. Marion sensed my discomfort, either from the way I leaned on him, or because he was getting tired himself. We took out across some open hills at a fast lope.

After a few more miles we came to a farmhouse set back amongst some trees, and he turned Mollie down their fence. We rode right up close to their porch, but there wasn't any lamp on inside. I reckoned it must be nearing midnight. We stopped at the barn and Marion got down, keeping hold on Mollie. There wasn't a sound from the house nor all around.

He took us into the barn. The door closed behind us. It was dark. The only lightness came from the night through the cracks in the wall boards. I was shivering so hard, my teeth clacked together. I eased off Mollie and the wet dress swished around my shins.

I could hear Marion moving close by. I reached for him but didn't hit anything but air. "Are you there?" I said.

"Ssh."

I heard the saddlebags and put my hand there, touched his arm.

"I'm getting a match," he whispered. "I don't think nobody's home."

"Maybe they're asleep."

"Where's their animals?"

I wanted my eyes to adjust to the darkness. I couldn't see a thing. I wanted to stop shaking. "I'm cold."

He rustled around some more. Then I felt his coat on my shoulders. He could see me but I couldn't him. It made me feel like a helpless child. I pulled his coat closed in front. One of the buttons was missing.

"Now you'll get cold," I said.

He struck a match. The fire flickered near his face. He cupped his hand around the flame and walked away from me to the other end of the barn.

"Either they ain't home or they left their animals out for the night," he said in a low voice. "This place's empty."

I left Mollie's side and went towards him. I just wanted to be where he was. It felt eerie in the dark barn. He didn't hear me coming and when he turned to get me, I was there and we bumped together. The match went out.

"Don't be scared, Lily. It's gonna be all right here."

"I ain't scared."

"There's some hay piled over here in the corner. I'll check it for rats and then we'll sleep there. It'll be warm."

"I ain't sleepy."

He moved away from me again. He had cat's eyes to be able to see in there. Without the match flame, I was lost. I inched in the direction I thought he'd gone. I could hear his steps crunching straw, his spurs, to my left now.

"I can't see a thing," I said, hating the whine in my voice.

I heard him again and then his hand clamped on my arm. "Over here," he said, taking me with him. When we got where he wanted us, he let me go. "Sit down here. I'll be right back."

"Where're you going?" I said but he walked away. I smelled the hay under me, felt its prickle through Estelle's dress. "Marion?" I called out, but keeping my voice as low as I could. "I'm sorry this's been such a terrible day. Az and Jack . . . and Haywood . . ."

He came back to me then. "Shh, Lily. We gotta be quiet. In case there *are* folks in that house." He did some more moving. I was starting to see a little. He was bent down beside me. I caught the liquid flicker of his eyes in the dark.

"Can I ask you something?" I whispered, touching his back.

"Now then," he said. "Take a look at that."

"I can't see it."

He grabbed my wrist and brought my arm downward. I felt where he put my hand. He'd spread the saddle blanket over the pile of hay, the bedroll folded back on top like a quilt. "Pretty soft, huh?" He sounded pleased with himself.

"Did Haywood kill that man?" I said as he settled beside me. "That Lee County deputy? That Heffington?"

He reached around my shoulders and tucked his coat up closer to my chin. "Why do you wanna know that? It wasn't me. I didn't even see it."

"But you were there."

His arm stayed around me. He pulled me next to him and his thumb rubbed back and forth on my jawbone. "Only for Jack. He said he needed me to go. In his stead cause of Estelle. It's the only reason I was there, Lily. Haywood was outside keeping watch. Fitzpatrick and Goodman, they were all out there keeping watch."

"Today Jack said Haywood was innocent. He told Mister Milton that. I heard it."

He didn't answer for a second, and I worried that I'd made him sad bringing up what'd happened in town this morning. His thumb kept rubbing, back and forth, at the same spot on my jaw. I felt a ragged edge on his nail.

"I didn't see it," he said finally. "Haywood swears he didn't do it. Claims he took the man outside town so's he wouldn't be just lying there in the street. Sometimes Haywood gets a little weak between the ears."

"If he didn't do it, who did?"

"Jeff Fitzpatrick, I guess. Goodman saw the whole thing. He said Heffington pulled a gun on them. Said they were outside the saloon by a tree, minding their own business, and he came up to them with his gun drawn. I don't know. I didn't see it. I wasn't out there. They said Fitzpatrick fired first, but he ran off before we could get his side of the story. Wouldn't none of it happened like that if Jack'd been there." Marion laid back on the blanket. "I don't know. I don't wanna talk about it no more, though."

"Even if you did know what happened. Even if you saw it for yourself. It wouldn't change anything for me. I know you were just there for Jack."

"That's right. That's the only reason."

His hand came up the back of my arm to my shoulder, and he pulled me down beside him. It felt queer lying next to him, but also safe. He raised himself over me. I could see the outline of his face now.

"You got the softest skin, Lily." His fingers touched my chin, then moved over my cheek. "I don't know what to do with you. Whether to take you on back home, or keep you with me."

"I ain't going home."

His lips pressed my forehead, then my eyelids one at a time. He smelled like sweat and raw nerves, and that mixed with the horse smell of the saddle blanket and the hay. I could hardly swallow.

He moved to my lips, kissing me just lightly a few times, so's I almost couldn't feel him. My arms went around him and he kissed me harder, longer, his mouth kind of open. His breath rushed into my lungs.

I ain't excusing what we did next. But I felt so full and wanting of him. And it had been too long since we held each other and kissed. And so many things had happened to us that day and I knew he was grieving. When his kisses moved down my jaw, and his fingers started working the buttons on the front of the dress, I let him. Not only let him, but helped him, since he was so fumbling with it.

When we got the buttons open, he rolled to his back, taking me with him and over him, kissing me still. His hands pushed the dress down my back to my waist, and the chemise I had on under, and his breath started coming funny. The cold air in the barn hit my bosom and then the warmth from his mouth.

It wasn't how I expected. It didn't feel sinful letting him touch me where nobody else ever had. It felt sweet and natural, and the wanting need from him gave me a thrill in the pit of my stomach. He pulled off his vest, the over shirt of Jack's he was wearing and his undershirt. And he pressed me flat against him. He had a thatch of hair on him I hadn't known was there, and a solidness to his chest and belly. When I ran my hands on him, he rolled me over again to my back. I felt the heavy weight of him on me and his fingers moving at the front of his britches. It broke the spell I was under.

I didn't know that he'd want more from me than our bare flesh pressed together. I didn't understand then about the carnal instincts of a man, though I'd read of it in the Bible. Nor did I know it was the woman's duty to keep that instinct at bay and not give it cause to rear its head. For it will, and does, take hold of a man's soul, and make him act in ways that's dark and unlike his normal self.

I heard the threads in the dress pop as he pushed it past my hips and my drawers with it. Shame and cold washed over me, and I didn't have my mouth to speak. The saddle blanket and his coat crushed under me, felt itchy and rough. I tried to move away from him, but he wouldn't let me go. His knees came between my legs and forced them apart. His tongue touched my neck. I felt his stiffness, and his hand there, guiding himself to me. The hot pain of it tore from my throat.

His palm covered my mouth. "Ssh, Lily," he said with more breath than words.

He kissed me, wet and slippery, under my ear.

His hand fell away from my mouth just as a cry came from his own throat, louder than mine had been, and I wondered if it hurt him, too. Then he got still and heavier on me, and quiet. But he didn't pull himself out from me, and I was stinging down there, like a swarm of ants were on me.

I tried to move and he rolled away, not far, just to his back. I reached for the dress and got it up to my waist, before he caught me and scooped me to him. The skin on his arms felt cool and clammy like after a fever. I pulled his coat around me, and he wrapped me in the bedroll.

"I didn't mean to hurt you," he whispered. He spoke so soft I thought I imagined what he said.

"It wasn't bad," I answered, but felt tears come to me.

He tucked my head closer under his chin, and his hand stroked my hair. Gentle again. "I guess we better get ourselves married now," he said. "We'll go to Austin tomorrow. We can do it there and nobody won't ask questions."

He sounded lazy and half-asleep. When I tried to move again, he kept me tight against him. I felt myself bleed—thought I did—and I wanted to do something about it, but he wouldn't let go of me. So I stayed there with my dress and my chemise all a tangle around my waist.

In a few minutes, he was snoring soft, and that kind of comforted me, made me think of my own room at the farm, with Dane and Nathan in their bed making the same sounds. I laid there against him, gathering in his heat, imagining what it would be like with us married. Having babies. It was what I'd longed for since I'd known I loved him, but somehow now, I couldn't get a picture of it clear in my mind.

I envied him his sleep. I knew it would never come to me. Not in this barn, with me half-naked inside his coat. Not with him lying so close beside me, and with the knowing of what we'd just done.

19

Sleep did take me off some time during the night, because I roused with a start at the gray sunlight coming through the board cracks in the barn. For a second, I didn't have my bearings, then I remembered where I was. Marion was gone. So was Mollie. When I saw that, fear leaped inside me like a bullfrog. He'd left me. Had me last night and now left me just like Mrs. Kennedy said any man would do if you gave them too much too quick.

It was frosty in the barn, but he'd left behind his saddle blanket and the bedroll. They were wrapped all around me. I groped for my drawers, pulled up the blue dress and my chemise, pushed my arms into the sleeves. I gathered a handful of straw and scrubbed at the crusty stain on my thigh. A little blood. Mostly something else. From Marion. I bit down on my lip.

I would not cry. I would not let myself. He left for good reason. To protect me because he cares for me. Because he saw it clear this morning that he's in big trouble and they're going to come for him. He saw himself dangling from that oak tree back home and knew it could have been him as anybody. Still could. He left to keep me from getting hurt. It didn't have anything to do with what we did last night.

Shivering, I straightened my clothes and planned how I would find my way back to the road. Maybe come across a good soul going close to McDade. I didn't want to go back and face Papa, but I didn't think that far. Didn't let myself. I wondered if Marion had put a child inside me. I felt sore and achy all over.

I pulled the bedroll blanket around my shoulders and went the length of the barn to the door. The hinges squealed open. I peeked outside. Smoke billowed from the stove pipe on the roof of the house. My breath caught. The people were home now. I'd have to sneak extra careful. Trespassing was near about as serious a crime as robbery.

Every step I took I expected to run into somebody. I hugged the outside of the barn. There was a line of myrtles that I might could duck behind to block me from view, if I could get there without being noticed. I wasn't sure which direction was the road. And then I stepped around the corner and scattered a bunch of barred-rock hens. They squawked and flapped about, making a racket.

A door slammed shut around the side of the house, and somebody came my way, whistling, never once expecting to run into a strange girl, wrapped like an Indian in a blanket, outside their barn. I lunged for the myrtles, caught my hem under the heel of my boot. The dress ripped. The blanket fell off my shoulders and to the ground.

"Lily? You're up." Marion's voice shook me. My hand went to my heart. He laughed. "What're you running for? Did I scare you?"

I took a look at the torn hem. My chest kept heaving. "It ain't funny. I thought you left me." I bent for the blanket, hung it over my arm.

"I was just coming to get you," he said, walking towards me. He was all smiles. Pink cheeked. You could have looked at him and never guessed he lost two brothers the day before, or that he was on the run himself now. "You didn't see the saddle still laying in the corner?"

I shook my head, feeling stupid then. My eyes moved around him. "What're you doing in those folks' house?"

"They ain't home. Just like I figured. I found some sausage they left." He rubbed his hands together. "I got it cooking. And there's a warm fire in there. Come on."

I glanced at the smoke again, fluttering from the chimney. "You broke in?"

"I was hungry. It'll be all right, Lily. They won't even know we've been here."

"You shouldn't just go inside people's houses."

"It'll be all right. Come on." He held out his hand to me. "Come on, now. If these folks were here I bet they'd let us in, give us some food, and let us warm our feet. Wouldn't you do that for a traveler? Now, come on. Let's go inside before that sausage burns."

I took his hand. I knew it was wrong to do, but my belly was grumbling and I was shivering cold. My teeth had started chattering again like they had last night. There was a small pasture close to the house and Mollie was out there, grazing. I tried not to notice the broken windowpane beside the back door where he'd reached in to unlatch the lock. I draped the blanket over the porch rail and climbed the back steps behind him.

Inside, the house was cozy warm and smelled like frying sausage. I stepped over the broken glass on the floor as Marion moved to the skillet on the stove. He pushed the link around in its grease, whistling again. Happy.

I wandered through the other rooms, two of them. One held evidence of a child, had a tiny bed nailed into the wall. The other room had linen curtains and a real bedstead, needleworked pillows. I fingered the dresser scarf, the tatting edge, and looked at the jewel box near the mirror. Seashells were stuck on top of the box, in a shape of a starfish, and the words "Galveston Island" spelled out with tiny black stones. I felt wicked and sinful poking around in other folks' stuff, and I hurried back into the room with Marion.

"We shouldn't be inside here without their permission," I said.

"Think of it like it was your own house," he said, and he didn't sound the least bit concerned. He pulled the skillet off the fire and forked up the sausage. "See if they got some bread somewhere."

"I can't think of this like it was my house. I won't ever own nothing this fine." I gazed around the ceiling. There was picture-hanging molding at the top of the walls, and portraits of family members strung on wire, strangers in Sunday clothes and stern faces.

"Yes you will. I'm gonna get it for you." He cut himself a piece off the sausage and, chewing, looked at me. His eyes were sparkly.

I couldn't help but grin at him. "How're you gonna do that?"

He shrugged his shoulder and cut himself another piece. "I don't know yet. But if I get my mind set to it, I know I can. I got good luck. Always have." He quit chewing and smiled broad at me. I realized it was last night in the hay giving him that smile. I felt myself blush. He held out a forkful of sausage to me. "You better come get you some of this before I eat it all."

I went over beside him and took the slice of sausage with my fingers. There was a pot of coffee on the stove top and two crockery cups. He poured both of them full.

"I didn't know you were handy with a skillet," I said, taking the footstool that was setting next to the stove.

"I can do better than this, except I forgot my apron."

He handed me one of the cups and laughed. I laughed too, because he was acting so giddy, then dipped my face into the cup. The steaming coffee felt good to my cheeks. We ate the sausage off the same fork.

After a while he said, "You feeling all right? I mean . . ." He motioned at me, at the skirt of the dress. Then he blushed himself. "We're gonna be riding a long way today. Are you gonna be able to do it?"

I looked away from him, embarrassed at the question, and felt the soreness again. "I'm just fine."

"Because what I was thinking is, we could just stay here for a day or two if it suits you. Since you like it so much. I figure these folks is gone someplace visiting for Christmas. They probably left their animals with a neighbor and won't be back for a while."

I cupped my hands around the mug. I guessed he'd forgotten about the posse, and about Austin and his proposal of marriage last night. "I couldn't do that," I said. "I just wouldn't feel comfortable being in somebody's house like that without them knowing."

He nodded and looked towards the front windows. They showed out onto a wide gallery with turned-wood pillars. "Well, then ... we'll just let this fire burn down some and be on our way."

"Where're we going?"

"Austin," he said, like I should have known.

I sat there warming my hands on the cup, and smiled.

While we were letting the fire die down, I started cleaning up the mess we'd made. Marion brought in a pan of water and went out to fetch Mollie from the pasture. I heated the water over the coals to get it hot enough to wash up the dishes we'd used, and threw the coffee dregs out back for the chickens.

There was a bar of soap on a tin can lid just outside the door. Marion wasn't in sight, so I snatched up the bar and hurried back inside. I took the water off the fire and set it on the table. I soaped my hands and washed my face, took down the top of the dress and washed my neck and arms. I wished I had time for a real bath. I hadn't even brought along a hair brush, but did what I could with my fingers. There were tangles all in my hair, and leaves and pieces of hay.

The spit bath made me feel better, and I looked out the window and saw Marion leading Mollie to the house. There wasn't anything special about it. Just him walking along in the sunshine, his coat breezing back, and his horse in his hand, bringing her up for her saddle. But the sight stirred something in me, made me go to the window and watch him, just how he moved, the swinging of his arm. I thought about lying with him last night, curved in next to his shoulder, listening to him sleep. And the memory of it filled me up with something I didn't understand, something so powerful it liked to burst right from me. When he got beside the house, I rushed outside onto the back porch.

"Marion!" I said, and he looked up like I'd startled him with my tone. His eyes on me made me forget what I had to say.

"What is it?" His voice was excited, a little breathless.

I stood there with my mouth hanging open for a second or two. Then I came back to myself. I pointed behind me. "This fire's almost down."

"OK." He acted confused that I'd rush out just to tell him that.

"Maybe you better come check it."

A frown wrinkled his brow and he hesitated. Then he looped Mollie's lead around a fence picket. "If you say it's down, it's probably down," he said, coming through the chickens to the steps.

When he got to the top one, I didn't move aside. He stopped there, and I guess he saw what was on my mind then. He reached out with one arm and pulled me to him. And when he came up that last step, my feet left the ground.

He carried me easy to the room with the fancy bedstead. It was nicer in a bed with a warm house around us, and with the daylight so's I could see his face and know it wasn't something evil inside him making him sound so rough. It was *me* doing it to him, and I understood some then about the carnal instinct.

It didn't hurt so much this time, though it still did some. But it was worth the pain of it with him whispering, "I love you, Lily," over and over in my ear. I couldn't remember ever hearing anybody say that to me. Not like that. With so much meaning in it. And when he cried out, this time it was me who did the petting, holding him close to me and stroking him, till his breath stopped sounding like he'd been running.

We took our time about leaving that house. Too long as it turned out, but we were both of us in some kind of dream with each other that day. It was the house, I think, and us playing like we were married before we went off to really do it. Practicing-like.

We stayed in that bed for a couple of hours, under those people's covers after the fire burned out, and neither of us with a strip of clothes on. And got used to each other that way. Marion had a long scar down his back to the left of his spine and kind of jagged. And another one, half-moon shaped, behind his thigh. That one came from a horse kick and the jagged one on his back from a barbed-wire fence. He had a birthmark on his hip, and the crookedest little toes I'd ever seen. He said he couldn't find anything wrong with me. That I was just perfect as far as he could tell. But then, I couldn't get over being shy, either, so he never got to look for long.

When we got up finally, we were both hungry again. There wasn't much food in the house, a box of oatmeal but no milk to make it with. We checked the yard for eggs but since we didn't know the hens' laying spots, and since the weather was still cold enough to have them shut down, we gave that up pretty quick. Marion found a jar of honey on a top shelf in the cupboard. It tasted bitter, like it had been drawn off persimmon blooms last spring. We ate it with our fingers and laughed at the sticky mess we made.

It came time Marion thought we should go if we were going to make it to Austin before dark. He figured we were a few miles south of Elgin, almost to the county line. And he didn't think we had to worry much about the posse. "They ain't looking for me," he said, and his eyes clouded over for the first time all day. It was Haywood, I knew, that he was thinking about then.

He went out to get the saddle on Mollie. Through the windows, I saw him go towards the barn as I was spreading up the bed. I even dusted off the tables, leaving everything nice since we'd had such a good time there. I wished I could do something about that windowpane by the back door. I made a pile of the glass pieces on the sill and swept up the flinders so's nobody would cut their feet coming inside the door.

We hadn't used but a few dishes. I swished them in the pan of water from my spit bath and put them away where I thought they belonged. I even emptied the ash from the stove, and took it in a dustpan to spread on the garden out back. There was a puny, frost-bit tomato plant there. Some winter squash that looked like it still had a chance to make. That was when I heard Marion calling me.

I went around the house, ran playful at a couple of hens that seemed frisky as I passed. There was a clump of sweet pea that didn't know it was December, growing up under the southern edge of the house. I stopped to pick one of the fading blooms before I went on around to see what Marion needed.

When I turned the corner to the barn, what was there brought me to a dead stop. A man, an old man in coveralls and with tobacco stains on his beard, was holding a shotgun. And the barrel of it was pointed straight at Marion's chest. My ears took to ringing. The flower fluttered out of my fingers.

"There she is," Marion said when I appeared. He had his hands out, not really up in the air, but enough so's the man knew they were empty. The saddle and saddle blanket were on the ground at his feet. "Darling, will you please tell this gentleman that you're Miz Gazway's niece come to visit unexpected?" Marion was smiling as he said this to me, but it wasn't a real smile.

"That's right," I said quickly, hoping I didn't sound too caught off guard. I wasn't sure what was going on yet.

The man looked at me doubtful and kept the gun covering Marion. "Miz Gazway didn't tell me a thing about no niece."

I took another step and glanced at Marion. He still had the smile pasted on his lips. He had on his vest, and the pistol was tucked in there, which was why, I suddenly realized, he wasn't holding his hands up real high. The old man hadn't thought to disarm him.

"That's because she didn't know I was coming," I said, thinking hard. "We were on our way to Austin and we just stopped."

The man narrowed his eyes on me. They were old eyes and nearly hidden by bushy gray brows. The gun nudged closer to Marion's chest. The hand at the trigger was missing two fingers. "Who's this?" the man said.

"My husband," I said. "Galveston. We come from Galveston Island. Here, I'll prove it to you."

I turned and rushed back into the house.

Through the bedroom windows, I could see Marion and the man. They weren't either of them moving. I snatched up the shell-covered jewel box off the dresser, and dumped out the things inside it. Then I ran back out. When I got around the side to the barn, I slowed down to a walk and put a smile on my face, too.

"This is what I brought her. For a Christmas present." I held the box out in my hand and went close enough so the old man could see. "Do you think she'll like it?"

He jutted his woolly chin out towards me, and peered down his nose into my palm. The shotgun inched just slightly off of Marion. "Mmm," the man said. "I 'spect she will."

Marion moved like lightning. He grabbed the barrel of the gun, wrenched it from the man's hands, and used the stock to club him on the head. I jumped back and dropped the jewel box, shocked to the core by the quickness and violence of what Marion did. The old man fell hard to the ground. I thought he looked dead.

"You didn't have to do that," I cried out. "He was just about to let you go."

Marion knelt and put his hand on the man's chest. "He shouldn't of come creeping up here like that."

"He was being a good neighbor. Checking on things for these folks. Marion? He's just an old farmer."

He looked at me and stood up. "He'll be all right. Let's get going before he comes to." He retrieved the saddle and blanket from the dust.

I bent to pick up the jewel box. Some of the shells had broken off and one hinge on the top had pulled loose from the wood.

"Leave it," Marion said, and I saw he was emptying the shotgun. He stuffed the two cartridges into his pocket, looked the gun over close, like he was thinking on taking it with us. Then deciding against it, he dropped the shotgun across the old man's legs. "Let's go," he said to me, and the words came out like a bark.

The man was groaning when we went back by him, riding Mollie. I wanted to stop and make sure he wasn't hurt bad. Marion didn't even break stride. In half an hour we passed out of Bastrop County and into Travis. By then, the saddle was already rubbing corns on my backside.

20

We spent the night in Manor, in a corner hotel across from the blacksmith's shop. It was Mollie throwing a shoe as we crossed Wilbarger Creek just outside town that caused us to stop. But by then I was worn out with the saddle, anyhow.

Marion left me in the hotel room and took Mollie over to the smithy. When he came back, it was dark and he had two plates of hot food with him. We were both hungry and ate fast, then we went to bed.

As soon as we were on the hard horsehair mattress, he rolled me under him. But it wasn't the same as it had been in that house back before he knocked that old man out cold. The Gazways' house. It would have be better if I never learned their name. Would have kept it more a dream to me than real. A real house belonging to real folks with a name.

We were up early the next morning and rode most of the day over rougher ground than we'd come to yet. Twice we used railroad trestles to cross steep, gorged-out creeks, before we finally came to Austin. It was a real city and like nothing I'd seen before. People were everywhere—walking, on horseback, in carriages and buggies, and even some in fringe-top surreys like we never had in McDade. All the traffic kept a cloud of dust hanging over everything, and there were more buildings than I had thought could fit in one place.

We saw at a distance the lunatic asylum, a big building with bars on the windows, more like a jail than a place for poor, pitiful creatures of God. We passed the spot where they were putting up the new capitol building. And then we passed the university, not even completely built yet, but still grand and tall, looking like a spired castle to me. It made me think of Daniel O'Barr, and I felt strange knowing he was back in McDade and I was here, like we'd exchanged places, though had come about it in different ways.

There were men in suits and bowlers. Fancy ladies wearing crinolines and gowns, lacy bonnets on their heads. Streets lined with gas lamps, and telegraph wires stringing everywhere. I did so much straining and looking that Marion finally switched with me and let me ride in front of him.

He knew his way through the streets, and once we got into the business district, he even tipped his hat at a few people, like he knew them well enough to say hello. I felt proud to be along with someone so worldly. Riding into town that way, like we belonged and had a right to be there, made me forget I was angry with him.

We stopped at a livery to put Mollie up. Marion gave the stable boy instructions about how to feed her and what her temperament was like when being handled certain ways. And he said he wanted her kept in the saddle, which I thought a mite strange till he looked at me and said, "I used to have one made of the finest soft leather you ever felt. And it up and walked off from me when they stowed it away at a stable in Giddings." I noticed he had to dig deep in his pockets to find money enough to give as payment for Mollie's care. He took his saddlebags with us.

When we left there, he steered me down the street to a rooming house that had a saloon right next door. This one looked more civilized than the rock saloon back home. There were bronze lanterns fastened to the wall by the door. No old drunks sitting around outside. Piano music came through the windows, and the sound of female laughter. I craned my neck to see, but Marion pulled me into the rooming house before I could get a look.

The rooming house wasn't fancy but it was clean inside and run by a snuff-dipping woman who looked to be about forty or so. The front hall had been turned into an office, and she sat behind a desk in there. When we walked in the door, she got a big smile on her face and said, "Well, if it isn't the young Mister Beatty, and with a little lady friend at that. What brings you here?"

He took his hat off his head and laid his saddlebags at his feet. He was smiling back at her. He held onto my arm. "This here's Lily. Ain't she pretty?"

"Marion." I gave him a nudge with my elbow,

then smoothed at my hair and face, felt the dust there. I blushed. The woman's eyes were on me.

"This is Miz Avant," Marion said.

The woman put her hand across the desk at me. "Pleased to meet you, Lily. You can call me Irene."

The way she smiled and said my name made me like her right off. It was good to see another woman, even an old woman with snuff on her breath. I shook her hand.

"You never said *I* could call you Irene." Marion laughed.

"*You* can't," she said. She looked up at him. "How's Jack?"

"Oh, I expect he's fine," Marion said, and he never even flinched.

"Tell him to come see me. I miss him around here," she said.

"I'll do that," Marion answered, and I was starting to get real uneasy about the conversation.

Mrs. Avant raised forward on her elbows and said, "Well, what can I do for you young folks? Do you wanna register?"

Marion let go of my arm, fidgeted a little. "Well . . . yes, we do." He glanced towards the parlor where two old men were playing dominoes on a the table beside a stuffed sofa. "But I need to talk with you about how we're gonna pay. I seem to be flat broke."

Mrs. Avant leaned back in her chair and crossed her arms underneath her bosom. "Well now, that *is* a problem."

Marion slid his hands around the brim of his hat, holding it at knee-level. I hadn't noticed before the tear at the back of his coat, on the shoulder seam. I looked down at my own ripped hem.

"What I was thinking is . . ." He put his fist to his mouth and cleared his throat, giving me a quick sideways glance. "If you don't mind going ahead and giving us a room, I can probably pay you by about seven o'clock. Eight at the latest. And then I'll give you the rent for two days at once, and we'll be all square."

I touched the back of his arm, and was about to ask him how he planned to do this, when I heard Mrs. Avant give him a coy laugh. "If you're flat broke, Marion, how're you gonna get in the game?"

He stuck his hand in his pocket and came out with a coin, which he held wedged between his first and second fingers. He grinned and let the coin roll over his knuckles. "I saved back one dollar."

She laughed again. She seemed to get a big kick out of everything he said. "Feeling pretty lucky, are you?"

"Yes ma'am." He tucked the dollar back into his pocket.

She reached into her desk and pulled out a tin cash box. She lifted the lid, took up one bill, and flipped it on the desk in front of him. "Here's another. Play a hand for me." She looked at me then, and I hoped she didn't see the dismay I was feeling. They were talking about poker, and gambling.

"I'm gonna agree to it," she said, shaking her finger at him. "But only because of Lily here. If it was just you, Marion Beatty, I'd let you sleep out in the street."

She showed us up a flight of stairs to a small room at the end of the hall. It had a pitch to the ceiling that ended too low to stand under on the east corner. But there was a brass bed, a ladderback rocking chair, and a mirror on a pedestal that I tried not to look into. I didn't want to compare myself to the fancy ladies I'd seen on the street.

"You'll be needing a second room, I gather," Mrs. Avant said to Marion. "There's one available down behind the kitchen."

"No ma'am," he said. "Me and Lily are on our honeymoon."

She frowned at him like she didn't believe a word of it, then shot a quick look my way. I nodded so she'd think it was the truth. But even then, the way she studied my torn hem and dusty boots, I knew she still had doubts. She tossed the key at Marion. He caught it one-handed.

"Whatever you say, *Mister* and *Missus* Beatty. Supper's in the kitchen at six-thirty." And then she turned on her heel and shut the door behind her.

"That's that then," Marion said after she was gone. He hung the saddlebags around the foot post on the bed, and when he turned to me, he looked kind of sheepish, like he knew I wouldn't be happy about what I heard downstairs. "I'm good at cards, Lily. I almost don't ever lose. You saw Miz Avant give me that dollar. She knows it's so."

"But Marion? Gambling? Poker?" I felt my nose wrinkle up. I couldn't hide my distaste.

"You knew I wasn't no saint. Now, if you're gonna be cross with me about it, I'm just gonna have to go on down to that saloon and let you be that way. Cause we need some money, and I can't think of no better way to get it right now."

I just couldn't pretend I wasn't disappointed in him. I stood there in the middle of the room and looked at him, not saying anything, feeling selfish about it. I wanted him to stay there with me and do things my way.

He gave me one of his crooked grins, only this one had a touch of sadness to it, and then he let out some air through his nose. "All right. I understand how you feel about it. I won't be gone longer than I have to be." He reached for the doorknob.

"Wait." I stepped after him. "Are you sure it's safe for you to go down there?"

"Course it's safe." The back of his hand touched my cheek. "This here's a big town, Lily. Ain't nobody down there cares about what happens in a hole-in-the-road like McDade."

He left then, telling me to sit tight while he was gone, and not venture outside without him along. He seemed distant to me; not cold but just off into his own thoughts. I was bone-tired and I laid on the bed, on top of the chenille spread so's I wouldn't dirty the bed linens underneath. My stomach was growling, but I tried to ignore it and fall asleep. About five minutes later, somebody tapped on the door. It was Mrs. Avant.

"Just saw your bridegroom heading over to the saloon," she said. She said bridegroom kind of snidely, but I didn't make mention of it. "If you'd like a bath, I've got one drawn up," she said.

A bath. The thought of it made me nearly swoon. We'd been on the road two full days, with all that grime accumulating. My hair felt like broom straw. "Oh, yes ma'am," I said.

She smiled at me, and there was a speck of snuff on her upper lip. "It's Irene," she said, and took ahold of my hand.

There was a bathing room downstairs with a steel tub and mirrors and hooks all around for towels and fresh clothes. I'd have to put back on my same ones, but at least my body would feel clean. She laid out a bar of sweet-smelling soap, but she didn't leave. Fact is, she helped me to undress. I was timid about it at first, but she didn't make any bones about my nakedness. As I slid into the water, she stoked up the fire in the stove and then sat down in a rocker with a needle and thread to mend the tear in the hem on Estelle's dress.

I wasn't used to having a person make such a to-do over me, and I started bathing quick till she said, "Take your time, honey. Just lay down there a while and soak." So I hunkered down till the warm water came up to my neck. It felt like pure heaven. I unclipped my hair and let it float down around me.

Mrs. Avant started talking as the needle in her hand worked through the dress. She told me how she'd been married herself once to a man who got himself killed fighting the Yankees at Sabine Pass. She'd been living in East Texas then and had come to Austin during Reconstruction. She told me how hard it as for the first couple of years until her hotel got going good. She called it a hotel. I didn't fuss with her about it. I was too busy luxur'ating in my bath.

When she finished with my dress, she broke the thread in half with her teeth, then said, "How come a little snip of a girl like you to end up with that rascal Marion Beatty?"

I soaped up the rag she'd given me and laughed. "He ain't bad as all that."

"The hell he ain't. Him and his brothers come ripping in here ever other month for the past year, causing trouble. We got us enough trouble without outsiders bringing in more."

An uneasy feeling churned in me. "He ain't riding with his brothers anymore."

"You figuring on reforming him then?"

I gathered my hair behind my back and nodded at her. "We're gonna find us a place to settle down. Maybe here. Maybe somewhere else. He's gonna get an honest job. Maybe farming." I just said that because I couldn't think of anything else to defend him with.

"A farmer? Marion Beatty?" Mrs. Avant found that real comical. Then she must have noticed my face. She quit smiling. "Men like him don't change that easy. I ain't saying they can't. I'm just saying it's hard for them. But he's young. Maybe he ain't too spoiled yet."

I felt my face get hot. I scrubbed at it hard so's she'd think it was just the cleanness making me red.

She laid the dress aside and came over to help me with my hair. She told me to tilt backwards and then she soaped up my scalp. Her breath smelled sour, from the snuff maybe. She said, "I didn't see you bring in any extra baggage."

"We're traveling light," I answered.

"So you got no other dress to put on while I wash that one?" She ladled water onto my head. I closed my eyes to keep the soap out. I shivered, her hands felt so good.

"It doesn't need washing."

"Honey, that thing smells as strong as clabbered milk." Her fingers raked through my hair as she ladled on more water. "You run off with him, didn't you? I bet your folks are worried sick over you."

Tears sprang to my eyes so quick I choked. I scrambled up and free from her hands, sloshing water out of the tub. Soap ran down the sides of my face. I wiped at it and also at my eyes, and smeared the soap in them by accident. That made the tears well up even more.

"Don't fret, child," she said, soothing. "I ain't gonna tell nobody. If Marion Beatty's what you want, why, who am I to stop you from having him? I can't even say as I blame you. I'd probably go for him too, if I was your age."

It didn't matter what she said to me, though, the tears kept flowing. I hadn't even known they were back there waiting to spill forth. It was as if once they'd started, they weren't going to quit till they were all out.

I thought about Papa. And little Dellie. Wondered how they were getting by without me. I hoped they weren't going hungry for lack of cooking skills. I figured by now Papa probably *was* worried sick, like Mrs. Avant said. For my safety and for my soul. I felt sinful and wicked for causing him grief.

Mrs. Avant held me against her bosom. She crooned, "Now, now," and patted my shoulders with a dry towel. She didn't seem to care that I was getting her clothes all wet.

"We ain't got married yet," I sobbed. "Marion told you a lie. He's on the run and we ain't had time for a marriage ceremony."

"I know that, child. I already know. I made that calculation on you both soon as you walked in the door." She let me go then and raised the towel. "Stand up now and let's get you dried off before you take a chill."

I hadn't even noticed that the water had gotten cold. I stood naked, no longer shy with her, and let her wrap me in the towel. My tears trickled down to a sniffle.

"What's he running from?" she said as I stepped onto the mat she spread beside the tub.

"The law?"

"That I figured, child. What do they want him for?"

"Robbery. But he was just helping Jack out. And then they shot them all down. Except Marion. And that's why we had to leave. If he went back to McDade they'd kill him sure. They got up a lynch mob, and they hung his cousins—"

Her hand on my shoulder stopped me, and I realized I'd been babbling. "Jack's dead?" she said.

"Jack and Azberry both. And Haywood's all shot to pieces. They got him over in Rockdale. We came here to get married and then we're gonna go there to get him."

She patted my shoulder again, then she leaned down and picked up my dress. "I'm gonna go find you something else to wear while I wash this. I'll be right back."

She moved the rocker closer to the stove, then handed me a silk wrapper to put on until she came back. I sat there and looked at the embers in the stove, thinking about how I'd blabbed to her. Told her everything we'd been trying to hide from people. And though Marion clearly knew her pretty well, he himself had chosen to lie to her about Jack, so I knew he must not trust her much, either.

The longer I sat there, the more worried I got about it. For all I knew she could be down there right now sending word to the sheriff. For all I knew there as a bounty on his head and everybody in the whole state was after him. I didn't get to feeling any better about things either, even after she brought me a pretty green dress to wear till mine was clean; not even when she looked at me and winked, and said she'd have a surprise for me tomorrow, and for me to get plenty of beauty rest. I tired to think of how I was going to tell Marion what I'd done when he came back.

21

Marion got back even sooner than he said he would. When he came in the door to our room, I was sitting in the ladder-back rocking chair, watching darkness settle on the street outside. I had on the dress Mrs. Avant lent me. My hair was loose and still damp against my back. I felt clean and all cried out. But by then, I'd worried myself silly over everything I told her.

He took a look at me and shut the door behind him. "Where'd you get them clothes?" he said. I told him. He nodded and laid his gun down on the chester-drawer, pulled off his vest and hat and put them there, too.

"Did you win?" I said, trying to think of how to start explaining what had happened with him gone.

He came to the rocker and knelt in front of me, taking up both my hands. "You look real pretty, Lily. Smell nice, too. Did you miss me?"

He reeked of whiskey and his eyes seemed darker, as if the pupils had grown and taken in all the color. He brushed my fingers against his lips. I felt the stubble on his chin.

"You've been drinking."

"A little bit. Fellas in a card game won't trust you if you don't take a sip." His hand moved to my arm, rubbed and squeezed me a little. "You still cross with me?"

I shrugged. Now I felt anger for the whiskey. It was just one more thing I didn't know about him. A drinking man. A gambler. What else was there? I'd seen him at the rock saloon back home, but I'd never thought about what he'd been doing in there. He was there with his brothers. That was as far as I ever conjectured. Disappointment settled on me again. It took my mind off what I wanted to tell him.

He squeezed on my arm for another second or two, then he sat back on his knees, digging in his pockets. He pulled out a wad of bills and some silver, laid it all on my lap. My mouth fell open.

"There's thirty-six dollars there. I had forty-five before my streak ended. I had to lose a little so's I could walk outta there with my back turned" He grinned and spread the money out. "Count it, Lily. I told you I was good at cards. And I already paid Miz Avant what I owed her. And won some with the dollar she gave me besides."

"Did she say anything to you?" I studied his face. He looked so pleased about his winnings, I didn't have the heart to ruin his mood.

"Just that we should come down pretty quick and eat some supper. Are you hungry?"

I nodded and he gathered the money out of my lap. I went to the chester-drawer to clip back my hair, but he followed me and took the hair clip from my hand.

"Leave it a-loose this one time," he said. "You look like an angel with your locks hanging down to your waist." He turned me around and his hands cupped my face. I let him kiss me. I tasted the whiskey on his lips.

When we went downstairs, Mrs. Avant had my dress ready, ironed and folded. She told me don't worry over the one she'd given me to wear. She said it didn't fit her anymore, anyway.

The supper was sweet corn bread and chicken stew, gotten up in country style, with lots of onions and peppers cooked in. Apple cobbler for dessert. Marion ate like he was starved, and the color came back to his eyes.

Mrs. Avant bragged on him for winning ten dollars for her with the one she gave him, and for doing it so fast. She called him a lucky cuss and said she wished he'd teach her his card skills so she could go over to that saloon some time herself and win a pile of money.

My mind began to rest easier about her. It seemed to me that she liked him right fine, and didn't have any plan of turning us in to the sheriff. Every time she looked at Marion, her eyes twinkled a little brighter. Before we finished with the supper, I stopped worrying altogether.

The other boarders were mostly old men. There was one other woman, Shoney, a Mexican girl who was a lot closer to my age than Mrs. Avant was. For doing kitchen work, Mrs. Avant didn't charge

Shoney rent. And while Marion used the tub room, and I was helping with the dishes, Mrs. Avant pulled me into a corner. Shoney was in the dining room clearing of the big table.

"Don't mention Jack Beatty around Shoney, now," she said to me in a quiet voice. "That girl had a tender spot for him, and it'd kill her soul to know he won't be coming around here no more."

What she said gave me pause. I looked through the kitchen door into the dining room at Shoney gathering the dishes in her arms. I thought about Estelle and how much they favored each other, save for the darker color of Shoney's skin. Jack would have never struck me as the kind to have a woman in every town. It made me wonder about Marion then, and how many others he'd known besides me.

"Miz Avant," I said before she could walk away from our private corner, "you ain't gonna tell anybody what all I said to you today, are you? About Marion being in trouble?"

"Don't you worry your pretty little head about that. Every one of my boarders are always safe inside my house." She gave my cheek a tap. "And call me Irene now. Hear?"

After his bath, Marion sat with two of the older men a while in the parlor, smoking cigars and playing Moon on the tea table in front of the sofa. They used Mrs. Avant's domino set made of real marble from down Mexico way. Marion was still on a lucky streak. He laughed and talked and seemed to be having fun. He beat the two old men five games in a row. They weren't playing for money. Cigars were all he won. I figured then he must just have a weakness for game playing. Brother Parkins always said it gets into your blood, like the pox or scarlet fever.

By the time we climbed the stairs, I was feeling easy again and Marion's humor was high. He seemed more relaxed than I'd seen him in weeks. He'd had a bath, shaved his face clean. He was back to being the old Marion. And it felt to me then like all our bad times were over. When he pulled me to him for a kiss, I forgave him for the whiskey drinking and the gambling, and for hitting that old man over the head back in Elgin. And for not mentioning us getting married again, though I was thinking about it every minute inside my heart.

The brass bed in that room was a noisy one. It rattled and creaked and thumped against the wall. I reckoned the whole house knew what we were up to. It didn't make a difference to Marion. He woke me up three times during the night. Woke a few others too, I expect.

By then, I'd gotten over the pain of it. Fact is, I'd gotten to where I liked the strong force of him and the way he whispered love words to me all through it. I felt a sort of control over him then that I didn't feel other times. Like I could bend him to my will if I wanted to. Make him into the man I wished for him to be just by letting him into my body. He seemed to need it from me, as much as he needed food or rest. More maybe. I didn't ever push him away. Never once.

The next morning it was dark and rainy outside. Cold seeped through the windows and walls. We slept through breakfast, snuggled together under the warm quilt. I dozed in and out for about an hour, before Marion banging around on the pot-belly stove in the corner woke me for good.

"I can't get this thing lit," he said when he saw my eyes open. I couldn't help but laugh at the sight of him in his long johns and boots. "You ain't gonna be laughing here in a minute. We got us a blue norther blowing in out there." He said it angry-like, but when he looked at me again, he was smiling.

At that moment, with that smile on his face, I loved him as much as it's possible to love a man you ain't been raised with. I didn't think none about Papa neither, nor of little Dellie and the boys. Marion smiling at me could make all my worries go away. Especially when he looked so fresh and clean, and sleepy-headed handsome like he did to me in those long johns just then.

"I guess it don't matter," he said, coming to me. He tugged off his boots and crawled underneath the quilt with me, pulling me over next to him. "We just won't get outta bed."

His hands were cold and I giggled, wiggling away, but he wrestled me back, laughing too. And we rolled around playful like that, twined up inside the covers, until he held me down on the pillow and kissed me tender. He raised his face over mine and traced his finger down my nose.

Seemed like I always had to mess up a sweet moment like that one. I don't know what it was inside me that made it so. Some deep embarrassment that came up whenever we were eyeball to eyeball like that. I said, "Jack had lots of women, didn't he?"

"Hmm?" He gave me a mystified look. His finger quit drawing on me. "Who told you that?"

"Nobody. Miz Avant said something to me about him and Shoney." I hated myself for bringing it up, especially right then. I hadn't even realized it was bothering me so.

He moved away from me, sudden-like, and laid his head back on the pillow, staring upwards. "Shoney was a saloon girl before she came to work for Miz Avant. Everybody liked Shoney."

"Did you?"

"I didn't mean me."

"No, but did you?"

"I never went to her bed if that's what you're asking."

He sounded disgusted with me and I didn't blame him for it, but I couldn't stop. I put my hand against his arm. He didn't respond to my touch.

"Did you anybody's?"

He let out a sigh and laced his fingers behind his neck. He rolled his eyes heavenward and shook his head like he was having a private word with the Almighty about me and my curiosity. "You're just trying to get mad at me for some reason."

"No, I ain't." I sat up and turned around facing him, my knees tucked under me. I pulled the quilt around myself. The chemise wasn't enough to keep away the cold in the room. "It's just some things I need to know about you. Sometimes I feel like you're a stranger to me, and I don't like feeling that way—"

"A few." He took my arm, pulled me down on his chest. His fingers combed through my hair, caught on some of the tangles from sleep. "There was a few times. All before I knew your sweetness."

"How many's a few?"

"Lily . . . it ain't important."

"I just wanna know. You can ask me any questions you want to. I ain't got anything to hide. You were my first."

He chuckled and drew me up to his shoulders, turned his body towards me some, so's our heads were resting together. "I already know that. I knew it before, even."

"How could you know before?"

"Cause you got quality. I seen it in you from the start." He was smiling again and I was glad. His finger ran a line at the edge of my hair, laced a strand behind my ear. "I know it was only since it was me you done it."

I felt my face turn pink. "You think you're so special?"

"I ain't bragging. You and me were meant for each other. It's just a pure fact. And you know it too." He put his hand on my cheek. "I love you. I ain't never loved nobody else."

"Me neither," I said, half whispering. "I love you, too." And it took something out of me to say it like that. In words and to his face. I thought I might bawl.

I think he saw how hard it was for me. He pulled me to him, both his arms around me and tight. My ear rested against his heart, listening to it thud. And that's how we were when somebody knocked at our door.

Marion sprang out of the bed and jerked his gun off the top of the chester-drawer. Then Mrs. Avant's voice rang out, "Lily? Are y'all in there? I got your surprise downstairs."

Marion looked at me, a question creasing his brow. I looked at the gun in his hand. "Be right out, Miz Avant," I said, and even to me, my voice sounded wooden.

"Make it quick," she said through the door. "This surprise seems to be in a bit of a hurry."

We heard her move away, and then her footsteps on the stairs. Marion laid the pistol down on the bedside table.

"Why did you go for your gun?" I said.

"I didn't know who it was."

I sat up in the bed. "And if it had been somebody else? You would've used it on them?"

"No I wouldn't. Just to scare them maybe." He got his britches off the rocker where he left them last night, and stepped into them. The worry lines were back on his face. "What's this about a surprise? Who's she got downstairs?"

"I don't know what it is. She said something about it yesterday but she didn't tell me what."

He reached for his shirt. Jack's shirt. "All right. You go down first. See who it is. I'll wait."

I got out of bed and started dressing myself, too. "I thought you said nobody was looking for you here."

"They probably ain't. It's just for caution's sake. There was a couple of fellas in the saloon yesterday acting kind of fishy." He shrugged into his vest, and put the gun inside its loop. "Don't get nervous, Lily."

But I couldn't help it. Just him saying for me not to, and the way he was acting, made my hands shake like the glass panes in the windows were doing with the norther blowing outside. He had to help me with my buttons. And he talked calm to me while he did it, and kissed my head before I left the room. I took a deep breath and raised my shoulders straight before I went down the stairs.

Mrs. Avant was in the parlor. Shoney was there and the two men Marion played Moon with last night. There was also another man, in a dark frock coat made of homespun, like the undertaker had worn at my mama's funeral.

"Lily," Mrs. Avant said, taking my hand. "This is Reverend Wiley Dinwiddie. He's the preacher over at the First Church of Christ. And a personal friend of mine. He's here to do that wedding for you and Marion. I thought we'd best get it outta the way."

My heart skipped over a beat.

Mrs. Avant had flowers and she'd made a white sheet cake with a pink candle in the middle. Shoney had a white dress with lace on the collar, and all kinds of tucks and embroidered ruffles. She made me put it on, and she twined my hair up in a comb. Marion wore his same clothes, but he took off his hat, and he let Mrs. Avant tie a wine red scarf around his neck. He had a weak smile through all the vows we said, but he wasn't backing out of it. I think maybe he felt embarrassed because Mrs. Avant had caught him in a lie.

She gave him the ring that had been her own to put on my finger. It wasn't flashy like the one Jack had given Estelle. Just plain gold and darkened with years. It fit loose but I thought how I could drip wax on the bottom to make it snug. When Marion kissed me, all the folks in the room—excepting Reverend Dinwiddie—clapped their hands. That gave Marion and me both a case of the blushes.

Reverend Dinwiddie wrote out the marriage certificate. Then he gave us the pen to sign our names at the bottom. I wrote Lily DeLony by habit, then squeezed in Beatty at the end. Marion squinted and held his tongue in his teeth while he signed. Carefully, he lettered Marion Simon Beatty in longhand. Mrs. Avant and one of the old men, Milford Johnson he was, witnessed our signing. Mr. Johnson drew an X-mark for his name. Reverend Dinwiddie put his signature in the corner, folded the paper and handed it back to Marion, who tucked it into his breast pocket.

The reverend wasn't a friendly man in particular. All business. But I guess that was just the way of a Cambellite like himself. He left as soon as he finished with the witnessing.

When the preacher was gone, Mrs. Avant went

upstairs and came back down with an accordion box that she played pretty good. It was a kind of polka tune that she knew, and one of the old men had a mouth harp he drew out of his pocket. Milford Johnson took Shoney up for a dance. Marion pulled me in to a waltz, even though that step didn't match good with the music. I think he just wanted me to see that he knew how.

"I guess you're my wife now," he said to me as we were dancing. "I knew someday you would be. From that first time I saw you after you'd grown up. Outside Billingsley's store."

I laid my head against his shoulder and kept dancing. He wasn't too good at it. His boots kept stubbing my toes, and the rowels on his spurs clinked. I held onto him and wished he hadn't mentioned Billingsley's store. I didn't want to think about that, or anything at all to do with McDade right now. It was my wedding day. Not exactly all I ever imagined it would be, but fine enough since it was Marion I'd taken for my husband, and not Daniel O'Barr or one of those others I could never have loved so much.

We filled up on cake and a ham Mrs. Avant had baked and left sliced up on a platter in the kitchen. There was potato pie and sugar beets, and flufftop yeast rolls with creamy sweet butter. It was the finest-cooked meal I'd ever eaten, and I couldn't resist picking at the leftovers even after we'd stacked away the dishes. That's where I was, in the kitchen with Shoney and Mrs. Avant, when somebody banged on the front door glass.

I'd left Marion sitting there, smoking cigars with

the old domino players. I got to the archway between the dining room and parlor just as Milford Johnson went to answer the door. The two men outside burst into the front hall with their pistols drawn. One had a badge on his breast. That man said, "Marion Beatty," and leveled his six-shooter in front of him. I gasped, and I guess I swerved his attention.

Marion leaped off the sofa, pulled his gun before I could blink, and fired off two shots. One hit the lawman in the wrist and the gun that man held clattered to the floor. The second shot thudded into the other man's knee. Blood spurted out in a stream and splattered on the floor. The two old domino men dove behind the furniture. I covered my mouth to keep from screaming.

I didn't have time to move or even think before Marion was grabbing me, shoving me back into the kitchen. A bullet hit the wall beside us and he turned, fired twice more. I cried out at the noise of it, and didn't see what he hit.

Mrs. Avant held open the back door. "This way," she said.

Marion pushed me outside and swept me down off the stairs. He said, "Run! We gotta run!" His voice was excited.

Rain poured down. My ears pounded, breath came short. I lifted my skirt and kept up with him best I could down the alleyway between the buildings. He ran fast. I could hear him huffing. The comb in my hair jostled loose and fell to the ground.

No shots came after us, but I expected to get hit

with one in the back. And he kept holding up for
me, then dragging me along with him, the gun still
in his hand. Smoke spun hot from the barrel. His
head whipped back to see if they were following.
I hardly recognized his face. He was pale and
hard-jawed, his eyes like stones.

He ducked me through an alley door into the
back of the livery where we'd left Mollie. He
shoved the pistol at the stable boy, who crouched
down, hands up, pointing towards an end stall.
Mollie was there in her saddle like we left her.
Marion climbed on and held his hand down for
me to take. He swung me up in front of him and
nearly pulled my shoulder out of joint doing it.
The instant I was set, he dug his spurs into the
mare's flanks.

We rode on a gallop out into the street. No coats.
All our things still up in Mrs. Avant's room. Saddlebags. Estelle's dress. Marion's hat was laying on
the tea table in the parlor. He hunkered low and
over me until I was flattened on Mollie's neck.
And I knew he did that so he'd be the one to take
any bullets that might have come flying at us. But
they didn't and we rode away. Out of Austin. But
not out of danger. They *were* looking for him. In
Travis County just like in Bastrop. I was too scared
to cry.

22

We rode Mollie hard for ten miles, then Marion stopped just before nightfall at an abandoned store he knew about somehow. It had been built on an old branch of the Chisholm Trail before fences came up to block the way. The building wasn't much more than a mud-and-rock hut. What windows or doors it once had were long since busted out. It gave protection from the rain, but we were already both soaked to the bone. Shoney's cotton dress stuck to me like it wasn't even there. I couldn't remember ever having been so cold. I felt numb all over.

Marion pulled Mollie into the building with us, and she stank of wet hair and her lather. Her breath made a fog around her head as Marion took off her saddle. He brought the blanket to me to wrap around my shoulders. It was damp and heavy, but warm from her body heat. Somebody before us had moved a big log inside the store, and Marion sat me down there and tucked me all in. His face looked gloomy and hollow-eyed, like he hadn't had any rest for a week. Rainwater dripped from his hair.

"Mollie can't go no further," he said. "Not with both of us on her. We'll let her rest a while, and then we'll head on. Maybe we can make it to Round Rock tonight. I hadn't been hearing horses behind us."

He poked through the remains of an old fire somebody had built, until he came up with enough kindling to stack under the small end of the log, just down from where I sat. From his vest pocket, he dug out two matches left from the cigars he'd been smoking with the old men at Mrs. Avant's. Both were soggy, and the sulfur crumbled off the first one he struck against a dry place on the log. The second one sparked, and he cupped his hand and shoulders, and whole body around it, shielding any draft, intent on nursing the tiny flame to life. He won, and in a few minutes, had the kindling burning.

The fire gave us some light if not much heat. He stood back and watched how much smoke was billowing, and the way it left through the busted-out windows. He didn't seem happy about it. He didn't look happy about anything.

I huddled inside the saddle blanket and tried to shake the image from my mind of the blood spewing out of that man's knee, and of the hard set to Marion's jaw when he jumped off the sofa, and how he drew so fast and hit where he aimed. I remembered him telling me once that he wasn't any good with a gun. And that it was why all his brothers called him Shot. I knew now the real reason for that nickname.

I watched him catch rainwater flowing from the

roof, inside his cupped hands, for Mollie to drink. And it hit me suddenly that he'd been a full-fledged member of the Beatty gang all along. I twisted the ring on my finger.

"It's gonna freeze over tonight," he said, looking outside. He still had on the scarf Mrs. Avant had given him, tied limp and wet, to his neck. "We gotta get somewhere outta this weather. Somewhere we don't need an open fire."

He shifted around and saw me watching him. Then he came back and squatted down to warm his hands. He didn't have on anything but his shirt and vest, and his lips were turning blue. I couldn't stop staring at him and thinking how I hardly knew anything true about him at all. I guess he read from my face what was on my mind.

He rocked back a little on the heels of his boots and his spurs dug into the dirt floor. "I had to do it, Lily. You know I had to. They give me no choice. If I'd missed, we wouldn't of got away."

I held the blanket tight around me. "It wasn't your first time to shoot somebody, though. You did it too easy."

"But I ain't ever done it when I didn't have to. And I ain't ever killed nobody. And that's a fact, Lily."

"I can't believe you anymore." My voice wouldn't go above a whisper. "All this time you've been lying to me. The same way as Jack did to Estelle."

He picked up a stick laying off the edge of the fire and chucked it into the flames. It popped and sparkled and sent up a plume of gray smoke. He swallowed hard and let out a breath, staring into the fire. The yellow light flickered on his face.

"You remember a while back?" he said slow. "That shiner Az gave me? Well, that's how come he done it. Cause I didn't kill this fella. A stage driver. We had him stopped, and all of a sudden he pulled a shotgun out from under his seat. Well, it was me closest to him so I gave him the butt of my pistol right quick. It done the job. He was knocked out cold. But Az, he didn't like it. He called me chicken-livered, and then he shot the man right through the heart. With him already out on the ground."

He picked up a twig and began to draw circles in the dirt between the fire and the toes of his boots. I couldn't speak. The doubt that had been gnawing at me seemed like it had froze to a small, hard spot in the middle of my chest. I could only just stare at him, and keep on twisting the ring around my finger.

He was no longer defending himself to me, but had sunk deep into the memory of the story he was telling. His voice went thick. "Well then Az, he came at me with his fists, still calling me names like that. Coward. Yella-hearted. Worse things. But I got in a few good swings at him and I think it surprised him. So he tore the brake lever off the coach. And then he came at me with that. And when he did, I drew my pistol on him. Cocked back the hammer. And I asked him did he wanna be my first."

He kept his eyes cast downward, still scratching circles in the dirt. "It was Jack broke it up, but it was the closest I ever came to killing a man. And that my own brother. Az was always pushing people too far. Just like he done with Tom Bishop." The twig snapped in two between his fingers, and he dropped the pieces into the dust. "He hated me. Claimed it was me turned Pa to the bottle. Me. Like I could help it I got born."

It was the nearest he ever came to mentioning his dead mama, and if Mrs. Kennedy hadn't ever told me of how she died, I wouldn't of understood what he was trying to say just then. That Az hated him for it. That maybe their pa had blamed him too. Because he'd been spared and she was lost.

"Was it Az that killed Eppie?" My voice had gone high and unnatural.

He shook his head. "That was somebody didn't want him going to your church no more. But it wasn't us. I swear to you. We wouldn't of done that. Not even Az. Cause that boy didn't have no money. You gotta understand . . . we were robbers. Not the Ku Kluck Klan."

I covered up my ears. "I don't wanna hear anymore."

He came to me on his knees, and took my hands down from the sides of my face. "I know you don't, Lily. And I knew you wouldn't wanna be my girl if you knew the things I'd done. I ain't no good for you. I know that. And I know I should of kept away from you after I saw the trouble I was bringing to you. But I couldn't do it. Cause I love you. You're all I got. And I ain't ever gonna lie to you again."

I felt my chin quiver, and bowed my face away

from him to keep him from seeing. "I told Miz Avant we were running from the law. I told her about Jack and Az getting shot down. I told her everything. It could of been her that sent for those men. It could of been my fault they came after you. I could of got you killed."

His hands were in my lap, and they were freezing. I drew them under the blanket and held them in mine to warm them. His clothes were wet and cold. I smeared my cheek against him, then opened the blanket and wrapped him inside with me. His arms came around me and he held me to his shoulder.

"Don't cry," he said. "Please don't cry. You wanna go home? I'll take you home to your pa if you want to. It'd be the best thing, Lily."

I shook my head, and gripped him harder. "Don't you ever go anywheres near McDade again. Not ever. They'll hang you sure. Or shoot you one. We can't either of us go back there. Not ever again."

"You can. You still can."

I raised my head to look at him. His eyes were on me and sorrowful. "I ain't going back," I said. "Even if you say you don't want me with you anymore."

"I ain't saying I don't want you. That ain't what I'm saying at all." The blanket slipped off my shoulder. He caught it and pulled it back up to my neck. "I'm gonna get outta this mess, Lily. Somehow I'm gonna do it. I'm gonna take care of you. And I ain't gonna let you get hurt."

I couldn't help but believe him. He sounded so

sure and true. And we were married-folk now. I had to stick by him. No matter what.

We made it on to Round Rock and spent the night at an inn. The rain stopped but I was nearly frozen before we got there. We went in to pay for the room, and he gave the landlady a false name. He was afraid somebody might see him and know who he was now. He said we had to be careful. Round Rock was where they'd caught up with Sam Bass, and though five years had passed since then, the citizens in that town were still on a law-and-order binge.

We slept hard and didn't do any lovemaking. It wasn't how I'd dreamed my honeymoon night would be.

23

*B*efore dawn, Marion left the room. He came
back in an hour with heavy coats for both of
us, a tan hat for himself and a woolen blanket for
me. He also had a bay mare for me to ride. He said
Mollie needed a rest and we could make better
time on two horses. I didn't ask where he got the
bay. I knew he had the gambling money but I was
scared he'd used it all on the clothes. I didn't want
to know for sure.

We rode out before the town was good awake.
The rain had left ice that crunched under the
horses' hooves. The bay was skittish about it. Neither was she too fond of Mollie. She kept shying
away from the commands I gave her, till finally
Marion took her on lead.

We were headed for Taylor. He said he had some
relations there. Farming relations. He stressed the
farming part so I'd know there wouldn't be any
stage robbing or store holdups. He thought he
might could help around the farm. I knew I could.
We only had to convince them, he said, to take us
in.

Their farm was on the other side of Taylor, in

the Blackland clay off the road to Rockdale, which was where we figured Haywood was by then. Marion thought we needed to wait a while and let Haywood heal up before we went for him. It wasn't said, but I knew Marion was scared we'd lead the law right to Rockdale if we went straight there. He spent a lot of time looking behind us, like he thought we were being tracked.

We got to their farm before noon. It was all flat land around, no trees save three big oaks stuck right up by their house. I'd gotten so's I couldn't look at a big, spreading-branch oak anymore without cringing.

The people weren't Beattys. They were Mercers. The brother of Marion's dead mama. An uncle Franklin and his wife, Violet. They had one boy about Dane's age, named Reese, but no other children. All this Marion told me as we rode up their road.

It was Frank that came to the door, and he didn't seem too happy to see us on their front porch. He said, "What you want, Marion?" and he didn't act af if he noticed me standing in the back, huddled in the heavy coat.

"We're hungry," Marion said. "And we need a warm place to sleep tonight."

"Who's that with you?" Frank said without looking at me.

"Lily. My bride."

The woman came to the door then and pushed it open. She had three warts on the skin between her lip and her nose, and she looked plumb worn out from years of farm work. But she had kindly eyes, and she drew me out from around Marion and inside the house without any more questions from her husband.

The house was simple inside, set up like our house in McDade with a bedroom off either side of the main room, east and west. But their kitchen was separated from the rest of the house, and the walls were covered with old newspapers to seal up what cracks there were, since the kitchen faced north.

Violet took me in there, away from the men. I could hear them in the other room, talking in low tones. She warmed a pot of beans and turned out a pan of crusty corn bread. She gave me two bowls to fill. One for me and one for Marion, for since I was his wife now, it was time for me to take care of him.

By the time we sat down to eat, Frank seemed used to the idea of having Marion there, and they were talking pretty good, mostly about work to be found in Taylor. I noticed Reese got an idolizing look on his face every time Marion spoke. It was that look, I think, that had Frank worried at first. He didn't want Reese following his cousin's example.

They moved Reese out to the main room to sleep on a pallet on the floor beside the wood stove. And they gave us his bedroom, which looked to me like it had been added later to the rest of the house. The floor in there had an inward slope so steep a cup of spilled water would have flowed into the front room and all the way to the far wall before it stopped rolling. A straight chair and wardrobe cabinet were the only furniture besides the bed. But Violet freshened the linens for us, and a small stove in the corner gave plenty of heat. I hung our coats on two of the hooks inside the cabinet.

After the oil lamps were doused, and the doors between the rooms closed, Marion laid down with me on the bed, and in whispers told me what all Frank had said while I'd been in the kitchen with Violet.

"He hinted we might could stay a while. Till we get our feet on the ground, he said. He's got a leaking barn he needs help fixing. I think he wanted to talk with Violet before he said for sure."

"Did you tell him we were on the run?"

"No." He put his hand to my mouth. "I didn't say nothing like that. And I don't want you to either, Lily. If he thinks we're hiding he'll turn us out." He pulled me to rest on his shoulder. "I did tell him my lawless days were behind me. I said I had a wife now, and I was ready to settle down. Become a farmer or whatever it took. I said that to him, and now I'm saying it to you. I mean it, Lily." His lips touched my head. "We'll have us a whole passel of babies. Raise up some wheat. Some corn. Maybe cotton. I can do that. I used to help Pa before he died."

"It's hard work, farming."

"I ain't afraid of work."

He sounded dead serious. And he *did* work for Frank. He worked hard.

They got the barn roof fixed, and made some new winter stalls inside for the animals the Mercers kept. Marion was good with a hammer and nails, and with the shaping of wood. He was especially good with the animals, and good with fixing Frank's broken-up farm equipment, too. It struck me that he'd be good at anything he did once his mind was turned in the right direction.

Frank seemed glad for the help. His fields of wheat and oats were growing fast with the rain that had come. Together, he and Marion walked the rows every day, and from the windows in the house, I saw them talking a lot. It was a good sign, I thought, and I hoped it was Frank learning Marion on ways to bring in a good crop.

At night the men played dominoes while Violet and I did her mending. She was an expert with a needle, and taught me things my own mama never had a chance to. She sewed me two dresses from some scrap fabric she had, and made work shirts for Marion from the linsey-woolsey she kept in a trunk. She told me how she used to weave her own cloth till the money gave out and she had to sell her loom.

Cooking was my best skill and so I did that while Violet sewed. Marion bragged over every meal I fixed, said how he'd never put his mouth around such delicacies, that he'd surely found a prize in me and that he'd already begun to put on weight, though I couldn't see it. He made such a big fuss at the supper table every night that I walked around with a red face all the way through cleaning up afterwards.

I knew it was mostly just him trying to keep my humor high and it worked pretty well. But sometimes, as I watched Violet sew, I fretted over that pair of pants for Nathan I never finished hemming. I thought too, about the sweater for Dellie half-knitted, and worried how she was getting by with all those men, nobody to understand her girlish needs. It was Dellie who caused me the most torment.

Violet tried to keep my mind off my gloom with her constant woman chatter. She'd been in sore need of company before I came, and she made me feel right at home. Frank too, though he wasn't big on small talk. Too much attention made him nervous, I think. He reminded me of Papa in some ways, though not how he tolerated laziness in Reese. I never saw that boy do much work. He mostly just trailed behind Marion, mouthing like a medicine-show drummer; or else stood around out by the barn chunking clods at the mockingbirds that sat squawking on the gabled roof.

To me it seemed the Mercers surely knew, someplace inside themselves, that something wasn't right, for us to come without clothes or belongings of any kind. Marion thought up a tale about how we'd been robbed by highwaymen outside of Austin. And he told it so good, and with such convincing detail, I knew he was recollecting a hold-up he'd taken part in himself, though on the other side. But Frank knew Marion had his gun, and he also must have known that Marion was a crack shot. I figured Frank didn't really believe that highway robbery story, but maybe he just wanted to and so he let Marion lie. Myself, I could understand that line of thinking. It was just easier to believe whatever Marion said than not to.

After the first week or so of looking over his shoulder, Marion finally took off the gun and left it lay in the bedroom we were using. He let his beard grow, and it came out a darker shade than his head hair. It changed the look of his face some. Both of us started to feel easier there at the Mercers' place. We took to laughing with each other again, and loving at night, quietly, so's the bed wouldn't creak. He tacked our wedding certificate to the wall where we could look at it whenever we took a notion.

He was changing. I knew in my heart he was. I prayed to God to give us more time together and not take him from me too soon. I asked for the Lord to look at the good part of Marion and see he wasn't beyond redemption. There were lots worse living with a lie of salvation on their lips, swearing by a Christian life, but without a hope of purity in their souls. I asked God to look at those folks, to compare them with the natural goodness inside of Marion, and to forgive him for his sins. And I prayed for Dellie to be safe and happy without me.

The second week in January, the coldest winter I'd ever known fell upon us. Artesian wells froze up. Cattle died. Children ice-skated on stock ponds. The oats and wheat in the fields froze stiff, then fell over and laid down flat.

Frank brought in a bottle of corn whiskey he'd had hidden in the barn. He and Marion drank the whole thing in one night. They sang songs I'd never heard. Saloon songs. And Frank knew the words as good as Marion, so I suspected Frank might have a past worth hiding, too.

Violet kept Reese out of the room with them best she could. She said it wasn't any place for a boy his age. But us women both knew it was just heartsick men letting off steam. With the oats and wheat frozen out, Frank wouldn't make any money before spring planting. I wondered quietly inside myself how Papa's crops were doing.

For Marion, the drinking soothed a different kind of sadness. That night in bed, instead of the whiskey putting him fast asleep as I expected, it loosened his tongue. He laid there well past an hour in the darkness, me with my back curled against him, and talked in my ear.

At first, it wasn't much I wanted to hear, reliving memories—card game memories mostly. Beating "Ace High" Kendricks in Hempstead with a bobtail flush. Things like that didn't mean anything to me, nor soothe my soul.

But then he got onto Jack and his voice turned more whispery, and he rubbed on my arm as he spoke. He told me how Jack had used to say there wasn't any way he was going to struggle just to have nothing like their pa had done, busting his back forty-eight hours a day for beans and corn bread. And then losing it all anyhow to a freak weather storm like Frank had just done. Said life was just too short and precious to spend it that way.

Towards the end, though, Jack had changed his mind on things. He really had been planning to make a cotton crop this summer, and maybe feed corn if the rain had held. And Marion said how it was Estelle that got Jack to thinking that way. That farming was a noble thing for a man to do, and took more courage than holding up a storekeeper or emptying out a cash drawer. And Marion said that it just didn't all make sense for Jack to die right then, when he was trying to get his life straight.

"He wasn't even carrying a gun when they went into town. I found both of them laying on the mantelpiece when I got back from the McLemores' place. I didn't think they'd gone looking for trouble. Not with Jack's guns just laying there like that. It was them two guns that fooled me. If he hadn't left them there, I'd of gone up town after them. You'd of seen me right there too. And Tom Bishop wouldn't of got away with what he done."

Maybe it was the liquor in his voice, but I could have sworn I heard a sob come out of him. It scared me to think he might be weeping there in the darkness beside me. I rolled myself towards him and put out both my arms around him.

"And you might've got killed, too. It ain't your fault, Marion," I said. "Maybe Jack didn't want you along. Maybe that's how come he went without you."

He snuzzled his face against my bosom and he put his hand there, so I felt easier, like maybe I just misheard that sob. Still, I stroked on his hair, smoothing it back from his face, and also trying to feel if any tears were on his cheeks. I couldn't tell anything. His whiskers pricked at the skin on my wrists.

"You know what I keep thinking about?" he said. "All them pups. Helped birth half of them myself. Docked their tails to keep them healthy. I hope they found somebody to take them in. It's the most ignorant things'll keep you awake nights."

He laid there quiet for a while, so I thought I'd put him to sleep with my hair rubbing. Then he shifted his position and I knew he was still awake.

"It's time I tried to see about Haywood," he said. "I bet he's up and walking by now. Maybe ready to ride. He's too full of spit and vinegar to stay down long."

"The roads are froze. You can't get to Rockdale. That's twenty-five miles from here."

"I ain't talking about this minute, Lily." His fingers touched my face. "I'll send him a wire. Just see how he's doing first. Tell him I'll be there to get him in a week. This cold won't last longer than that. Just to see what message he sends back. I'll sign myself Shot and call him Peckerwood like we done when he was a kid." A little laugh came from him then. "Nobody but him and me'll figure that one out."

"What if they're watching the telegraph offices? Expecting you to go there?"

"I'll send Reese. He'll do it for me."

"And then what?"

"I'll go to Rockdale and fetch him." He moved away from me and back to the pillows. His hand rubbed my shoulder. "They're giving away land in

Idaho. Frank was telling me about it. Staking out homesteads. I figure we could all go there."

"Where's Idaho?"

"Up north somewhere. Up by Canada, I think."

"It snows in Canada. You can't grow crops in the snow."

"Yes you can. Different crops than here maybe. I don't know. Maybe I'd like to raise cattle. Land up there wouldn't be all fenced up yet like it is down here. I can see myself on a big cattle ranch."

"Do you know anything about that? Ranching? Raising cattle?"

"I done it before. Worked a couple of round-ups for Mister Holman down in Fayette County." His voice was getting slow and softer. "I reckon I know enough."

"I ain't ever thought of leaving Texas before," I said, feeling a shaking start on me for no reason. I reached out to him and gripped him around his middle.

He didn't say anything, and after a while, I noticed his hand had gotten heavier on my shoulder. Pretty soon, it fell off onto the bed and I knew he'd gone to sleep finally. But he'd left me awake with all these new worries. I thought about snow and cattle and Idaho, and then about Haywood and that pack of cur dogs. It was a fine thing Marion had done, springing all these new thoughts on me, then taking off into dreams himself.

24

Reese sent Marion's wire. It took a full day of warmer weather before the ice on the roads began to thaw. Frank had need of provisions, and Reese begged to be the one to go along. When I heard him sound so eager, I knew Marion had arranged for the wire to get sent. I felt uneasy that this was to be done without Frank's and Violet's knowing.

All morning, Marion chopped wood. It was mostly an excuse so's to be outside when Frank and Reese returned. For Violet's sake, Marion kept his spirits high, but I knew by the way his eyes were jumping, over-excited, how anxious he felt, though he didn't confide in me.

When the men returned close to noon, I watched through the windows as Marion raced to meet them on the road. It was Frank who came inside first, then Marion and Reese a few minutes after. It wasn't until evening, when we were alone, that I learned what happened.

Reese had sent the wire while Frank was in the general store. No message had come back through the telegraph lines. Marion took this as positive news. He began to make plans to ride to Rockdale the following Saturday.

In the meanwhile, the time for my monthly cycle to begin had come and gone. My body swelled up and ached but no blood flowed. Violet said it was probably due to the cold weather. Me and Marion both knew what it meant. He began to look at me with a new softness and wonderment in his eyes. I tried to think which time it was that made the child I knew was growing inside me. I hoped it was the one night in Austin we'd had so sweet together, or the morning at the Gazways' house outside Elgin.

During the evening of January 18th, a day before Marion planned to go for Haywood, a letter came marked "M.B." on the outside and delivered to Taylor, care of Frank Mercer. The boy from the general store brought it to the farm. It came postmarked from Rockdale. That much I saw as Frank handed the envelope to Marion.

Both Violet and Frank waited, while Marion opened the letter, for him to say what it contained. His lips moved silently as he read to himself. I saw his eyes glaze over but I don't think they did. When he looked up he had a smile planted on his mouth, a smile about like the one he'd given that old man outside the Gazways' barn.

"It's news from Jack and Estelle," he said. "She says they're doing well."

It was the first time I remembered him not having ready a convincing lie. Violet especially wasn't satisfied and wanted more details. But Marion left her questions unanswered and disappeared into Reese's bedroom, closing the door behind him.

"He's always private when it comes to his brothers," I said to Violet, like it wasn't anything for her to worry over. Then I myself hurried after him.

When I came in the door, he was sitting on the side of the bed, holding his head between his hands, staring at the floor between his boots, trance-like. The letter laid on the quilt beside him and I went there to pick it up. The handwriting was flowery and hard to read at first for the flourishes. It said:

January 12, 1884

Dear Marion,

It is with great sadness and trepidation that I send this news to you. Your brother, Haywood, is not here as you had reason to believe, but is presently at the county jail of Bastrop, along with R. Stevens and C. Goodman. All three were taken by sheriff's posse on the morning of December 26th last, less than twelve hours from the time you left McDade. They are being held on large bonds for the murder of Willie Griffin, whom, as you know, they all loved and trusted as a brother unto themselves.

By the time you receive this letter, I will be in Bastrop, called as a witness in the examining trial beginning Monday, the 14th. It was my heartfelt desire to see Haywood to safety here in Rockdale but, alas, it was not to be. You will be pleased to know, however, that I was able to recover the remains of your brother, Jack, and he has been laid to rest near my family home here. I weep daily for his memory.

Marion, let this letter serve as a warning to you. Do not venture from your safe haven. Do not send more wires. There have been men here seeking you or information as to your whereabouts. These men, G. Milton and T. Bishop, your brothers' murderers, will not rest until they track you down, too. Take heed. I fear danger even in writing this letter to you. But I wanted you should know the fate of poor Haywood and the others. My heart is heavy with the burden of sending this news.

Your friend and sister,
Estelle Beatty

I read the final part of the letter over twice. The part about Mr. Milton and Mr. Bishop. Panic rushed upon me. I dropped the letter back on the bed where it was when I came into the room.

Marion grabbed the paper and wadded it into a ball in both his hands, so quick it startled me. "All this time," he said, "while I've been running free, they had him locked up in their jail like a circus animal."

He chunked the wadded ball across the room, where it thumped on the wall and fell behind a chair. Then he flopped backwards on the bed with his arm thrown over his brow. I retrieved the letter.

"Let's go ahead up to Idaho," I said, opening the grate on the stove in the corner. The paper took the fire and flared. "We ain't got that much to pack."

"No money, either," he muttered.

"We don't need money. We can make do some way."

A breath of hard air came out of him. "No, Lily. I can't leave him there."

"You can't pay his bond, either." I just said it. I didn't really think that was what he meant. My heart was jumping with fear. "Maybe they'll find him innocent. Willie Griffin just got caught in the cross fire. I saw it. They can't prove it was Haywood's gun that killed him."

"They'll find a way to. They ain't gonna let him out. You know it and I do."

I went to his side. "Maybe they will. Let me ride to town and get a newspaper. Maybe they got something in there so's we'll know what's going on."

He didn't look at me, but he reached into his pocket and pulled out a coin. He flipped it at me. I didn't catch it and had to chase it across the floor. A ten-cent piece.

"That's it," he said. "That's all the money I got left."

I took the bay. Violet and Frank tried to ask me where I was headed. I left it to Marion to explain. The weather was still cold enough to freeze the breath inside my lungs. I hadn't gone a quarter mile when Reese came galloping up behind me. He said his mama sent him to give me an escort.

We rode along side by side a ways, then Reese said, "Why are you going into town? Did Marion send you in for something?"

"He wants a newspaper."

"He's in trouble with the law, right? Oh, I know you can't tell me. But I know there's some reason he won't ever leave the farm." He sounded almost excited about it. I glanced at him and thought how unlike Dane he was, and how much older than just a year or two I felt. He said, "Maybe he wants us to pick up a box of cartridges for his gun. I know the kind he needs. Winchester .44."

"All he wants is a newspaper."

"Well ... I happened to notice he was empty and thought I'd mention it. If money's the problem, I got some of my own. I earned it right before Christmas working down at the gristmill."

"Just a newspaper is all we're after," I said, firmer this time, and Reese shut up. I couldn't imagine him doing work for anybody, but especially not the grueling kind of work like at a gristmill.

The story was there all right, on the front page. Even in Williamson County. With the name Beatty spelled wrong. And with Charlie Goodman called Goodwyn. Bob Stevens they got right. And all three were charged with murder and attempted murder. Haywood's bond totaled $7500, Charlie's $5000, and Bob's was set at $4000. Huge sums of money, I thought. Nobody'd been brought to account for the death of Jack and Az. And nobody would be.

I stood on the street outside the general store and read the sworn statements of the witnesses. Even Dane gave one, saying how Az had come up to Tom Bishop on the gallery and started the trouble. All the statements were for the State. All save Estelle, who claimed only that Jack had not been wearing a gun when he left his house that morning. And Bird Hasley was hardly mentioned by anybody. Bird Hasley, I figured, must've gotten away, since he'd been the only one not wounded.

As I read, there was movement all around me, buggies and wagons passing, men on horseback, some afoot. But to all of it, I was deaf. I was thinking how they'd needed my statement at that trial. How I could have told them that Haywood, and Mr. Bishop, and Mr. Milton all three had been shooting when Willie Griffin ran out of the rock saloon. It could have been one of the other two guns as easy as Haywood's that took him down. And that neither Charlie Goodman nor Bob Stevens had even been there at all by then. It seems so unfair and unreal to me. I couldn't move from that spot on the street, nor my eyes off the newsprint that smeared when I touched it.

Reese came up beside me and shoved a box of Winchester cartridges at me. He said, "Here. Put these in your coat."

I blinked at him a second before I remembered who he was. I looked at the box in his hand. "I said I don't want that."

"You will." He took me by the wrist, my hand still gripping the newspaper, and he dragged me into the store. He stood me in front of the near wall, his hand holding my shoulders square, and pointed. "Look."

It was Marion's face staring back at me from a sign six inches by twelve, tacked among and over those of other men and notices of land sales and animals astray. It was the picture of him from the church fair from my Bible, and it said, "WANTED for robbery, abduction, and assault with intent to kill."

And there was a hundred-and-twenty-five-dollar reward posted and a description of "18, 19, 20, or 21 years old, 6-foot, 150 pounds, brown hair, black eyes, armed and dangerous." And there on that sign, they had the name spelled right, even if it was the only thing they got right—MARION S. BEATTY. I had to hold onto Reese's arm to keep from falling over.

"At least he's got his whiskers now," Reese said, and I thought he was talking too loud.

I collected my balance and reached up to rip the paper off the wall. Then I moved to leave the store.

"Hey! Young lady!" the clerk called to me. "What's you take down from there?"

I didn't turn around. I heard Reese say, "We seen a horse we think is our lost Shadow," and he came running after me. I stood out on the gallery, rending that paper sign into bits.

25

When Reese and me got back to the house, Marion was gone. Violet met me at the door to tell me. "I didn't go in there till an hour after you left," she said. "I'd started to get worried over him. He must of went out through the window."

I headed that way, to see for myself he was gone. A sick feeling flushed on me and I thought I might puke. Frank's voice came before I could get to the bedroom.

"What's going on here, Lily?" he said, sounding grave.

I turned around, flashed a look at Reese, who was still just inside the front door. "We had an awful fight this morning, Frank," I said, amazed at how easy the lie came to me. "It's the first one we've had yet, and I guess we ain't taking it too good."

Frank and Violet exchanged a glance. She came to me and put her hand on my shoulder, then walked me over to a chair, patting at my back. "Poor thing," she said. "Just sit down here and talk to Aunt Violet about it, now."

Frank turned for the kitchen, like he didn't have time for a whining woman. Reese gave me a grin and a wink, and went after his papa. My whole insides were shaking. The box of .44 cartridges in my pocket was pulling my coat sideways towards its weight.

"I don't wanna talk, Violet," I said, sitting anyway. "It's just trifleness."

"Well, he's probably gone right now to try and find you. Men can be so misunderstandable sometimes." Her hand patted me some more.

My mind was in such a state, I couldn't do more than stare at Violet, where she sat across from me, our knees touching, and gave me womanly advice on how to handle a new husband. Marion wouldn't get far if those signs with his picture were hanging all over Texas. I tried to think of what I should do if he didn't come back. Where he'd gone. Why he'd done it so secret.

The evening crept by. I was keyed up, jumping over the least noise. After supper and the dishes were done, I tried for a time to concentrate on an old copy of a fashion magazine Violet gave me. She leaned to whisper to me when she did it, "It's a woman's lot in life to wait for her man. That's why I took up needlework. It helps pass the time." She gave me another pat. She'd been patting on me for the last few hours. I thought I must have looked a pitiable sight for her to keep on doing that. "He'll be back," she said, "by and by." Then she sat down to darn a pair of Reese's socks.

Frank and Reese tried to lure me into a game of checkers. I didn't have the stomach for it. Directly,

I yawned big and headed for the bedroom. I kept a candle burning, and though I changed into the nightdress Violet had made for me from some flour sacks, I didn't try to go to sleep. It wasn't but about eight o'clock when I went in there, and time moved slow staring out the window.

The longer the night grew, the more sure I became that Marion wouldn't be back. He'd either run into bounty hunters or the law, or he'd headed off to Bastrop and to Haywood. I couldn't come up with a plan for finding him. I didn't know my way good around this part of the countryside, and I had a dread fear of getting lost without Marion to lead the way.

I cried and paced, and wrung my hands. I prayed. As the night faded into wee morning, I got numb. The candle burned down to a nub. I blew it out and sat there in the dark. He was gone sure. I couldn't think what I should do.

I woke with a neck cramp from dozing in the chair. Then I heard the noise that must have roused me in the first place. It came from the front porch way, through the walls of the house. The sound of a door, opening quiet and shutting. I scrambled out of the chair and rushed from the bedroom.

He was there, creeping in the darkness of the front room. I knew his shape. Heard his spurs. I sprang to him, and threw my arms around him.

"Thank God," I breathed, drawing him tight.

I held onto him and pulled him into the bedroom. He closed the door behind us. My hands groped his jaw, felt the beard under my palms. I wished it was thicker, longer. I wanted it to cover up his whole face.

"I've been so worried," I said. "I didn't think I'd ever see you again. Where'd you go? Why'd you sneak off like that?"

He moved away from me, went to the bedside table, and lit the candle stub with a match from the box there. The light was dull and I knew it wouldn't be but a few minutes before the wick was gone completely.

He sat down on the bed. The bags under his eyes made shadows on his cheekbones. "I went to bust out Haywood. But then I came back cause of you."

"Thank God you did. They've got your picture on a proclamation in town." I went to sit beside him. He was turned facing the center of the bed, just one foot resting on the floor, so I couldn't get up as close to him as I wanted. "They got things about you on that sign. Things like 'armed and dangerous.' They're offering reward money. A hundred and twenty-five dollars." He was digging in his pockets and didn't seem to be hearing me. I touched his knee. "Marion? It's that picture from the fair. I guess Papa found it and gave it to them. It says 'wanted for abduction.' I think that means me. That you stole me away. Reese saw it, too."

"They're gonna convict Haywood." He had his gun out on the bed and kept riffling around in his pockets. "I saw a newspaper in a store where I was. Ever one of them people testified against him.

Said he aimed his gun at Willie Griffin and shot him down in cold-blooded murder."

"I know. I read it too. I brought one of them for you." I started for the wardrobe cabinet where my coat hung with the newspaper folded in the pocket. He clutched my arm and held me back.

"I gotta go get him out, Lily. You know that, don't you? I can't just leave him there. He's my brother."

"What if you get caught? What am I supposed to do then?"

I felt tears wanting to come again and knew my eyes were already red. I struggled to hold them back. He looked at me for a spell, and I tried to read the unfamiliar set to his mouth.

"That's why I came back. I don't want you left with nothing." He reached into his vest pockets again. "I got almost five hundred dollars here."

My eyes slid down with his hands, to the bed where he laid a pile of money beside his gun. All bills. He reached into his coat pocket, brought out more, stacked it with the rest, then started emptying his other pockets.

"I wanna give some of it to Frank," he said, fanning out the bills with his fingertips. "To see him through spring till he can get his crops planted and brought in. For helping us out like they done."

My voice had gone down to a whisper. "What did you do?"

"And if it works out and I get back here in a couple of days with Haywood, we'll use this to get us to Idaho. Or maybe old Mexico. Wherever we end up going. Someplace they ain't heard of Beattys."

I put my hand on his, stopping his sorting. "Marion? I asked you a question."

"I heard it."

"You said you'd never lie to me again."

He raised his eyes on me. "I hadn't. Lying and just not saying ain't the same thing."

I looked down at the money again. "Did you win all this playing poker?" I knew I sounded hopeful.

He shook his head. "I thought of that. But I needed the ante. And I gave you my last dime to buy that newspaper."

We stared at each other. It was me who turned away first. He went back to shuffling the money into piles, like he was dealing cards.

"What did you tell Frank and Violet?" he said. "About where I went?"

I watched his hands. I'd never seen that much money all together at once. The candle nub had started to sputter. "That we were fighting."

"That was a good thing to say." He picked up one of the bigger stacks and patted the edges so's they were neat. "I want you to take this. It's two hundred dollars. I'm gonna give two hundred to Frank, too. And I'll keep a hundred in case I need it for something while I'm gone."

He held out the pile he'd neatened up. I wouldn't take it from him. He grabbed my hand, turned it palm up, and put the money in it, closing my fingers around the stack.

"Take it, Lily. It ain't gonna do either one of us

no good you refusing. They already got me down for everything I ever done or thought of doing in my life, so this can't make it no worse."

My hand cradled the stack, but loose. He went back to sorting the other piles on the bed. I said, "You saw the reward signs, then?"

He nodded and set aside Frank's money on the bedside table. The rest he stuffed back into his vest pocket. Then he took off his hat and tossed it on the floor beside us. "Does this look like brown hair to you?"

A laugh escaped me. It was nerves and relief that he wasn't dead or caught, that he was back here sitting next to me, even if just for a short time. I covered my mouth to stop the laughter. The smell of the money in my hand came to my nose—ink and rag paper, the flesh from a hundred hands.

"No. It ain't brown," I said. Another giggle glimmered from me.

He smiled and took the stack away from me. He flipped through it, counting it again. I think he liked handling it, rubbing it between his fingers. His face went kind of moony for a second. Then he gave the bills back to me.

"Put this somewhere it'll be safe," he said, and watched me as I moved across the room to the wardrobe cabinet.

I squeezed the wad of money into a roll and shoved it down in the pocket of my coat. The box of cartridges was there, and the newspaper. I took both to him. His eyes lit on the box.

"Reese said you needed these. He said forty-four caliber."

Marion snatched the box eager from my hand. The newspaper he didn't touch. "He was right. I didn't have but one left."

I stood there and watched while he broke open the gun. The cartridges made a clinking sound sliding into the cylinder. The one bullet was still in its chamber. That gave me some relief seeing it wasn't gone.

"Was it a store?" I said. "Where you got that money? The one that had the newspaper you saw? Was it here in Taylor? Or did you go someplace else?"

He closed the gun and spun the cylinder, and he looked at me while he did it. Then he set the pistol and the box of cartridges on the table beside Frank's money. He wasn't going to tell me anything. I could see it on his face. He took off his boots, then his coat and vest, and pitched them onto the chair where I'd waited all night. He reached for my arm.

"C'mere," he said, lying back on the bed. He took me with him. "Don't get so worked up over everything, Lily. I'm gonna come back for you. I got it all planned out smoothly in my mind. I ain't gonna let them catch me."

I reached for his mouth, kissed him there and all over his face, his neck. After the long hours of worrying, and with the fear still screaming inside me, a hunger for him rose that I'd never felt in just that way.

He pulled my nightdress over my head. Both of us tugged his galluses off his shoulders, yanked at his shirt and the buttons on his pants, until he was down to nothing, same as me. He moved on top of me, sideways across the bed, us not even stopping to get our heads the right direction on the pillows. And the breath came out of me hot and needful like it did from him.

We weren't either of us quiet about it, and it wasn't till later I wondered about Reese on his pallet in the next room. Probably even Frank and Violet heard us, and thought we were making up from the fight I told them we had. There was no shame in me about it, though. I wasn't thinking of anything but Marion and of how I wanted to hold him there, locked within my body and safe. He knew my thoughts. He always did. When it was over, he whispered, "I gotta go, Lily. He's my brother. I gotta take the chance."

"You ain't leaving now, are you?" I said.

"Sunday." His fingers on my spine brought up chills. "I'm going Sunday."

26

Saturday passed by in half the time the night before took, even without sleep and with the worry growing in me, for Marion was with me then, and happiness speeds by, while misery lingers.

He didn't give Frank the two hundred dollars yet. He was afraid Frank wouldn't take it. He said we'd just leave it somewhere before we left. Someplace where they'd find it but not too quick. Like under Reese's pillow. Marion thought it was the best way so's they couldn't get in trouble for hiding a fugitive. He thought he could get Reese to stay quiet about seeing the proclamation in town. And I noticed the two of them later, out by the barn talking.

Sunday morning, I woke up sick. Not just since it was the day Marion planned to leave, neither. The first second I raised my head, I knew I would puke. I ran through the house in my nightclothes, my hand clapped over my mouth, and barely made it to the back porch before it came out of me. After the first heave I sunk to my knees, and holding onto the stair rail, emptied my stomach till there wasn't any more.

Marion rushed outside after me, and when he saw what was happening to me, went back in for my coat to wrap around my shoulders. I shrugged it off, though, for I was sweating hot and wished he would leave me out there alone. I hugged the porch post. The wood felt cool and good to my face.

"You eat something bad?" he said. He sat down beside me and I gave him a sidewards glance. He was in his long johns, hair messy and curling on his forehead, concern in his sleepy, morning eyes. I hated the thought of even one hour without him.

My shoulders quit heaving, and I spit to get the taste from my mouth. "I gotta clean this up before the hens get to it," I said.

"I'll do it. You stay still." He moved quick before I could say a word. But it wasn't in me to argue with him just then. The back door shut behind him.

The cold air felt good on my body and the sun was peeking up, turning the sky to fire. One of the roosters started crowing and it seemed like a lonely sound to me. I tried to think how I would get through the next two or three days, waiting to see Marion back here and safe. With Haywood or without.

Marion came out with his boots on, his coat, and no pants. He loped down the steps and over to the cistern. While he was drawing up a bucket of water, he started in whistling. He sounded right jolly over there and it made me cross with him since I felt so low. He whistled the whole time he came to throw water on the mess I made off the porch, and whistled going back, a smile kind of playing on his pucker.

The second time he came with the bucket, he saw my frown and quit his tune. He emptied the water on the ground and figured, it seemed, that he'd done enough, because he didn't go back for another bucketful. He looked at me, then at where I was staring, out at the red sun boiling up from behind the earth.

"Guess we're gonna have us a baby for sure," he said, coming around the steps. He set the bucket down and reached for my hand like he wanted me to stand. "Lemme see you."

I shook off his fingers, peeved that he'd thought of why I was ailing quicker than I had. "You can't see nothing yet."

He sat down on the top step then, and rubbed his hand up my back. "Ain't you cold?"

I shook my head and kept staring away from him, at the pilings underneath the house, the frost on the windowpanes, anywhere but at his face.

"You ain't happy about us having a baby?" he said, leaning around in front of me to make me look at him.

"I ain't happy with you leaving."

He glanced at the door. We could hear Violet and Frank stirring around inside. He drew his feet up on the next step under him and rested his elbows on his knees. "I'll be back by tomorrow night. Tuesday at the latest."

"You act like it's just a trip across town and back. Ain't you even scared about it?"

"Yeah, I'm scared. Scared I won't get to see you with your belly swelled up or my son born. I'm chewing on it, Lily. It scares me plenty." He reached to tuck a strand of my hair behind my ear. "But I can't go on being cooped up and hid away like this, not able to go past Frank's land yonder. I just ain't made thataway. I gotta get loose from here. Go somewhere I can move around again. And I can't do that knowing my brother's stuck behind bars. I don't think I could sleep nights if I went off and left him."

I peered out at the fiery sun and at the sky with not a cloud one floating. The look of it reminded me of Christmas morning, of riding into town with Dane under the same kind of sky.

My arms were getting cold. I reached behind me to draw on my coat and he helped me with it. My hands shoved down into the pockets. The roll of money was in there. My fist closed around it.

"Don't go by way of McDade," I said. "Take an extra day getting there if you have to, but go around it far."

I felt him looking at me, and looked at him, too. The back of his hand touched my cheek. His eyes were soft. "I got plain lucky with you, Lily. I don't know how come, or what it is you see in me. I can't for the life of me figure it out."

The door above us opened, and Frank leaned out. He must have thought we'd gone plumb loony, sitting out in the cold in nothing but our

nightclothes and coats. He said, "Either of you care
for a cup of hot coffee?"

I raised my chin to him. "Marion's leaving us today," I said, calm. "He heard of work over in
Lexington."

"That a fact?" Frank said.

Marion grinned at me, and it seemed I saw
something I never placed before. It was a little,
devilish boy inside him and that grin. He kept his
eyes on me as he answered Frank. "It surely is.
Fella name of Dunnigan's breaking out some new
land. Said he needed help." I couldn't keep from
shaking my head at him in wonder. He was as
good a fibber as I'd ever heard. I wished like anything that this particular lie was the truth. He
looked up at Frank. "I'll be back in a day or two
for Lily."

He left around nine that morning. Frank lent
him a saddlebag and he packed it with the food I
fixed him, some candle stubs, matches, an extra
shirt for Haywood to wear. The box of .44 cartridges. He filled his canteen, looped a length of
rope on his saddle, and buckled on his spurs. He
planned to stop down the road in Coupland or another small town and buy a horse and tack for
Haywood. He thought I might need the bay.

I walked with him all the way down to the road
and would have gone further, but he turned to kiss
me and in that way, told me this was where we'd
part.

"Maybe you should wait till dark to go," I said,
holding onto his coat.

"I'll stay in the woods. I wanna be there and done with it before first light tomorrow." He put his hand on top of my head and gave me a shake. Then he patted my belly and a smile curved his cheek. He had on a pair of Frank's gloves, and the rough leather of them picked threads on my skirt. Then he took ahold of the saddle horn and swung himself onto Mollie's back.

I stood there watching, still feeling his hands on me, as he rode off. When he got down a ways, past Frank's land and the view of their house, he kicked Mollie up to a gallop. He disappeared into a line of cottonwoods that followed a creek for a bit. But I knew the trees gave out after a while, and that he'd have open land then until the other side of Taylor, where the post oaks started up.

My stomach rolled like it needed emptying again. I held it and stayed, waiting to catch another glimpse of him. It didn't come. After a few more minutes, I trudged back towards the house.

The Mercers went to church. They asked me to go along, but I chose to stay and make dinner so it'd be ready when they got home. Cooking kept my mind busy, but not enough. Every few minutes I thought of Marion, tried to imagine how far away he'd gotten by then. My stomach felt queasy still, and after peeling boiled chicken off the bones, I had to puke again. Nothing came that time but coffee, as I hadn't been able to hold down breakfast. I wondered if I'd packed up enough grub for him and hoped he wouldn't go hungry.

The Mercers got home from church just after

noon, and we sat down to the meal. Violet complimented me on the lightness of my dumplings. I'd warmed a loaf of her bread and it was all I could manage to swallow. I figured Marion might have already made it halfway to Elgin, and I thought about the Gazways' house and the few happy hours we'd had there.

It was while we were eating that we heard a rider come up outside. I looked through the windows and saw a sorrel-colored horse and a man with a badge seated on the saddle. I felt my breath begin to quicken.

Later, I told myself that it wasn't any surprise to me when that town marshal rode up to the house, that I expected it all along. But I was lying to myself more than I'd lied to God and to Papa when I'd promised never to see Marion again. It was a shock to me, plain and simple, when that lawman appeared out there. And I knew, by instinct and in my gut, that Marion had never made it to the post oak woods.

It was Frank who went out on the porch. I stood with Violet at the window behind the curtains, and watched the marshal get down off his horse.

"Had some trouble in town today, Frank," the marshal said. He came to the edge of the porch and stopped, stood there. "One Marion Beatty? Said he was your relation. Did you know he was wanted in Bastrop and Travis counties? For robbery and assault?"

"No, I didn't know that," Frank said.

"Is there a young woman named"—the marshal took a slip of paper out of his pocket and squinted at it—"Lily DeLony here with you? Seems Mister Beatty's been charged with her abduction."

"I didn't know that either, John," Frank said. "We give them food and shelter for a while. Boy's my nephew. But I didn't know he was wanted by the law."

I shoved myself out the door and I heard Violet behind me let out a gasp. "I'm Lily DeLon—" I held my chin up and stepped around Frank. "Lily Beatty. And I ain't been stolen. I'm his wife. What've you done with him? Is he hurt?"

The marshal took off his hat. "No ma'am. He's in my custody. He asked me to see you get home safely." He said it in a kind voice. I didn't want him to be kind. I wanted to hate him, but there wasn't any use in it. He looked at Frank again. "Would you be able to see to that, Frank? I got my hands full down at the calaboose."

Frank looked relieved that he himself wasn't going to be held to account for any crimes. He backed up closer to the door.

"Take me to him," I said to the marshal, and I surprised myself how peaceful I sounded.

27

The marshal waited with Frank at the front of the house for me to saddle up the bay. Reese helped me, and while we were in the barn, he told me that the marshal's name was John Olive, of the famous ranching Olives who owned a goodly portion of Williamson County. In the Seventies, him and his brothers drove 150 thousand head of cattle up the Trail to Kansas, Reese said. "He's the scrappy type. From a family of feuders. And he don't put up with much foolishness. Folks in town all like him real good." I didn't care to hear about it, though. My mind was on getting to Marion.

We rode, this Marshal John Olive and me, into town and I didn't have any trouble keeping up with him. He wasn't much for conversation and that suited me. He asked me one question, though: "Can you prove you're his wife?" I told him I had a certificate and that we'd have to turn back if he needed me to get it. But he didn't say anything more about it, and we kept on riding towards town.

The jailhouse was made of red stone and looked like it might have been something else at one time—a dry goods store or a tannery. It stood along the railroad tracks, with four saloons in the same line of buildings, a wheelwright shop stuck onto the end. Marshal Olive tied the bay to the hitching rail for me and helped me down from the saddle. Part of me dreaded going inside and seeing Marion locked up, but another part pushed me on.

Inside there was a small office up front, walled off with unpainted slapboards and a metal door from whatever was beyond. A man wearing wire spectacles and a badge sat at a cluttered desk. But the most horrifying to me—the thing that made all the breath leave my chest—was the sight of George Milton and Tom Bishop standing there waiting on us. And though it was Sunday, they weren't either of them dressed for church. They both had on riding boots and gauntlets, long dusters cut high in back for the saddle, wide-brimmed hats on their heads to keep off the sun. Traveling clothes. Tom Bishop wore a pair of shotgun chaps and his six-shooter strapped to his hip. I know my mouth dropped open when I saw them there.

"Praise the Lord . . . she's safe," George Milton said when I stepped in the door behind the marshal. He doffed his hat, showing the bald spot at the crown of his head. Mr. Bishop didn't say a word. Neither did I.

The man at the desk, the deputy marshal I guessed him to be, spoke next. "This just come in, John." He held up a scrap of paper. "It's from Sheriff Jenkins. He wants the prisoner delivered to

Bastrop. And these two men here say they'll take him."

John Olive glanced at Mr. Bishop and Mr. Milton, then went to reading the telegram.

"We'll see him there all right," Mr. Milton said. "That's what we came for."

"You'll take him to McDade," I cried out. I stepped towards the marshal and put my hand on his arm. "He ain't safe with them."

John Olive's eyes flicked at me.

"Now, Lily, you know that just isn't so." Mr. Milton made a laugh. "We're upstanding citizens, Marshal. We'll uphold the law. You can count on us."

"They killed his brothers," I said. "I watched it with my own eyes. I was there."

Mr. Milton tried laughing again. "Why, Lily! That's strong words you're using. You know it was self-defense."

Mr. Bishop stood there with his legs apart, arms folded. He had an angry glint in his eyes when he looked at me. I remembered how he shot Az and whirled for Jack with that same pistol he had hanging on his belt. I imagined he was a big hero by now back home. He stood there like he thought himself one.

"I've got two other prisoners I can't leave untended," Marshal Olive said to me.

"Marion ain't safe with them." I struggled to keep control of my voice. "I'm telling you the truth."

John Olive's eyes stayed on me a long time. They were hazel eyes, and I watched the pupils in them grow and ebb as he studied on me. I forced myself not to flinch away from that gaze. I looked him straight back till his eyes moved first, glancing towards Mr. Bishop and Mr. Milton.

"You men have a seat," he said.

He bent to scribble something on a sheet of paper. I peeked over his arm. He wrote down the date and Sheriff Jenkins's name, and then he wrote out a message. It said he would not release the prisoner to any individual or subordinate officer. It said if Sheriff Jenkins wanted the prisoner returned to Bastrop, to come himself or the prisoner would be turned free. Then Marshal Olive put down the pen and slid the paper at the deputy. "Take this to the telegraph office," he said.

Our eyes locked again and I knew he'd seen me read the message. I wanted to thank him but didn't know if that was the right thing to do. The part about turning Marion loose shocked me and gave me hope. I started praying Sheriff Jenkins wouldn't come. The deputy marshal went out the front door.

"Do you want to see him now?" John Olive said to me.

Mr. Milton stood up from the bench where he'd sat a moment ago. "Marshal, I must protest you taking this young girl back there with the likes of those rogues you have penned up. She is clearly overwrought at the ordeal she's been put through as it is."

John Olive faced the two men from McDade. "She's his wife," he said. "And now it seems to me you two fellas had better back off just a little bit on this."

Mr. Milton gave me a look that would have shrunk the thorns on a blackberry vine. He mouthed, "Lily . . .?" in disbelief, and I crossed my arms, my left hand out in front, in case he wanted to take a look at the wedding ring on my finger.

Marshal Olive turned towards Tom Bishop then. "If you think you'll be staying long here in Taylor, I'll be needing to take up your sidearm. While you're here, you'll abide by the gun ordinance."

Tom Bishop's face went as red as a bee sting, but he took his pistol out of its holster and laid it on the deputy's desk. The marshal stuck the gun inside a drawer and turned a key. It gave me a thrill to see Tom Bishop treated like a common gunman. Both the men sat back down on the bench, still thinking, it seemed to me, that the marshal intended to hand Marion over to them.

Marshal Olive took me through the door that led to the dim hall between a row of four cells, two on each side with a solid wall running between them. It smelled like a soured hen house in there. No windows. Just five wall lamps for light. I breathed through my mouth and willed my stomach quiet. My palms got sweaty and I kept my eyes off the two men in the other cells, once I saw they weren't Marion.

He was in the farthest cell, on the left-hand side. There was a bed in there, with canvas straps for a mattress, a chamber pot in a corner, and on the back wall, a wooden bench. That was where he sat, face in his hands, elbows on his knees, shoulders humped, and staring downward at his boots. His vest was gone, and his coat, his spurs and hat. Just shirtsleeves, galluses, and pants were all he wore. He looked cold and small, and he didn't raise his face when I stepped to the bars. I felt the tears well up in me right then.

"Marion?" I said, my voice all cut up with phlegm.

He lifted his eyes, then stood up and came the five steps towards the bars, but he didn't look happy to see me.

"Mister Beatty," Marshal Olive said, and I hadn't realized he was still behind me. His voice sounded loud and gruff so close, and echoed in the dampness of that place. "You have some men out here wanting to take you to Bastrop."

Marion looked past me. "I know."

"Your wife seems to feel your life will be in danger if you go with them. Do you feel such yourself?"

Marion's eyes struck mine for an instant, then moved back on the marshal. "Yes sir. I reckon it's possible."

"All right." John Olive nodded. "I'll let you two have a minute. I'll be right down here." He pointed to the middle of the hallway, and then went there to wait.

As soon as he moved away, I wanted him back. With him right there, I wouldn't have cried. It came on me in a wave I couldn't quiet. I hung onto the bars and let my shoulders shake out their grief.

"Lily . . . please," Marion said, his voice low and

private. "Hush up, now. I got some things I need to tell you."

I put my hand through the irons, reaching for him. He didn't move closer but looked towards the marshal, like he expected words to come from the man. They did.

"Ma'am," John Olive said. "I can't let you have contact with the prisoner."

A whimper escaped me as I drew back my hand. *Prisoner*. It was an ugly word.

"Listen to me, Lily," Marion said. "The marshal says I gotta chance at a light sentence since it's my first time. Maybe just two years. Five at the most."

"Five years?" More tears came to me. I put my hand at my mouth. I felt sick again.

"Shush, now. That ain't so bad. Here's what I wanna tell you. That land of my pa's. He paid for it square and clear. It's thirty-six acres, and by rights, it's mine now. And Haywood's. And that means it's yours too, since you're my wife. They can't take it from me long as you keep it up. I already asked the marshal all this and he said it's the law."

He moved up to the bars, so close I could smell him. It was a scent of sweat and sunshine. I had all I could do to keep my hands to myself. I whispered, "What happened? Who caught you?"

"I gave myself up." He said it slow. "I saw Mister Milton and Tom Bishop on the main road. I couldn't believe it. They knew somehow I was here. It was like somebody had told them I'd be by that way. My luck turned on me, I guess."

"What were you doing out on the main road?"

"Just crossing it. I hadn't been gone from Frank's more than twenty minutes. They saw me and they started chasing me. Bishop was firing at me. Their horses were fast. The only way I could of got away from them was to kill them both. Maybe I should of done it." He glanced up the wall of bars between us. "But I came here instead. And told the marshal who I was. And said if he cared to check, he'd find arrest warrants for me in two counties. So he done that and here I am." He let go a laugh without smiling. "Least I'll get to see Haywood. Find out if his leg healed up all right."

"The marshal ain't gonna let them take you back. He wired Sheriff Jenkins and said he'd have to come for you himself."

Marion glanced towards Marshal Olive. "He's fixing to make you leave. Did you hear all I said about the land? You can find a farmer to lease it for five years. Then when I get out we got someplace."

"Five years . . ."

"It'll go by quick. What horse did you come on? The bay?"

I nodded. "I'll never make it five years."

"One more thing, Lily," he said, his voice seeming urgent. "When the baby comes . . . if it's a son. Name him for Jack. Will you do that? Jackson Thurman. It's a good name, and it'll do him proud."

I couldn't answer. I was too choked up. All I did was nod and gasp, trying to force some air into my chest so's I could breathe. I heard Marshal Olive's footsteps coming behind me. His hands took my shoulders.

"I'm sorry, ma'am," he said. "That's all the time I can spare you."

"Can she take my horse?" Marion spoke up. "That bay mare she's riding ... I found her in an alley over in Round Rock, tied to a hitch-post back of a store. I sort of borrowed her." He glanced at me, then again at the marshal. "I reckon the owner would pretty well like to be getting her back about now."

"I reckon he would at that." John Olive gave Marion a long, scrutinous look like the one he'd given me earlier. "Seems to me like I might have to take you to Bastrop myself, Mister Beatty," he said. "To keep you from getting caught up in a necktie party along the way somewhere. I'll wire the sheriff. Tell him to meet us halfway. Fair enough?"

Marion nodded once, and the smallest flicker of a grin lifted the corner of his mouth. Then he reached through the bars, with the marshal standing right there, took ahold of my hand and brought it to his lips, brushing a kiss onto my knuckles. John Olive didn't say a word. I couldn't.

When it became clear to Mr. Bishop and Mr. Milton that the marshal wouldn't be turning Marion loose to them, they followed behind me to the Mercers' farm. I didn't invite them, nor did I give them the pleasure of knowing I recognized they were back there, a hundred yards or so to my rear. I rode Mollie and she felt like part of Marion with me, giving me some of his pluck.

Frank and Violet were waiting on the porch for me, it being a Sunday and a day of rest. Frank came to take Mollie, and I told him who was following me. "I'm sorry to bring you such bother," I said.

He looked off towards the gate, keeping a hold on Mollie, then started in that direction, where the two men from McDade had stopped their horses. "Get on inside with Violet."

"Frank'll send them on their way." Violet's hands took me.

I hadn't heard her coming to me, but just the sound of her voice sent the courage out of me. I turned into her arms. She led me every step to the porch, keeping a grip on me, and we went inside the house that way, arm in arm. She sat me down in the chair beside the stove and took the one across from me. She patted my hands in hers, and she felt to me then to be as near to a mama as I'd had in all these years.

"Now you just cry it out if it makes you feel better," she said to me, and I did like she told me. She pulled me across the space between us and to her shoulder, and she stroked my hair. "I know," she murmured. "Oh, I know what you're feeling, but the time will pass and it'll be all right. You don't believe me now, but this'll get behind you."

"Five years," I wept to her. "He said he'll likely get five . . ." I choked and couldn't finish.

"Five years is but a wink of an eye. Frank done ten and we got through it." I heard her but it didn't set in me for a second or more just what she said. Then I caught in my breath and pushed back from her shoulder. She nodded and cupped my chin. "And he's a better man for it. He don't do me like he done before no more. Causing me anguish for his safety. Wondering what saloon he's gambling in. Worrying he was lying dead someplace."

I wiped at my cheek. "I didn't know, Violet. Marion never said."

"It weren't Frank's wish that folks should know. It ain't something he's proud to tell. It were an accident but he killed a feller all right, and that's what took him under. But he done his time and he's a changed man. And the Lord blessed me with a child to tend to same as He's maybe done for you, to keep my time full while Frank was away. And it will for you, too. The Almighty never gives us more than we can bear."

But it seemed to me that He had. And it seemed He hadn't been listening to my prayers all these weeks, either. I felt completely forsaken by Him, even more surely than I had when Mama died. It seemed to me God was a ruthless taskmaster who'd thrown His own Son to the devils, and that I'd been foolish to expect any better treatment for myself.

Frank came in the door then, and took off his hat as he stepped inside. I looked at him anew, saw the weary lines and sadness about his eyes, and I wondered was it his prison term that had put them there? To me he seemed beaten down in a way I hadn't noticed before. I glanced at Violet and saw her looking at Frank too, and saw the love she had in her for him. It was like seeing me and Marion five years from now and it brought a great chill to my heart.

"These men out here say they're friends with your pa," Frank said. "And members of your church. They said they'd see you home in safety if you'd be so willing. It don't appear to me that they mean you harm, Lily, but if you want me to send them away, say the word and I will."

The way he said it I knew he had no desire to leave Violet and Reese just to tramp me home. I looked towards the windows but there wasn't anything to see. Just daylight shining through.

"I'll go with them," I said with a sigh. "Tell them to give me ten minutes to gather my things."

Before I even finished speaking, relief passed over Frank's features. I understood then what heartache we'd been causing him, Marion and me, by coming here and bringing back old memories he'd have rather forgotten. I thought of the two hundred dollars Marion had meant for Frank to have, and I knew suddenly where I'd leave it. Stuffed deep inside Violet's flour jar, where it would appear, as if by magic, the next time she baked bread.

Tom Bishop and George Milton gave me pleasant enough escort. There wasn't much talking done, nor anything I felt the need to say to them. I closed my mind to their company and focused my thoughts on Marion, knowing I'd given him a better chance of getting to Bastrop unharmed by taking these two with me.

We stayed overnight with farmer-folk outside of

Coupland. They fed us a meal and enjoyed the talk of Mr. Milton at their table. I couldn't eat or join in the conversation. I noticed Tom Bishop staring at me a lot, so I wandered outside away from his probing eyes.

I sat on a chair they had on their porch and took in the cold night, thinking how on the morrow Marion and Marshal Olive would be passing this way too, headed to Elgin, where Sheriff Jenkins would meet them. Four weeks was all the time we'd had together since that first stop we made, at Elgin too. In that four weeks a lifetime had passed for me.

Tom Bishop came out on the porch and let the door close easy behind him. I could hear Mr. Milton's voice inside, still babbling freely with the folks around their table. Tom Bishop moved to the edge of the steps, rolled himself a cigarette and lit it. Smoke came out of his nose in a stream.

I saw for the first time how short a man he was, barely taller than myself, and how his boots didn't look so shiny anymore on his little feet. He said, "Is there anything I can get for you?" But I knew he'd only come out to make sure I hadn't tried to run off. I shook my head and kept looking towards the road.

"You know," he said, casual-like, as if we were old friends having a chat, "we'd have gotten him to Bastrop safe. Ain't anyone holding grudges these days. That Beatty gang was bad business, Lily. But they're all closed up now. I think you'll be surprised at how peaceful it is around McDade lately."

I rose from the chair without speaking, and went back inside the house.

28

*I*t was late in the day when we rode up to the farm. Papa, Dane, and Nathan were all out in the fields. They saw us from there, where they were working among the rows of freeze-damaged oats. Nathan was the only one who came on the run. It seemed he'd grown four inches. As he raced past the barn, Knuck scrambled up from his warm place in the sun and chased on Nathan's heels.

I got down off Mollie and let him come into my arms. He didn't say anything, just clung to me hard, and I knew from that how much he missed me. Knuck sniffed at me like I was a stranger. Prickly-pear needles stuck from his nose and forehead, the tops of his ears, gotten from chasing critters into places he shouldn't.

Next came Dellie from the house, and I got down on one knee for her and hugged both of them up close. It was these two only I was glad to see. Mrs. Kennedy was there too, standing on the porch, watching the three of us with a mournful frown on her face.

"Is it Miz Kennedy who's been looking after

you?" I said low to Dellie. She nodded and bit her lip to keep from crying. At the sight of me, I guess. Her little arms held tight to my neck.

"Dane says her and Papa's been talking about getting hitched," Nathan said, and I wondered at the truth of it. Somehow the thought didn't surprise me, though Mrs. Kennedy was far too old for a man Papa's age. Nathan reached to stroke Mollie's nose. "This your horse, now?"

"Her name's Mollie," I said to him. "Take her to the barn for me, would you? See she gets watered and fed?"

I gave him the reins and he looked pleased to take the mare. I watched Papa and Dane coming nearer. Mr. Milton and Mr. Bishop went over to speak with Mrs. Kennedy, leaving their mounts loose, as seemed to be their habit.

Papa came up then and stopped in front of me. He gave me a long look, then moved past me. Dellie held onto my skirt. I heard him say, "Tom. George. Thank you for bringing her home."

Dane took his turn before me, searching my face. He said, "Glad to see you in one piece, Lily," and I thought how ignorant he was for thinking that of me. Him of all the ones around us should have known there wasn't but half of me standing there.

Papa didn't believe in the marriage. He ripped the certificate in two when I showed it to him and plunged it into the fire before I could wrest it from his hands. I burned my fingers going in after it, but Papa took my arms and held me back. I tried to twist away. His grip was strong.

"Let me say my piece, Lily," he said and turned me around so's I was facing him. He didn't look angry, only sad and filled with confusion. "Don't fight me like a wild coyote."

"You've got no right—" I watched the flames take the paper up in smoke, and I gave up my struggle against him. He kept his hands on my arms, though, not trusting me to stay still.

"I know it ain't been easy for you, being the oldest like you are," he said. Mrs. Kennedy was keeping the others outside, and I heard them talking on the porch. "And we ain't got none of the finer things it's natural a girl your age should want. I know all of it, Lily. It hadn't been nothing I could help. But you're better off without that ..." He drew in his breath, thinking it seemed, of a word that wouldn't rile me. "... without that boy. In time you'll see it for yourself."

"Marion, Papa. His name's Marion. And he ain't a boy. He's my husband. I'm married to him."

He flushed then, and his voice went down in tone. "You ain't married till I say you are. I didn't give consent to it and that means it ain't so. No court in the land will uphold a union with you but fifteen years of age, and with him locked up in jail."

I peeled his hands off my arms and slung them away. He looked like I'd slapped him. "I'm carrying his child inside me. And burning that paper won't change it."

I went from him then, out back behind the barn and found that hollow log there, alongside the creek. It was strange to me how I went by that log and saw it there for the first time, like it was waiting on me. The color of the bark had grayed with age, so I knew it must have been there a long while, though I'd never noticed it there before. It had a flat place along towards one end that made a perfect seat.

At one point during that first evening, I heard Dellie's footsteps in the fallen oak leaves behind me. But she must have seen me with my hands clasped in front of me, leaned forward towards that creek, and thought I was in the throes of a deep and soul-searching prayer. She didn't bother me, and I didn't let on that I knew she was there, though it pained me some later. She had missed me sorely and likely needed reassurance that I wasn't leaving her again soon. I couldn't have given her that, though. And it seemed best to let her be.

Truth is, I was inside myself mightily those first days back, as if a cloak was thrown around me, walling me off from everything but that creek gurgling by and the solidness of the log beneath me. My hands kept twisting the ring on my finger round and round, reminding myself that it was real and had happened, and wasn't just a dream.

I sat out there through drizzle and cold, hoping, I think, that I'd take a chill. And it wasn't until after nightfall that I'd venture back inside, to sit then in the rocker and stare at the fire. I heard Dane say, "What's wrong with her, Papa?" and I guess they all thought I'd seen such horrors in those four weeks that it had driven me insane.

Mrs. Kennedy kept coming and I smelled her

cooking, saw the plates she left for me on the sideboard when I came in. But I couldn't eat much. There wasn't any appetite in me, and the baby growing in my belly kept my guts churned up in a knot.

I spent some time in the barn with Mollie, for without the marriage paper or the photograph from the fair, or even the notes Papa'd taken from my drawer, she was all I had left of him. I gave her handfuls of grain out of my open palm and whispered to her. I rubbed oil into his saddle to keep the leather soft. I never noticed till then the initials carved into the cantle—M.S.B. My fingers traced over the letters a thousand times.

On the fourth day, when Papa came to me and said those words—"That's all the grieving you got time for ..."—I'd already realized how Marion had given me the way to freedom. I had his horse, a strong horse with steady feet. I had the land, the thirty-six acres and the broken-down house two miles towards the Knobs. And I had three hundred dollars, counting the extra hundred John Olive had given me from Marion's belongings, rolled up in the pocket of my coat.

I did the chores Papa requested of me, tended the hogs and baked four loaves of bread. It took until the noonday meal and I cooked that, too. For Papa and Dane only, since the young ones were off at school.

The men talked some while they ate. Not *to* me but *around* me. About the weather and when they thought it would break enough to plant for spring. About the likelihood of salvaging anything out of the fields of wheat. When they were done eating, I cleared the table and rinsed the dishes, just as if there wasn't anything changed in me.

After they were back in the field, I went to the barn and put the saddle on Mollie. She seemed excited to have it on her and raised her head to snort at me. I didn't try to hide that I was leaving, but neither Papa nor Dane saw me go.

The road looked different in the dead of winter, with the trees bare of branches and with the undergrowth frozen back. I could see up onto Mr. Grossner's place, past the big oak on the rise, all the way to the board fence around his horse get. Knuck followed along for a while, then got bored with the road and took off into the woods to hunt. The Knobs rose up before us.

On Mollie, the two miles didn't seem so long, and she trotted like she could smell where it was we were headed. She tried to turn in the gate with no command from me, but a heavy chain, wrapped over and under the rails and padlocked, barred our way. A crude-lettered sign said, NO TRESPASSING. FORECLOSED IN LIEU OF BACK TAXES.

Mollie bobbed her head and stamped, anxious to be on the move, but I held her in check and studied that sign. Taxes for what, I wondered. I didn't know anything about the laws on land tax, nor what kind of money was owed. There was a name there that I had to edge Mollie up close to read. MURRAY BURLESON—TAX COLLECTOR, it said. I looked over the fence at the weeds that had grown up high, then died in the cold, untrampled underfoot. Thirty-six acres of upright, crisp weeds.

I turned Mollie around and went back down the road a ways to give us room. I put my heels to her and we flew right at that gate. She cleared the rails easy, though I nearly bounced off her for my own lack of riding skills. We went past the rusting plow and the low stock houses.

The barn was still standing and the north wall of the house, but the rest of it was gutted by fire. The odor still clung to the air and my first thought was of lightning, though it wasn't the right time of year. Then I saw the blackened coal oil can laid over near the place where the door had been. And it came clear to me, sitting on the back of Mollie, staring at that burned-out house, that five years from now, even ten, there'd be no peace for me and Marion in McDade. Folks here would never forgive nor forget, not even when he'd done his time. Beatty would always be a name they'd spit off their tongues.

I wheeled Mollie around and headed away from that dark place.

I rode into town and tied the mare in front of Billingsley's store. I ignored the looks that came from people, Captain Highsmith and Wes Peterson on the bench out front of the barber shop. Mrs. Slater as she went inside the beef market. Things were quiet down at the rock saloon.

I stepped up onto the gallery and went inside the store. The hole from Mr. Milton's shotgun blast had been patched up but not painted. The glass in the cabinet above the counter had been replaced. Mr. Billingsley himself was there today, helping somebody I didn't know choose a pair of boots. I didn't see Mr. Milton around anywhere.

Lying on the counter, still strung and ready to be racked, was a bundle of Bastrop newspapers. And though it wasn't what I'd come for, I picked at the knotted twine and tried to read if there was news of Marion. I couldn't see anything but the top half of the front page, and I couldn't untie the twine, either. I reached for a pair of scissors I spied behind the counter, hoisting myself high on tiptoe.

"I'll be right with you, Lily," Mr. Billingsley said, and I looked over my shoulder at him. He seemed as friendly as ever, smiling my way and waving his hand at me a little. "Go ahead and open those newspapers. I just haven't gotten to it yet today."

I cut the string and took off the top paper, shaking it open, and seeing at almost the same instant, the article near the bottom of the page concerning Marion's arrest. It said all about John Olive and Sheriff Jenkins meeting in Elgin to exchange Marion, and about how he was charged with the robbery of the same store I was standing in now. It mentioned his brothers and their fate, and all their names were spelled right this time. I read the whole thing through while Mr. Billingsley sold a pair of new boots.

"Did you want to buy that newspaper, Lily?" he said to me when his customer was gone.

I looked up at his kindly face and the sight brought me out of my trance. "Oh ... no. Thank you." I folded the paper and put it back on the stack. "I'd like to look at that," I said, pointing at the snub-nose pistol inside the glass case on the counter by where I stood.

He gave me a funny look but he didn't say a word. He brought the pistol out and laid it in my hands. It was small, but heavy. And cold on the steel part. The handle was wood and sanded down smooth to a shine. There was room for six bullets in the chamber.

"I'll take this," I said. "And a box of cartridges to fit it, please." I used some of the money from the roll in my pocket to pay, and the gun fit in there, too.

"Good day to you, Lily," Mr. Billingsley said as I went towards the door.

I gave him a smile. "You too, Mister Billingsley."

For a moment, standing outside unlooping Mollie from the hitching rail, I stared over at that hanging tree across the road. The three pieces of rope were still tied to the lower branches. A reminder, I guess, to anybody who cared to remember. I glanced at the place where Jack and Az had fallen in the street. There wasn't any sign of that now. Old Captain Highsmith, down on his bench, touched his hat in my direction.

I swung myself onto Mollie and squeezed her with my knees. My eyes stayed straight on the way ahead of me as I rode away from there. Down Main Street, past the bank, past the schoolhouse. Crazy old Lucien Previne was standing there, waving at me as I rode by, headed towards the pine boughs at Bastrop.

Marion is there now. Behind the bars in the county jail. A thousand dollars bond posted on his head. Awaiting a trial, the newspaper said. Like it was some special day to look forward to. Awaiting a trial. Here first and then in Travis County on the charge of assault.

He doesn't have a chance. Not with trials and juries. Not when he's guilty sure. It's up to me to give him his chance. I'm the only one that cares.

I pull my coat tighter around me, and feel the weight of the pistol in my pocket. I wonder if I can get there before dark. Make it in time to see him and let him know why I've come. He'll tell me what to do. How to get the gun past the sheriff and his deputies.

The chill in the wind bites at my cheeks. I lean forward to stroke Mollie's neck, and wonder as I do, how cold it gets in Mexico at this time of year.

The End

Author's Note

The story of the Christmas lynchings of 1883 in McDade first came to my attention as I was reading a bit of Texas history. The details of the story were greatly exaggerated, telling of eleven outlaws who were hanged on Christmas Day in one wholesale act of vigilance. Upon further research I found nothing to corroborate that original story. Eleven hangings were, I think, a figment of a myth that got blown out of proportion in typical Texas style. Eleven men (probably more) were indeed hanged in that district, but over the span of six or seven years, not all at once. In 1883, on Christmas Eve not Day, there were only three men hanged, but they were executed in sudden and terrifying lynch-mob fashion—taken out in the night by a band of masked men and strung to a tree.

Although I have embellished and rearranged the actual events that took place, some of the people in my story really did exist. Their ages, physical descriptions, and personality traits, however, are all the product of fictional invention. There was a "Beatty Gang," more often referred to as the "Beatty Boys." Jeff Fitzpatrick did, presumably, kill

Lee County deputy Heffington, and in so doing, set in motion the events which led to so much violence. Goodman, Hasley, and Stevens existed. The McLemores and Henry Pfeiffer did as well, and were the unfortunate men lynched on that fateful Christmas Eve. George Milton, Tom Bishop, and Willie Griffin, in addition to several townsmen of lesser importance to the story, also were real people. There is some doubt as to the correct spellings of certain names since newspaper editors of that time seemed to have spelled phonetically, and thus, one name often appeared spelled in a variety of ways within a single issue.

Completely fictional characters are the DeLonys, Daniel O'Barr, Eppie, most of the townswomen, and Estelle Beatty (although Jack Beatty did have a wife). All of the characters in the Austin portion of the book are fictional, as are the people in the Elgin and Taylor sections, with the exception of Marshal John Olive, who really did threaten to turn Marion Beatty free rather than let George Milton and Tom Bishop return him to McDade to face a mob.

Marion Beatty's story was the one that intrigued me the most, since I found him in such an offchance way while scouring old copies of the Bastrop County newspaper. In a small article, buried amidst the sensationalism of the shoot-out trial and detailed statements from witnesses, I learned that there had been a brother not in attendance on the streets of McDade that Christmas morning. He skipped out while the fires were hot, so to speak. He did not turn up for over three weeks, and then in the small town of Taylor in company of Bishop and Milton, who had apparently been diligent in tracking his whereabouts.

That two-paragraph article inspired the fictional account of those three weeks on the dodge. In none of the accounts I have read of the McDade shootout of 1883 is Marion Beatty even so much as mentioned. Historians state that there were four Beatty brothers, and then go on to write of Jack, Az, and Haywood only, leaving Marion completely shrouded in mystery.

In my research, the only factual thing I have learned about him is that he was sentenced on June 3, 1884, to two years in the state penitentiary for robbery. This tidbit was noted in a listing of the Bastrop County court docket for that week. Since I was searching for clues to his life, his name flashed out like neon from among the dozens listed there.

And finally, places I have mentioned in the story really existed and still do to this day. In the words of the *Bastrop Advertiser* of 1883, McDade was a "hot town." Today, it is a quiet place off the highway between Austin and Houston with a few old buildings that have a history. The people there are open and friendly. They still sit on wooden benches along the covered gallery that runs the length of the stores. And if you ask, they will gladly point out for you the old hanging tree across the main street.